Posey's Peril

Jenny Wheeler

ISBN 978-1-067012-24-3 (Paperback)
ISBN 978-1-067012-28-1 (Large Print)
ISBN 978-1-067012-22-9 (Kindle
ISBN 978-1-067012-23-6 (E-book)

Published by Happy Families Ltd Copyright © 2024 Jenny Wheeler (E-Book)

Books by Jenny Wheeler

Of Gold & Blood Series
Poisoned Legacy #1
Brother Betrayed #2
Double Jeopardy #3
Tangled Destiny – A Christmas Novella and Prequel #4
Unbridled Vengeance #5
Hope Redeemed – A Spanish Novella #6 Tainted Fortune #7
Captive Heart – A Hawaiian Christmas Novella -# 8
Book Bundle Of Gold & Blood Series 1, Books 1 – 3.
Book Bundle Of Gold & Blood, Series 2, Books 1 & 4 – Elanora's Story.
Book Bundle Of Gold & Blood Series 3, Books 5 & 6
Book Bundle Series 4, Books 7 & 8.
Ancient Deception #9
Dangerous Desires #10

Home At Last series
Sadie's Vow #1
Susannah's Secret #2
Rosie's Rebellion #3

Sisters of Barclay Square series
Poppy's Dilemma #1
Posey's Peril #2

Posey's Peril

Jenny Wheeler

Prologue

January, 1841

Benedict always believed his oldest brother turned into the devil on that snow-locked night during one of the coldest Christmases England had ever known. Great chunks of ice floated in the Thames at Worcester Park, and by New Year's Day a strange dark fury infected the children at Worcester Park Lodge. For eight tedious days, the deadly freeze that stalked the land kept them inside. Even worse, in his mind, it invaded the playroom. Like a stealthy fog, it crept under doors, oozed down chimneys, looking for a way to kill and destroy.

Their gamekeeper narrowly escaped death as the polar storm prowled the forest outside their lounge windows, the forest where King Henry VIII once hunted deer. A lamplighter in a nearby village froze to death on his rounds. The ornamental pond in the garden iced over, and icicle fingers hung from the multi-arched bridge that traversed it.

Worcester Park Lodge was a medieval castle complete with battlements, and Benedict wished they had patrolling armoured knights, enlisted to rebuff the enemy. Little did he realise the threat would come from inside. From one of their own.

They were alone, playing quietly in the nursery when the attack came. Nannie had gone to visit relatives for Christmas Day and had not returned. Mother said she couldn't get back because all the roads were closed and, anyway, she wanted to make sure Nanny's mother had enough wood to keep warm. Otherwise, like many others throughout the realm, she might die from the cold.

He and his beloved younger sister were cutting out dresses for her paper dolls in the playroom, an activity considered unsuitable for a seven-year-old boy, but which was pure delight to his five-year-old sister. He put up with it because he enjoyed nothing more than pleasing Rosamunde. She was the only girl in the family, the apple of their father's eye and, ever since the famous *Angel Dreaming* painting went on show, the toast of the nation.

Captured by the famed portrait artist Sir Francis Grant, her innocent beauty had taken London by storm. There sat a four-year-old Rosamunde, in a blue velvet dress with lace collar, her treasured doll, Bubba, in her lap, gazing up with wistful blue eyes. Displayed in the National Portrait Gallery, the child's soft, haunting melancholy captivated audiences. "England's Mona Lisa" was how the critics described it.

Their big brother couldn't countenance his little sister outshining him, the heir to an earldom. As the dark afternoon edged into inky night, Gideon strutted in on them, a picture of haughty arrogance, and embarked on a session of torture. Usually, he confined his malice to annoying names and hair pulling, but tonight he was driven by an intense malevolence Benedict hadn't witnessed before. When his spiteful challenges didn't prompt the desired response, he grabbed Rosamunde's doll, the one featured in the painting, and held it aloft, taunting her, saying he was going to cut off her head, just like King Henry had Queen Anne's.

He snatched up the scissors his sister had been using for her paper dolls and wielded them threateningly. She jumped up, arms outstretched, squealing in protest, reaching towards him to rescue her prized toy. And he'd stabbed down viciously into her neck.

Nightmares of eleven-year-old Gideon's frenzied face haunted Benedict's sleep for years afterwards. His eyes gleaming with hate, an exultant smiling glee on his lips, as he raised the blunt-ended tool to strike again. Blunt-ended, yes, but when wielded with malignant force, deadly.

Propelled by a fury that came out of nowhere, Benedict rose to pull his sister out of harm's way. She was slippery, so slippery, as arms locked around her chest, he pulled her to him. And there was blood. So much blood. Rushing out. There was no stopping it.

And then came the pain: a shrill, piercing torment. He fell backwards, hauling his sister with him so they fell in a heap, him flat on his back, her lying on top of him. He couldn't reach his face or his eye, where the agony seared.

That was how Gideon's tutor found them when he came to investigate why the children had not reported to the dining room for supper.

Rosamunde was dead.

And Gideon? At first, he was nowhere to be found. And when they found him at last, in the dayroom practising his fencing moves, he denied everything.

Benedict woke up blinded. But worst of all, he didn't die. He was forced to live on.

One

Barclay House, late June, 1868

Posey Barclay rolled over, opened her eyes and blinked at the sun slanting through the French shutters on her bedroom windows.

I was so tired last night I forgot to close them. I wonder what time it is.

She exhaled a lingering sigh, flopped back onto her stomach and buried her head in her pillows.

Three months without Poppy. I'm not sure I can do it without her.

The family had celebrated her twin sister Poppy's marriage to her journalist beau, Thomas Yates, in recent fine style, before waving them off on a clipper to London. Posey could hardly believe they'd really gone. Truth be told, she wanted to miraculously swoop out over the oceans and beckon them home again. The thought of them passing out of Australian waters had opened up an abyss inside her and made her heart race.

Calm down. You're perfectly capable of running the household until she gets back.

She allowed herself the luxury of a few more minutes of inertia, before surfacing again to full consciousness, turning onto her back and listening for the normal sounds of the household waking around her.

The birds chimed from the treetops in the extensive orchard garden. If she crept to the window, she'd spot the currawongs and rosellas perched on the uppermost tips of the eucalyptus trees, gently swaying in the light breeze from the ocean, already going about their day.

She bent her ear to see if she could catch sounds of her mother, Arabella, always an early riser, venturing downstairs for her first cup of tea, and immediately pictured her falling on the stairs. Their once robust mother had become fragile in mind and body in recent months, and Posey feared the decline was accelerating with Poppy's absence.

The faint clanging of pots told her Geraldine Crowe, their longstanding cook who doubled as a housekeeper, was in the kitchen, no doubt already mixing up a batch of shortbread or cheese or date scones for morning tea.

If Mrs C is at her post, then all is right with the world.

She sat up and attempted to warm her day with a smile.

And then the memory of the approaching court case smothered her with its heavy weight

She'd be representing the family in court, in all likelihood before Poppy and Thomas returned from her brother-in-law's posting as the London correspondent for the *Sydney Herald*.

The disastrous collapse of the family business, Barclay Investments, the previous year, and their father James Barclay's subsequent sudden death, had led a posse of disgruntled investors to bring a damages case against the family, attempting to scratch back their losses by other means. Most of them fraudulent, in Posey's estimation.

But Poppy had always been the one to lead the charge on this, and she was no longer here.

We've all relied on Poppy far too much. Thank goodness I've still got Silas.

She swung her feet to the floor and perched on the edge of her mattress. She shivered, even though the mild Sydney winter didn't really warrant her trembling. July was the coldest month, but the day was already warming up. By late morning, it would no doubt be around 60 degrees.

She stood and quickly slipped into a velvet at-home day gown, padded to open the door onto the upstairs hallway, and listened for her mother, her focus intent. There was no sound from her room down the hall.

She tiptoed to Arabella's slightly ajar door.

Funny. I closed this myself when I tucked her up last night. She must be up already.

She peered into the gracious room. A four-poster bed covered in a pretty yellow-and-green floral duvet dominated the generous space. Wall and bedside table lamps lit the room with a pleasant pink glow. A long, low dresser ran against the wall abutting the hallway, under an eye-catching oil painting of an angelic child clutching a round-eyed doll. It had the look of an old master – like a Raphael, she'd always thought when she saw it. Inherited from Arabella's aristocratic English forbears, Posey knew little more than that about it.

Her mother's bed was empty, the white Egyptian cotton sheets thrown back in messy disarray. She tiptoed in, even though it seemed clear her mother was not there, and stood in the middle of the room, slowly turning in a circle, checking for any unusual signs or disruption.

Nothing.

Her mother's day dress, with its drawstring waist, was no longer hanging on the back of the wicker basket chair where she usually left it.

She's probably down stairs with Geraldine cadging an early pot of tea.

As if drawn by some unseen force, Posey stepped closer to the dresser under the painting. She then noticed something new. Something she was certain she'd never seen before. A China doll with large blue glass eyes clad in a blue taffeta dress trimmed with matching blue ruffled headband sat on the dresser top, propped up immediately below the painting.

With a start, Posey stepped forward to examine the toy more closely. She glanced up at the painting and her stomach lurched. The doll on the dresser looked identical to the one the child in the painting held lovingly in her lap. It was dressed in identical garb.

Oh, my gosh… they're a matching set…

She stretched out her hand, almost afraid to touch the doll, and then noticed a handful of old glass daguerreotype plates cast in a careless heap beside it, along with a sheet of notepaper.

A letter, or an invoice perhaps?

She tiptoed forward and uttered a superstitious prayer as she picked up the old pictures and shuffled through them. She recognised none of the portrayals: a refined gentleman in a military uniform and plumed helmet; a handsome full-bodied woman in a heavy brocade gown with mutton sleeves; and a dark-haired youth with a newly grown, pencil-thin moustache who looked vaguely familiar. She shook her head in confusion. *Who are these people? And why had Mother seemingly pulled them out of an old storage box?*

She picked up the sheet of notepaper. It was an invoice for the painting, made out to her Admiral of the Fleet grandfather, Admiral Sir George Fairfax.

> Angel Dreaming, A Portrait of Rosamunde Vane,
> 1839 By Sir Francis Grant (Scotland)
> Exhibited at the National Gallery, London, 1840
> Winner of the Grand Exhibition prize, 1841

She stared into the bottom right-hand corner of the painting. She could just make out the artist's faded signature: Francis Grant.

I've passed by this work daily, but never considered it anything more than sentimental romanticism. Chocolate-box art. If it's a significant work, how is it I didn't know? And why is Mother suddenly so interested?

Minutes later, fully dressed, Posey barged into the kitchen where Mrs Crowe was bending over the oven.

"Have you seen Mother this morning, Mrs C?" she asked. "She's not in her room."

"Arabella?" Mrs Crowe paused in pushing a tray of shortbread into the wood-fired oven and glanced up. She shook her head and the curls that escaped from the sides of her white cook's hat bounced around her flushed red face. "Not since last night. Why?"

Posey's heart raced. "She's not in her room," she repeated. "I thought she might have come down here and begged a pot of tea off you." She gazed around the kitchen, as if expecting to see her mother's slight form emerge from the adjoining scullery. "It looks like she's still in her nightwear. I don't think she's properly dressed to go out."

She sniffed in the citrus-spice smell of marigolds, mixed with the vanilla from the shortbread, and caught sight of her sister's bridal bouquet, lying on top of a fruit bowl on a dresser near the door.

Poppy deliberately chose a cottage-garden theme for her flowers, freshly picked from their garden on the day. It had been too early for orange blossom, so she'd settled for in-season blooms like orange marigolds, white cosmos, and red-and-white-eyed verbena.

"I'm worried she might be disoriented by Poppy going," Posey said. "You know how she's been in recent months. Not at all her old self."

"Maybe she's taken an early turn round the garden," suggested Mrs Crowe. "She loves to sit on the bench near the pond and daydream."

Posey bit her lower lip. "It's a bit cool for that right now, isn't it?" She whirled to the door. "But I'll go and look anyway."

When she got to the door it was already ajar. *Maybe she has slipped outside*, she thought.

She stood on the front porch and considered her surroundings.

The dew on the front lawn was drying fast, but no footsteps showed in the remaining damp areas. She made her way down the front path, thinking to glance out on the street. Barclay Square was a quiet cul-de-sac, with only a few neighbouring houses with park-like gardens similar to theirs.

She pushed open the pedestrian gate and within half a minute was aware of figures hurrying up the street, their legs and arms working in jerky movements.

"Posey!"

Her younger sister Petunia, wearing her riding outfit and boots, broke into a run towards her. Posey saw that Petunia's companion was Clarrie O'Reilly, a professional jockey who was a good friend of the family. His legs pumped with urgency as he covered the ground at high speed, his arms filled with a slumped female form.

Posey gasped and stared, her attention switching like a pendulum from her sister to Clarrie, whose shirt was covered in red staining.

Blood! Clarrie is saturated in blood.

Two

Petunia halted beside her, gasping for breath, and croaked, "It's Mother. I found her on my way to the stables."

Petunia's passion for horses was a family joke. She got up early several times a week to go out to Hugo's place, where their mother's lawyer friend had a riding track of near professional quality that local jockeys used for training.

"Thank goodness Clarrie was riding today, too. He came along just as I found her and helped. I'd never had managed by myself."

"What was she doing out there?" Posey exclaimed. "What was she thinking?"

Petunia brushed the back of her hand across her forehead. "I don't think she was thinking," she said. "You know how she's been lately. Away with the fairies sometimes."

Clarrie carried Arabella to a bench near the front door, his breath fast and gasping as he endeavoured to move her in a protective embrace

"She's unconscious, but her breathing and heart rate are both steady," he rasped between breaths. "She's had a nasty blow to her head, though," he said. "She obviously needs a doctor."

Posey leaned in and examined her mother's bedraggled head, streaked with blood draining from a gash across the top. She stroked the sticky hair, drew her hand away and her knees went weak. She grabbed at Clarrie's shoulder.

"Hey there, girl, go easy, or I'll have to hold you up too."

She stared into his kind, slate-grey eyes. "Thank goodness you found her."

Three

Silas Williams made his way up the path to Barclay Manor with a pulsing excitement that irritated him. He did his best to suppress it. The afternoon sun was at his shoulder and after nearly two months away in Victoria, he wasn't dressed for the Sydney temperatures, even in winter.

I've forgotten how hot it is here. I should've worn my waistcoat and shirt sleeves. Not the jacket, he mused as he reached the front door. An underlying niggle chewed at him as he raised his hand to rattle the bronze lion-head knocker, but he tried to ignore it. *It's not the sun that's getting you in a sweat. It's the prospect of having some relaxed time with Posey.*

Nonsense, the sensible Queen's Counsel voice inside chastised. *You know there's nothing doing here. She's already turned you down once. You're simply here to discuss the claims against her father's estate and give her a report of who you saw in Ballarat and Melbourne.*

He'd arrived back a few days earlier, but he'd had a lot to catch up on in the office after two months away, and they'd had no chance to sit down and have a proper conversation.

He thumped on the knocker and, after a long pause, Mrs

Crowe answered, her usually placid face looking harried.

"Oh, Mr Silas," she said with a breathy hesitation. "Is Miss Posey expecting you?"

The nature of the inquiry caught him by surprise. Since he'd agreed to represent the family in the looming court case, he'd been in and out of the Barclay home with no comment raised. So much so, he almost felt part of the family.

He raised his brow in a query. "Yes, she is, actually. We organised it yesterday. I haven't briefed her yet on my trip because of the excitement over the wedding. We said we'd sit down today and talk things over at length. I've got a lot to tell her after two months away."

The housekeeper stepped back abruptly and made space for him to step into the hall. "My apologies, Mr Williams. No offence." She glanced over her shoulder and up the stairs, her face crisscrossed with anxiety lines. "It's just there's been a family emergency. I'm not sure Miss Posey has remembered you're coming. She's been quite taken up, she has."

She glanced back up the stairs and then at the hallway floor. "Would it…" She cleared her throat and started again. "Could I show you into the drawing room and let Miss Posey know you're here? She's in her mother's bedroom."

Silas's stomach clenched with a sudden cramp. "Arabella? Nothing serious, I hope?"

Mrs Crowe's head bobbed, and her face reddened. "The doctor's been," she said. "In fact, he's still here."

Silas took a step towards the drawing room. "Of course I'm happy to wait. Let her know I'm here and I quite understand she's busy. I don't mind how long she is."

"I'll bring you a pot of tea and some shortbread," Mrs Crowe said with a relieved smile. "Hopefully, she won't be too long."

***

Several cups of Earl Grey tea and three delicious shortbread biscuits later, Posey swung into the drawing room.

"I'm so sorry, Silas," she spluttered. "It's been an unbelievable day." She collapsed into the armchair opposite him. "I'm glad Mrs C. has looked after you. So sorry for the delay – and for the fact that our meeting entirely slipped my mind."

"I'm sure there's a totally understandable reason," he said, head cocked on one side in question.

She shook her head. "So much of what's going on I don't understand. I've no idea yet of the reasons behind it. But Mother wandered off this morning, early, before I was up. She got out onto the street and ended up injured. Either she fell down, or she was attacked. We don't know. But Clarrie and Petunia found her lying in the road with a head wound, totally out of it."

Silas stared. "Oh, Posey, I'm shattered to hear that. I know it must be devastating for you. But she's going to be alright, isn't she?" He glanced down to his hands in his lap. "Mrs Crowe mentioned the doctor has been. What does he think?"

"She's regained consciousness now. She's still a bit woozy. Some things she says aren't making sense. And Doctor Appleton can't tell us anything about what might have caused her injury. She could have fallen. Someone's coach might have been frightened her in the early-morning light and she might have tripped. Or she could have been attacked. He can't say."

Silas consciously modified his breathing to a calm rhythm. "But otherwise, she'll recover? No lasting damage?"

Posey shrugged and nodded. "He's optimistic about a full recovery, yes." She reached out for a shortbread and waved it in the air. "I've just realised I'm starving. I have had nothing to eat today, what with all the excitement." She took a small bite. "We have to keep a watch for signs of concussion." She chewed slowly.

"But?"

They both let the single syllable hang in the air, and then Posey broke into a warm smile.

"You're so clever," she whispered. "You always know when you haven't been given the full story."

With you, I do.

They'd become close the three years she'd worked in his office as an articled clerk. She only left after things became awkward when she turned him down.

Become close? You fell in love with her, you dunce. You're still in love with her, though don't let her know that.

His good eye roved her face, taking in the drawn pallor around her eyes.

Working together on the case, trying to ensure the four Barclay women left behind when James died are protected – that's the role I have here now. Nothing more.

"So, what's the rest?" he asked.

She hesitated. "I'm sure you've noticed Mother hasn't been her usual self the last few months. She's vague and forgetful. She gets easily confused."

He nodded. "You have mentioned it."

"Well. There are a few weird things that have accompanied this latest mishap."

Another long pause.

"Like what?" he said, hoping he wasn't sounding too much like a probing barrister.

She took some while to consider the question and then stood. "Perhaps it would be best if I we went up to Mother's room and showed you," she said. "She's sleeping at present. I think she's in shock. We can tiptoe in there and I'll show you something, and then we can come back downstairs and discuss it. How does that suit? It's easier than me trying to explain it all down here."

He rose slowly from his chair. "Sure," he said. "If that's easier." He couldn't for the life of him think what it was he was about to see. He fell into step behind Posey and walked upstairs to Arabella's room.

Four

The curtains were drawn, and the rhythmic sigh of her mother's breath – in and out, in and out – lent a reassuring calm to the faintly scented air. Darling Mama's perfume – Old Bond Street – Posey thought. If only we could go back to when she got given that famous perfume on her sixteenth birthday, when she was fully in command of her faculties.

Halfway across the space between the bed and the door she paused and turned towards the painting. She lifted a hand and gestured for Silas to take it in.

Then I'll explain how it fits into today's events.

She glanced back to Angel Eyes, her name for the young girl in the painting. Now she'd given it her full attention, the work was growing on her. She was beginning to appreciate how it could have won the Grand Exhibition – whatever that was – more than twenty years ago. The brushwork was finely detailed, and the artist – Francis Grant, wasn't it? – had captured a rare sweetness in the child's face. She'd been hasty when she'd dismissed it as a sentimental pastiche.

A strange cry rose from behind her, interrupting her musings. She swung around to her mother, but Arabella rested just as she had when they entered the room, her chest rising and falling at a reassuring, gentle pace.

She glanced at Silas. He stood doubled over, one hand clutching his chest. And the anguished, strangled cry was coming from deep within.

"Silas," she whispered, "what's wrong? Are you ill? In pain?"

He attempted to straighten himself, and one arm over his brow, staggered for the door.

"Hawk Eye!" she exclaimed, calling him by his childhood nickname, gained because the boys at school said even with one eye he saw more than most others did with two.

"Let me."

Just as she had when they'd come upstairs, she took the arm closest to her – it happened to be on his left side – and gently guided him from the room. She'd come to understand in the years she worked for him that he managed his limited sight with extreme skill, but now and then, like on stairs, his impaired peripheral vision disadvantaged him.

They paused on the landing outside. She gazed into his face, taking in the familiar black eye patch, expecting some explanation, but he seemed unable to speak.

His face was a ghostly white, and his single eye radiated an intensity she hadn't seen in it before.

Pain? Fear? Anger? A mixture of all three emotions, perhaps. *And it's burning him up.*

She asked again, her voice an appealing murmur, "Silas! What's wrong? Have you got chest pains?"

His blue-lined lips held a tight line, but he shook his head. "I can't… I can't…" He gasped. Nothing more.

He turned for the stairs like a cat with its tail on fire, and she galloped to keep up with him.

"Stop," she said when they reached the bottom. "You're not leaving, are you? I thought we were going to have a meeting about your trip. And don't forget we've got the reception for the new Supreme Court judge tomorrow. We can't miss that."

He stared up at her, as if this was another unexpected hammer blow. "What Supreme Court judge? I don't recall."

She took a deep breath. "It was announced soon after you left for Melbourne. It probably didn't make the papers down there. Gideon Vane. He arrived a few days ago, and the New South Wales bar is all set to welcome him at a reception tomorrow night. Just for the legal profession. He might even be the one presiding over our case, so we need to be there."

His knees almost buckled under him as she spoke, and she reached out and attempted to grab him by the elbow to hold him up.

"Silas! Something is dreadfully wrong. Come into the drawing room and sit down."

He stiffened to his full frame and stepped away so fast she worried she'd offended his pride.

"I mean… I want to help," she said. "What can I do?"

"Nothing." The word was loaded with anguish. "There's nothing you can do." He backed off down the hall, gazing into her face as if he was uttering a last goodbye. "Not a damn thing."

He pivoted like a whirling dervish propelled by renewed volcanic energy and stormed out.

Not a damn thing?

Hawk Eye never allowed himself even the mildest of curses. He never lost his composure, either.

Oh, no. Poppy's only been in London a week, and already everything's going wrong.

Five

Not another Irishman.

Sydney's newest, not-yet-sworn-in judge, the Hon. Gideon Vane, Esquire, heir to an earldom, suppressed a shudder of irritation and shook hands with the fair-haired young man who introduced himself as "Alfred Morgan, notary of the Court of New South Wales and the chief justice's assistant registrar."

He'd barely been in this Godforsaken colony one hour, and already he'd heard more accents born within sight of the River Liffey than any blue-blooded speakers of his mother tongue.

That was the first surprise. The streets, the buildings, looked like the middling parts of London – nothing like the Tower or Windsor Castle, of course – but the speech! He could barely understand them. They either had the rolling burr of Ireland, or the shuffling, incomprehensible patter of the native Australians.

Not the black natives. He hadn't seen any of them yet. The white inhabitants who'd been here for a bit over one hundred years.

I suppose it's the nature of the place. It's for the world's outcasts, isn't it? The people no one else wants.

Along with the Scots, Gideon couldn't stand Irishmen, who, he'd found from experience, never knew their place.

But Morgan, the serene, erect officer of the court, seemed impervious to Vane's prickly rebuffs.

"Sir Frederick is detained by court business. He's unable to personally greet you off the boat. That's why he sent me. But he's formally welcoming you at the Officers of the New South Wales Bar reception tomorrow night."

"Tomorrow night?" said Gideon, unable to keep the aggrieved tone from his voice. After three months couped up on a ship with two hundred other passengers, the vast majority of whom held no interest for him whatsoever, he'd expected to at least be given a week or two to get his land legs before he started work.

Even as they stood conversing on the bustling quayside, he felt his knees weaken and sway. A giddiness momentarily assailed him, that anticipated sense of the wave roll that never eventuated that was becoming familiar.

"This is just a welcome. Not the swearing in," said Morgan apologetically. "But I'm afraid with the sudden death of the last judge, the courts have got badly in arrears with their business. Sir Frederick is set on getting you sworn in and set to work as soon as he can."

Morgan turned to the two baggage men who trailed behind them with a trolley laden with Gideon's suitcases. "I'll give these fellows instructions about where to deliver your bags, and we'll get moving. The court breaks for lunch in half an hour and Sir Frederick will see you briefly in the recess."

***

Five hours later, Gideon found himself installed in a comfortable suite in Petty's Hotel on Church Hill. His clothes were all unpacked and receiving the required attention from the hotel staff – being washed, aired, hung, or ironed as appropriate, and he was lying back in a hot mint-scented bath, relaxing for the first time since he'd set foot on land.

They'd explained that the hotel would provide laundry and meals, but he'd need to hire additional personal staff. A valet, perhaps, to take care of his personal needs. And a housekeeper to attend to domestic tasks, the ironing and so forth. On his salary here, that wouldn't be a problem. He'd talk to Morgan about getting that under way tomorrow.

Washed and dried, he lounged in an armchair with a brandy and a cigar and thought back to his earlier meeting with Chief Justice Sir Frederick Dooley, the second-highest officeholder in the state after the governor. He was another Irishman, a flinty, sharp-eyed fellow with a long white beard and a towering intellect. The twenty rushed minutes Gideon had with him were like being immersed in a laundry-house boiler, and he had no desire to repeat the experience.

With that penetrating intelligence, it's remarkable he doesn't seem to have heard about my unfortunate incident. Long may it stay that way.

Bile rose in his throat at the very thought of Miss Primrose Hetherington.

Dooley hadn't asked about her, but in that short meeting he'd put Gideon through a thorough interrogation about his previous court experience, the barristers he'd worked with and under, and his interpretation of arcane points of law. Gideon was relieved he'd swotted up on colonial cases and precedents. He'd held his own and kept the conversation away from delicate personal areas.

Failure isn't an option out here on the edge of the world. I've nowhere to go if this doesn't work.

Morgan then gave him a quick drive around town, and he'd been favourably surprised by the substantial public buildings constructed in the local sandstone – the Australian Museum, Government House and the University of Sydney, as well as the grand houses in Darlinghurst and Potts Point, many of them with impressive big gardens overflowing with imported trees and flowers.

I can have a fine life here, far from prying eyes. As soon as I've got established in the job, I must find a wife.

Six

Posey ate the beef sandwich Mrs Crowe brought her and watched her mother sleep, searching her blank face for any sign of change in her condition. Her breathing continued uninterrupted, and she showed no signs of nausea or vomiting. All danger signs for concussion, the doctor had said.

Did she have headaches? Confusion? They'd have to wait to check for that once she awoke.

Posey heard the enthusiastic clump of riding boots on the stairs long before Petunia entered the room.

"My turn to take over watch duties." She laughed as she burst in, face fresh and hair windblown. Posey guessed she'd been outside, probably helping the groom with their coach horse. Her green eyes sparkled, and her cheeks and lips glowed with rosy health. "You deserve a break." She paused and gazed at their mother's sleeping form. "How is she?"

Posey gave a light shrug. "She looks much the same," she said. "I hope that's a good thing."

"Perhaps we'd better wake her. See if she's thirsty or got a headache." Petunia settled on the side of the bed and stroked Arabella's brow. "She doesn't have a temperature, but remember, Doctor Appleton said don't let her sleep too long."

Posey's stomach turned over. He had said that, hadn't he? She'd been so immersed in thinking about Silas and his strange reaction to the portrait the day before, she'd completely forgotten.

She stood immediately. "Good idea. Let's wake her and then I'll go down and ask Mrs C. to bring up some of the chicken broth she's making."

Twenty minutes later, a still sleepy Arabella was propped up with pillows and Petunia was feeding her a broth that filled the room with the yeasty smell of poultry and green garden herbs. She blew on each spoonful to cool it before presenting it to Arabella's mouth.

Their mother chuckled. "I did exactly that for you girls, and now look. You're spooning food into me. Oh, how our lives change."

They laughed companionably, and then Posey struck.

"What made you go off like that this morning, Mother? You've never done that before."

Arabella's brow furrowed, as if she was mulling it over. "Ah. I can't recall," she said, glancing up at the painting.

Posey followed her eyes. "Did that painting have anything to do with it? And that doll? Where did the doll come from?"

Arabella's hazel eyes lit up. "Oh, I can answer that one. That's easy. The doll and the painting both came from my grandmother, Cordelia. My cousin Christina brought them out with some other precious things when Grandmother died: the silver tea service in the library, the silver cutlery set we use for dinner parties…" Her voice weakened and drained off. "And a lot of the paintings we display downstairs."

"So why is this one kept up here? And why are you suddenly taking notice of it? Bringing out the doll…?" Posey walked to the dresser. "And pulling out this old invoice? Did this come with the painting?" She crossed back to her mother and held the invoice under her nose.

Arabella screwed up her face and shook her head. "Oh, Posey, you know I can't see without my reading glasses." She fingered the paper between timid fingers, as if she feared contamination. "Possibly… probably… I dug out the box the doll came in when I got home from Hugo's."

Posey dropped the document to the side table and after a moment's hesitation, Petunia resumed her spooning duties.

Arabella swallowed, and her face clouded over, as if she was recalling a past conversation. Then she looked up, her face alive again.

"After I spoke to Minerva. She was such a good friend when we were girls," she said, her voice ringing with enthusiasm.

"Minerva?" Posey's pulse accelerated. "What's Minerva got to do with it?"

"You don't have to be like that, Posey," Arabella said, sounding every inch the reprimanding mother. "I can hear the condemnation in your voice. Minerva was at Hugo's dinner party. We sat next to one another, and we were reminiscing about when Christina was here. On the trip when she brought the painting. Minerva reminded me about it. She asked me if I still had the doll, and of course I said yes." Her brow furrowed. "It was all a bit strange."

Just as suddenly as she'd leapt into normal conversation, she reverted into reverie.

Posey shot a knowing glance to her sister.

Petunia nodded her assent. "She seems to slip in and out of the real world," she whispered. "Is that a symptom of concussion too?"

Posey shook her head. "I don't think so. But I don't like the sound of Minerva being tied up in this."

They had good reason to suspect Minerva Thorne held a longstanding grievance toward their mother and was involved in the claim against their family, but Arabella had been reluctant to believe her old friend guilty of disloyalty.

Petunia scooped up another spoonful of broth, but Arabella sighed and waved it away.

"It's delicious, but I've had enough," she said. "I'm feeling a lot better. Can I get dressed and sit in the garden?"

"Maybe tomorrow," Posey said. "The doctor was adamant you stay in bed for at least twenty-four hours."

Arabella pouted. "I'm fine," she whined. "It was only a bump on the head."

Posey leaned over and stroked her mother's arm. "We still don't know how you got that bump, Mother," she said. "It might not be safe for you to go out. We'll need to keep a close watch on you for the next few days."

She let a long pause follow as Petunia replaced the lid on the soup tureen and set it aside, ready to take downstairs.

"There's still hot tea in the pot, Mother," Petunia said. "Would you like a cup to finish?"

"That would be nice, dear." Arabella settled back on her pillows.

"You mentioned something was strange, Mother," Posey

interjected. "Can you think what it was? Did you see something odd on the street?"

Arabella's head fell back and she let out a peal of her enchanting clear-as-a-bell laughter. "Not my fall," she said, as if that should be obvious. "Something strange about what Minerva said."

"Oh," said Posey, masking her rising concern by speaking as lightly as she could. "What about it?"

Arabella leaned forward and said in a confidential whisper, "She reminded me. Your grandmother left written instructions about the painting. She said it was famous and valuable, but it could not be put on public display. It had to be for private appreciation only. And the doll too. I wasn't to show it around."

"Uh huh," said Posey, feigning mild interest when she was bursting to conduct a full interrogation. "Do you know why that was?"

Arabella gazed into her eyes and then squeezed hers shut. When she opened them again, they were wet with tears.

"Minerva says it's because that darling little girl was murdered." Her gaze flicked to the painting. "She says it's bad luck to even have it." She threw another pained glance at the wall and burst into quiet sobs.

Seven

The dream began with a familiar pattern. Someone knocks on Silas's front door. Unusually, he answers it himself, without any hesitation. His staff must all be on a night off. He swings the heavy oak panels wide open, without checking first who might be calling.

Three beautiful young women, one of whom reminds him of someone close to him, but he can't at this moment remember who, stand on his doorstep, confident and beaming, plainly under the impression he's expecting them.

He looks behind them as he's hit with a wave of cheers and muffled words, and sees a band of others: older men and women, and some young children, who are apparently related to him, all his family follows them. He swallows in shock as it hits him. He doesn't know any of them.

The lass at the door he felt he might know – he stabs a wild guess that she could be his sister's child, his niece – he acts as if that is the case and waits for her to make the introductions.

"I'm Kate, and this is Leslie and Penelope," she says with a smile.

He is too dumbfounded to do anything but pretend he

knows exactly who she is talking about, although he still has no clue.

Kate. Did his sister have a daughter called Kate?

He waves them all in and falls easily into the role of host. They surge behind him, fully at home, laughing and talking amongst themselves as if they're in a familiar club they frequent every week. Except he is falling deeper into a swamp of confusion every minute.

How come you don't know these people?

Are you losing your mind?

What's wrong with you?

They all obviously know you.

And then, just as suddenly as they swarmed in, they're gone, and he's left with lingering smells of tobacco smoke and floral perfume, spilt brandy and heated savouries.

Where did I get all the food?

He doesn't have time to find out before he's in another room he knows only too well.

It's the nursery at Worcester Park Lodge, his childhood home in Surrey.

He and Rosamunde are playing one of her favourite games, cutting out paper dolls their mother buys from the Temple of Fancy. Their favourite sets are for the English Kings and Queens. Silas shivers with pleasure at the memory of his fingers on the heavily embossed garments – the imagined touch of ermine and brocade – as they chatter and laugh their way through an afternoon.

It's not a game considered suitable for seven-year-old boys, he knows that, but he adores his younger sister so much he doesn't mind playing along when they're locked in by a winter gale that's frozen the road to the village.

He's laughing at one of Rosamunde's little jokes and then he's seized with a terror that catches his throat so tight he can't scream. When he opens his eyes, one hand is sticky with blood and the warm air in the closeted room stinks of something too evil to open your eyes to.

I can't open them. I won't open them.

Silas Williams, respected Queen's Counsel, a few years away from his fortieth birthday, lies rigid with terror in his Hunters Hill bed. When he finally opens his eyes, he's convinced his hand is sticky with blood and that the vile coppery stench of it fills the room.

He slides out of bed and vaults for the water closet, only just making it before he spills his guts into the porcelain bowl. He hangs over the basin for a long time afterwards, his face clammy with sweat, his head pounding, and his knees too weak to rise from the floor.

And this is just the start of it. Tonight I've got to face Gideon.

***

"So. What am I to do, Jeavon? You can see that in the circumstances, there's no way I can continue with the Barclay case. But how am I going to explain that to Posey?"

Former police superintendent Jeavon Yates glances up at his lawyer friend, Silas Williams, over a cup of steaming black coffee, his first of the morning. He is savouring it. He scans Silas's face without speaking. His friend was one of the most composed, buttoned-down professionals in Sydney town, always immaculately dressed and so assured and well-informed in his opinions some regarded him a legal oracle.

On the way to the top. To Chief Justice.

Not today, though. This morning he looks like a towel that's been ravaged in a midnight storm and wrung out to dry. It isn't as if his clothing is awry. He wears with flair his trademark morning coat with the wider sleeves and tucked in waist that's become the style. His hair is parted down his scalp, from forehead to neckline, right across his head, in the current fashion. But his mood? His composure? Over many years of acquaintanceship and then close friendship, Jeavon hasn't seen Silas so rattled. He sits opposite, tapping the edge of the small round café table incessantly with his index finger. His good right eye burns with a fervour Jeavon has never seen in him before, a combination of iron-willed determination and panic.

Limited by his peripheral vision, he turns his head from side to side, checking out the room as if expecting the very devil himself to materialise in their midst. And his face! Overnight, everything about him seems to have plummeted into despondency. His tight mouth has turned down at the corners, his cheeks are sunken, and his skin lined and pasty. Even his strong eyebrows seem to droop.

Jeavon decides on the path of least resistance. He shrugs lightly and says, "I don't know, Silas. How are you going to explain to Posey you're chucking it in?" He flashes a wry grin. "I wouldn't want to be in your shoes when you do it."

Silas checked himself for a moment, as if registering Jeavon is playing with him, and then shoots back in a raw voice, "What do you suggest then?"

Jeavon regards him steadily over their empty breakfast plates. "Suggest? Well, now. Maybe that you conduct yourself in the manner you've cultivated to date. To outstanding success, I might add. You walk on in your deliberate, restrained and brilliantly intelligent way, and wait for opportunities to open up. It may not be comfortable or predictable, but I am confident if you proceed as you always have, you'll win through."

"But what about Gideon?"

"What about him? He's the newcomer here. You're the respected counsel. He may even see you as more valuable as an ally than an enemy. Who knows?"

Silas gave a dry, bitter laugh. "Oh, I know all right. Without a doubt. He'll never see me as an ally."

"More fool him then," Jeavon snaps.

Eight

Arabella patted the turquoise-blue mohair rug wrapped around the lower half of her body and gazed up at her twin daughter – the only one of them here with her now, with Poppy off in England with her new husband.

"Posey, I really don't know why you're making such a fuss about all this. I took a tumble yesterday, and now I'm fine again. End of story."

Sunshine streamed in through the window behind her, warming her shoulders, and a fire burned in the sitting room grate. The rug was an unneeded luxury. She rested her hand on it once more, savouring the softness. On the occasional table at her right knee, a cup of hot black Assam brew rested, but she decided not to risk reaching out for it and spilling it on the rug.

She resumed the declaration she'd pondered on when she'd first woken that morning. "I've survived Hong Kong riots and the death of two husbands," she said, charging her voice with irony. "It will take more than a banged-up head to keep me down."

Posey and Petunia gazed back at her from the table where they sat finishing lunch. Posey smiled, her dark eyes shining with understanding. Relief, too, Arabella noted. The poor child was terrified her mother's life was in danger.

"I know, Mother. Forgive us if we're making you feel too cosseted. Understand, you're precious to us." She hesitated, and the smile broadened. "And if anything happens to you while Poppy's away, I'd never live it down," she said. "There is that."

Arabella laughed. She could still recognise irony. Her twin daughters were so temperamentally different, with Poppy the Queen of Society, delighting in balls and the social life of "the first 10,000", while Posey had never been interested in "frivolity", as she called it. Instead, she'd pursued serious ideas, questioning the very foundations of society. She craved change. Better equality for women. Education for the children of the working-class poor. Help and comfort for disadvantaged women.

Arabella was frankly relieved she hadn't taken it into her head to join a religious order. She'd worked with Hawk Eye as an articled legal clerk, even though women were not supposed to work, let alone allowed to become lawyers, and now she gave a lot of her time to the Female Refuge Society, providing succour for women in distress.

Posey rose from her chair and went to her mother's side. "Is that tea going cold, Mother? Do you want me to get Mrs Crowe to freshen it up?"

"It's fine, dear girl. You just relax and stop worrying about me."

"You are looking much better today, Mother. I do grant you that," Posey murmured. Then she hesitated.

Here it comes, thought Arabella. *The inquisition.*

"We are still rather in the dark about that painting, though. Do you think you're up to giving us some more information about it? I know it's hung on your wall for years, but none of us have thought to ask you about it. It was just part of our surroundings. Now we discover it's by a famous artist and may be valuable. I know you say you inherited it from your grandparents. But how did they acquire it? Do you know?"

Arabella thought back to the days when her cousin had arrived with the treasure chest of delights bequeathed to her by her grandparents. She was recently married to James. If she was honest, still grieving the loss of Sir Robert and the other boys, the family they'd built together in Hong Kong. He'd had two sons already when they married, and then they'd had Nathan together. She'd thrived on being the mother of three sons. When Robert died, Sebastian had gone to his maternal uncle in Boston and the oldest John, to California to extend his father's business. She'd come home with Nathan, then ten years old. The painting had filled an emotional gap for her that remained, despite her new life in Sydney with James and their newborn twins.

"My grandmother included a note explaining some of the background," Arabella said. "It will be somewhere in the papers upstairs."

"Who was the little girl in the painting?" Petunia chimed in. "She has a radiance that shines through."

Arabella frowned. "I don't think they ever mentioned any names. All I know is she came from a well-known family in London. It was painted when she was about four years old, and displayed at the National Gallery in London. The Gallery was new then, and was attracting a lot of attention in the art world. All the most acclaimed artists wanted to show their works there, and Sir Francis Grant was one of them.

"I gather he displayed half a dozen original works. He was one of the most praised portrait painters of his day, you know, but *Angel Dreaming* was the one that was an instant hit. The National Gallery wanted to buy it, but the family wouldn't sell it. After it had been on public display for some years, they requested its return, and they kept it private from then on."

"Why was that?" asked Petunia.

The girls had settled close to her on a small settee.

Arabella shrugged. "This all happened after we came to Sydney." She let out a long sigh, suddenly overcome with a foggy fatigue. "The letter Grandmother Cordelia wrote does vaguely hint at some upset or secret. All I know is my grandparents were asked to look after it. They bought it, I understand. But it was all confidential. All I knew was that Grandmother thought it should come to me at her death."

A heavy hammering at the front door interrupted the peace of the breakfast room, and a minute later Mrs Crowe was at the door, followed by Hugo Davenport. At the sight of her lifetime friend and companion, Arabella's tiredness vanished, and her veins pulsed with fresh energy.

She raised her hand and gave him a flippant wave. "Hugo," she called. "How wonderful to see you!"

Petunia and Posey both rose to greet him, but Arabella could sense their lack of enthusiasm. For reasons she couldn't fathom, they were down on her friendship with Hugo, who had been her best friend since James's death.

"We were just chatting about my last unfortunate little escapade and the painting that played a part in my downfall," she cried. "Come and sit down." She pointed to the settee beside her. "I'm sure the girls won't mind resuming their chairs at the table."

"Actually, Mother…" Petunia glanced at the door. "I'd like to get away. I'm meeting Clarrie for a ride in an hour." She flicked her attention to Hugo. "That's okay with you, isn't it, Uncle Hugo? If I take advantage of your wonderful track yet again?"

Hugo was halfway into the room as she spoke. He paused in his progress and gave her a paternal smile. "Of course, Petunia. You're welcome anytime." He fixed his eyes solely on Arabella. "Just like your beautiful mother. How are you, Arabella? I came as soon as I could."

She acknowledged as he stepped across the room that he was no longer the dashing aide-de-camp she'd met at the governor's dinner just before she sailed for Hong Kong. His gait had changed from a graceful stride to a clumsy wobble, his body tipping slightly forward to counter the weight of his girth.

"I knew you would," said Arabella with a warm smile. "You always do."

He sat down with a grateful sigh. "And you're looking so much better than I feared you might," he said. "I see you've still got the bandage on your head. How are you feeling?"

"I'm in great shape," Arabella said bravely. "All the better for you being here."

"And what's this you're mentioning about a painting? How on earth is a painting mixed up in this?"

Arabella glanced at Posey, who was slumped at the table, watching. At the mention of the painting, her face lit up with alarm.

"Mother," she reprimanded. "It is meant to be confidential, remember?"

"Oh, tush," Arabella replied. "Hugo is practically family. I've known him longer than I've known you."

Posey's mouth tightened.

Arabella glanced back to Hugo. "I've got a painting upstairs in my room that I inherited when my admiral grandfather died. It's been on my mind since dinner at your house last week when Minerva mentioned it."

Her eyes roamed the room. She suddenly felt unsettled again. Maybe even a little queer inside. "It's a harmless piece. A portrait of a little girl. Just a pretty little girl. And Minerva said it was bad luck; it was cursed." Her face crumpled again, although she tried to keep it untroubled.

"Oh, Arabella, I'm sorry if she upset you," said Hugo. "You know how she is. She gets funny ideas. You shouldn't take her seriously."

"I know, but somehow I can't help it," she said. "I had horrible dreams after that. Nightmares, really."

Posey jumped in. "Mother!! You didn't tell us about any nightmares."

"I didn't want to worry you. They were nothing!" Arabella exclaimed.

"Minerva's put ideas in your head. I'm sure there's nothing wrong with the painting," Hugo said. He spoke with such force, the jowls beneath his chin wobbled in agreement.

The room fell to silence and then Arabella said, "Posey, why don't you take Hugo up to see the painting? I'd like to get his opinion on it."

She gazed into her daughter's mutinous face. They'd had this argument once before, she and the twins in particular, about including Hugo in "family secrets". They didn't like her doing it.

"Posey?" she said, a warning tone in her voice. "I'm speaking to you."

Posey rose slowly. "Of course, Mother, and I hear you." She turned to Hugo. "Let's go, Hugo. No time like the present."

Nine

"Posey. I'm trying to explain something. Will you listen?" Silas regretted that his voice carried a sharper edge than it should, but he couldn't help that, dammit. This was probably the hardest thing he'd ever faced. Harder even than losing an eye when he was seven years old.

He didn't understand then what the full repercussions would be. This time he understood only too well what might happen, not only to him, but in this case, to Posey, to the whole Barclay clan. They could all be ruined.

Posey's face blanched at his tone, and she covered her mouth with one hand, as if suppressing a response.

Silas sighed loudly. "I'm sorry, Posey. I don't mean to sound angry. But we're facing a highly unusual set of circumstances and I am trying to get that across to you."

They were sitting on a bench in the garden at Barclay Manor. The late afternoon sunlight filtered through the trees, and a butcherbird scuffled at their feet, its smart-aleck jauntiness and pert eye announcing its confidence the world would deliver up what it wanted.

If only I could be that certain.

They were dressed ready for the Law Society reception, him in an austere black-tie ensemble he hoped made him as anonymous as possible. Posey always insisted she didn't care about clothes, but to his eye she was perfectly turned out, as usual. Tonight, she was wearing a slim Ming-blue tunic with a slit to her knee. The matching blue silk stole she'd flung across her shoulders and wound around her neck enhanced her dark hair and flashing deep-brown eyes.

On any other occasion, in any different circumstance, he might have been tempted to take her hand. As it was, they left a long silence, as if each was fearful of offending the other further.

"Then why don't you do that?" Posey asked in a sharp whisper.

"Do what?" Silas retorted. He was losing track.

"Explain," she said in a gust of energy. "Explain everything. Not give me this dillydally, whitewashed version of things which makes no sense." She glared at him. "I know when you're holding back on me, and what you've said so far makes no sense. None at all."

He took a breath to answer. She was right. What he'd told her was fiddle-faddle.

But I can't tell her the whole story. I just can't.

"Your inexplicable reaction to the painting," she continued. "You looked as if you'd seen a ghost. And then this piffle about how you might have to withdraw from our case, that you can't really explain why, but you may be compromised as our lawyer. That you've had dealings with this new Supreme Court judge in the past and he may not regard you with favour."

She shook her head vigorously from side to side, as if flicking water out of her hair. "For goodness' sakes, Hawk Eye. Have you forgotten we tried practically every barrister in town before you agreed to take it? I wasn't exactly keen on the idea of asking. It was only because Poppy pushed it. If you back out now, we'll be totally in the lurch. And, as far as I know, you've been practising law in Sydney since you were eighteen or nineteen years old. If you've 'brushed up' against this new big wig in town, it must have been when you were a mere boy. A little kid. That just doesn't make sense. No one holds grievances that long. Do they?"

You don't know my family.

But all he said was, "I can't explain anything further. But if this new judge acts strangely around me, at least you've been warned." He stood and offered her his arm. "I guess we'd better step out and see."

She took it gingerly, and despite their angry words, her touch sent a warm charge up his arm.

If only I didn't feel like I'm walking to the executioner.

Ten

Silas had been preparing to face the man he hadn't seen for over twenty years from the minute Posey had uttered the words 'Gideon Vane' the day before. But when it came, it was like what he'd heard people say about the long-expected death of a beloved one. No amount of planning and forethought equipped you to handle the real thing. It was always a lot more terrible than you'd imagined.

A selection of Sydney's most celebrated and illustrious citizens gathered in a grand salon at the Royal Hotel in George Street to welcome Mr Justice Vane, otherwise known as the Hon. Gideon Vane, heir apparent to the sixth Earl of Worcester, and entitled to call himself Lord Brook through other convoluted family links.

He was thankful like never before to have Posey at his side, her quick intelligence monitoring the circling crowd; her tall, slim form dressed in the blue silk brocade patterned with swirling red dragons that set her apart from every other woman in the room. Her piercing dark eyes gazed out over the robe's high Mandarin collar with steely resolve, as brilliant and unique as ever.

The official hosts for the evening, the New South Wales Law

Society, had turned on the best of Sydney hospitality, the black-tie waiters circulating with champagne and a selection of hors d'oeuvre featuring local delicacies like angels on horseback (grilled local oysters wrapped in bacon) and roast wallaby tarts. A string quartet provided soft background music to the conversation, which rose in volume as the champagne went down.

The society had been formed more than twenty years before by a group concerned about rogue lawyers, and they enjoyed a warm relationship with the chief justice, who encouraged their activities. It was an informal group with a rather formal name, and the guest list was made up of members of the association – most of the city's top legal men were members – as well as legions of prominent politicians and businessmen, including newspaper owners like the *Sydney Herald*'s Clifford Gilbert. Law and journalism had always enjoyed close links in London and Sydney, with several of the most respected men here tonight, including the chief justice, starting out as journalists.

They'd already talked to Hugo, Clarrie and Rupert Bellamy, a principal in McAllister and Bellamy, another prominent law firm that had refused to take their case even though Rupert was squiring Poppy around town at the time. Too unpopular and damaging, they'd said. Too many important people who want their money back.

Silas experienced a rising dread as they awaited the arrival of the guest of honour. His heartbeat was sluggish, and his chilled fingers were not warmed as the crowd heated the room. He'd withdrawn into his shell, and left all the social effort to Posey. When spoken to, he replied quietly in one-word responses, leaving his companion to catch the conversational ropes.

The spectre of meeting this man who'd changed his life forever, and having his carefully constructed new identity outed in one handshake, possessed him.

Then the moment was upon them. He stood pressed against a back wall, rocking on the balls of his feet, as Sir Frederick entered with Gideon at this side, and the crowd broke into a smattering of applause.

Gideon – Lord Brook, if you will – was of course taller and matured now. The last time Silas had seen him, he'd been eighteen or nineteen, but he would have recognised the familiar emu-like walk anywhere. The man's head sat on top of a long neck that moved in a subtle rhythm, just like the big bird's, eternally positioned to probe its surroundings with a predatory air. When Silas had first seen emus in the northern grasslands, he was mesmerised by how much they reminded him of Gideon.

"It's uncanny," he said to himself now, and momentarily, he felt his inner tension ease.

The impression of quiet suspicion the man gave off was heightened by a long nose in a narrow, serious face that rarely brightened. Gideon's world, it said, was populated by those who wanted to best him, or betray him.

Just as he always had, Lord Brook, the Hon. Gideon Vane stood at Sir Frederick's side, head erect, his neck and body swaying as if responding to an invisible breeze, seeking, searching, always on the alert for enemies.

Nothing's changed. He's still on the offensive. The son eternally ignored. Overlooked. Forgotten. Even with all the titles.

Silas had vowed ahead of time that when it came to their face-to-face moment, he'd direct his one good eye over Gideon's shoulder, avoiding visual contact altogether. Hoping maybe that Gideon would somehow miss him.

But when the moment came, he could not deny his curiosity. Had this man who'd changed his life irrevocably, remade his own? Twenty years had passed since they last saw each other. Had time moulded a different Gideon? Surely, life's inevitable storms would have curbed his arrogance, scoured out his cruel determination to always get his way?

Ten seconds of being locked into Gideon Vane's appalled stare told him all he needed to know about the last twenty years. He felt Posey's light grip on his arm tighten. She'd picked up on the silent fury that charged the air.

His eye patch was always going to be an immediate giveaway. Even if Vane had only scanned him with cursory interest, the black patch would have immediately alerted him to something, someone, out of the ordinary.

Gideon was clever at hiding his shock, however. His wrist had jerked in the handshake as the understanding of who he was meeting burned up his arm and into his brain, but his outward demeanour gave nothing away.

He'd leaned forward into Silas's blind side and said in a quiet but theatrical baritone, "Mr Silas Williams, did you say? I must get the name right. And you're a leading Sydney barrister?" And then he'd leaned back out of the intimate radius he'd created and said, "Well, I never. Life is full of surprises, isn't it?"

After years in Australia, Gideon's enunciation sounded

especially formal and plummy to Silas's ear. He instantly recognised it as the new boy's way of asserting his dominance, even here. The Eton-educated judge, claiming superior status and social ranking over all these former convicts.

Gideon glanced at Posey, hanging silently on Silas's arm, and with an affected courtly air inquired, "And is this Mrs Williams?" with a cutting emphasis on the "Mrs".

Silas gamely followed his lead. "Not my wife, no."

He stepped aside, and Posey's arm slipped clear of him. She hated even seconds in the limelight, but she stood tall and proud, staring Gideon down from her high-cheeked beauty.

"Miss Posey Barclay, meet Mr Justice Vane," Silas said, not attempting to sound in the least bit English.

Posey bobbed in a hint of a curtsy.

"Miss Barclay is a former articled clerk in our law firm, a role she carried out with distinction, I might add."

Gideon's brows climbed to his hairline. "Really?" he said in the same deep, tragedian voice.

Silas thundered on. "And you, Lord Brook? Will Her Ladyship be joining you here in the sub tropics soon?"

Already they were back in the one-upmanship race he could never escape from with Gideon, who, wherever he perched, had to rule the roost.

Gideon jerked back, as if not expecting the question, but quickly adjusted back into his stance of aristocratic superiority.

"No ladyship, I'm afraid. Maybe I will find a candidate in the colony?" He grimaced at Posey and then glanced down the receiving line.

Out... and in... Out... and in... The neck danced

infinitesimally and Silas suppressed a smile.

The waiting line had a long tail that curved through the salon, and Silas grasped his opportunity to escape.

"Mustn't hog all your attention, Judge. Half of Sydney is here hoping for an audience." He glanced pointedly at the people waiting patiently behind them and stepped out of Gideon's orbit. "We need to make way."

***

"What on earth was all that about?" Posey exclaimed as soon as they found a quiet corner in which to perch and recover with a stiff drink. Brandy for him, sherry for her. "That was the most coded conversation I have ever witnessed in my entire life."

She let out a huff of astonishment. "What's gone on between you two? And why did he seem surprised at your name? If he knew you so well, he wouldn't forget it, would he?"

Trust our ever clever Posey to pick up on that.

Silas shrugged. He was swimming in a wave of euphoria, dizzy with light-headed relief. At least Vane had not made a public spectacle. He'd worry about what was still to come tomorrow.

"An old grievance," he said, sipping his brandy. "Let's leave explanations for another time. I just want to enjoy the reprieve."

"Reprieve from what?" said Posey, her dark eyes bright with questions.

He sighed and appealed with a quick smile. "I should have remembered Gideon would never make a public display of emotion, no matter what. That doesn't mean he won't cause trouble."

She regarded him with a measured stare. "This hasn't got anything to do with that painting, does it?"

He wanted to feign ignorance. To widen his eye and ask, "What painting?" But he knew that would never go down with Posey. She was too smart to swallow it. His stomach turned over. Sometimes it was inconvenient to love an intelligent woman. He thought of his malleable French office assistant, Amelie. The question would never have occurred to her.

He looked over her shoulder, unwilling to meet her eyes. "What if it does?" was the best he could summon up.

"Oh, Silas," she whispered in exasperation. "It's not good to have secrets. We've always been honest with one another, haven't we? We've got this enormous case looming that's critical to my family's future. I need to be reassured you're all on board with it."

She turned back to her sherry and placed the glass down on the small table with a definitive clink. "I don't want the rest of this. If you don't want to tell me what's going on, I don't want to sit here sipping sherry and making small talk for the rest of the night."

She drew the silk stole that matched her dress around her shoulders and rose from her seat. "I imagine you probably feel the same way. It feels like we've attended a momentous occasion." She shrugged as she nestled into the wrap of the silk. "Momentous for what? I do not know. But for whatever reason, let's leave."

For a few seconds he was tempted to break his silence and try to explain. That's exactly what Jeavon had urged him to do earlier.

She's going to find out eventually. Either from me or Gideon.

He shuddered at the thought that it might be Gideon, but he still couldn't rally the reserves he needed to tell her the whole sorry saga. Even the thought of Rosamunde and that painting raised a lump in his throat.

"I need more time, Posey. That's all. Please, grant me that."

She shook her head and shot him a glance that said, "I don't know you anymore." Then turned for the door, leaving him to follow.

Eleven

Back in his third-floor Petty's Hotel suite on Church Hill Gideon Vane's equilibrium was rocked by much bigger waves than the unsettling motion of sea legs and imagined swells.

Silas Williams. He's calling himself Silas Williams. And he's very much alive.

Most inconveniently alive, despite what his father had told him. He threw himself onto the luxurious eiderdown, then rolled over on his back and stared up at the apricot silk canopy.

Betrayed again. My father lied to me.

Percival Augustus Vane, the sixth Earl of Worcester and Lord Brook, no less. Who can you believe, if not an earl?

He swore to me he was dead.

Lost at sea. On a stormy channel crossing on his way to France. That's why there was no grave, and no funeral. My mother was told that by the sheriff.

His stomach roiled at the sense of exultation the news had given him at the time. His entire body had hummed with triumph.

I won. At last, I've won!

Did someone make a mistake? Did the constables give his

parents the wrong information? Or is this another one of their little conspiracies to protect the family?

"I don't believe it," he hissed at the overhead hanging. "I just don't believe it."

The empty room returned no answering shout.

How long have they known he's alive? Why do this to me?

And the biggest, most worrying question of all.

How much does he know? And will he tell?

He cast his mind back to his last audience with the earl before he boarded ship for Australia.

"You're my eldest son and you'll inherit this title one day. But until that day comes, you'll not get another penny from me."

According to his father, his adventure with Primrose Hetherington was the last straw.

"I'm not covering for your folly anymore," the old man had said.

Gideon didn't understand why the Hetherington chit had put up such objections to their marriage. He was the best offer she could ever hope for, and he needed a rich wife. They were entirely suited, so he really couldn't understand why her father had raised such a hue and cry.

But never mind. He'd noticed in the brief time he'd spent at the reception that night that Australian women seemed a lot more robust that English ones. They stood firmly planted on the firmament, with something spirited about them. Their confident fashion sense matched their boldness of attitude. They weren't afraid to stand out.

He thought of the wench at Benedict's – Silas's – side, with her Chinese tunic and matching stole. She was a looker.

This judgeship here in Sydney. It's my last chance. I knew that before I got here. I have to make it work. The alternative doesn't bear thinking about.

And I can't risk Benedict spreading spiteful rumours. It would be just like him to spoil things for me.

Look how he's done it before.

He pitched off the bed and sauntered over to the decanter that sat on a silver tray in the corner. He poured himself a drink, letting the amber liquid trickle out as he ruminated.

A thought struck him. *Eternal tarnation! I'll have to get used to calling him Silas. Silas! What sort of a name is that?*

And that woman he had with him? An articled clerk? Never. It shouldn't be allowed.

I'll have to talk to him. Find out what he knows, and get him to agree to keep our little secret.

But what if he won't agree?

Well then, you'll have to find another solution. You've never had a problem with doing that in the past.

His head stopped swimming. His breathing calmed to below its usual frantic pace. His legs were heavy and eyelids drooped. For the first time since he arrived in Sydney town, he felt in control of his destiny.

Everything will work out. It has to.

And Lord Brook, the Earl of Worcester's undisputed heir, fell into a deep, contented sleep.

Twelve

Posey Barclay paused in front of the white villa at 86 Elizabeth Street. It was a traditional Victorian villa, opposite Hyde Park, with a glass-panelled front door and double-hung windows either side of it. A barrister's shingle hung out the front. She stopped and read it, though she'd been here enough times to know it by heart.

Silas Williams, Q.C.
Barrister and solicitor
"Let justice be done though the heavens fall."

She was nervous about this meeting, she admitted to herself. Ever since Silas had viewed the Angel Eyes painting, he hadn't been acting himself, and she didn't understand why. She'd worked with him for three years, and got to know him well. He was nearly twenty years her senior, and she'd discovered in the last couple of days that she relied on his steady authority, his integrity, above almost anything. Call that into question and her world tilted on its axis.

Yes, she'd turned down his proposal of marriage a year ago,

but not because he wasn't dear to her heart. If she was going to marry anyone, it would be someone like Silas. But she was not going to marry. It was a statement of her beliefs. Women did not get a fair go in this world, and married women were even worse off than single ones, with fewer legal and property rights. Just ask the women she'd seen come through that very door in front of her, desperately seeking protection from their husbands.

Even a woman with a loving husband could find herself cast out when he died. Unless he'd specifically named her as their children's guardian before his death, even her children could be taken away from her.

She shivered as the anger that always boiled deep down in her bubbled up again.

Forget it, Posey. This topic is not for today.

She closed the parasol she held for protection against the strong southern sun and marched up two wooden front steps. As she opened the door, a brass bell announcing her arrival chimed cheerily, and Amelie, Silas's new office attendant, glanced up from the desk at the back of the room and smiled. Posey responded with a businesslike nod. As usual, Amelie wore a pretty pastel dress patterned in spring flowers – daisies and the like – that added to her refreshing appeal.

"Miss Barclay," Amelie called. "Our ten o'clock appointment. Mr Williams is expecting you, I believe."

Mr Williams, said with the hint of a French accent, and was that a barely audible lisp she hadn't noticed before? *She's not his articled clerk though*, a grumpy internal voice huffed.

"Thank you," she said. "I know my way in."

Silas rose from his desk with a frown as she entered. "Posey," he said. "You really didn't need to make a formal appointment."

"Oh, I think I did," she said. "You are our solicitor. And there are things we need to discuss." She hesitated behind the chair placed right before his desk.

"Of course," he said, "Do sit down, please."

In the significant pause that drew out between them, she studied his face. Its well- proportioned planes were pale and drawn, the lines in his forehead below the dark cowlick that often stood up at the front of his crown were deeper than usual.

Poor man. Stressed out and not getting enough sleep.

"We haven't really talked about the case," she began tentatively, when he still didn't speak. "There's been so much else going on. How did you fare in your Victorian travels?"

What with his trip, Posey's wedding, and the furore over Arabella's injury, the painting and Gideon, they still hadn't had a detailed talk about strategy.

He swallowed hard. "As you might expect, some promising evidence, and a few possible stumbling blocks. Which would you prefer to hear about first?"

She let out a relieved breath. Hopefully, they were back on their normal track.

"Tell me the good news first. We've had enough bad news to handle the last few days." She shot him a weak, apologetic grin.

He didn't seem to notice, preoccupied as he was by papers on his desk.

The main purpose of his trip south was to prepare their defence against the claim losers in the Barclay's collapse were attempting to bring against other assets, including a productive gold mine in Ballarat owned by the sisters' half-brother Nathan Russell. They suspected the claimants were trying to make a case for Nathan being tied in with his stepfather's affairs, or for James to have been entangled in Nathan's mine ownership. Either way, they wanted to claim the mine as an asset they could use to recompense them for their losses in the bank.

Silas reached over and grasped a sheet of paper from his desk. "A chap called Jeremiah Hawkins has been Nathan's mine manager since almost forever. I understand he's a good sort and they get on well, but I haven't interviewed him. However, he is willing to testify, and he's coming to Sydney next week, so you'll have a chance to meet him."

He reached across to another pile of documents. "And I've tracked down the original mining licence. It was registered solely in Nathan's name. No one else's. That has to be good for us."

He glanced up; his face still troubled. Posey realised he had hardly met her eyes the whole time she'd been sitting there.

"And the not-so-good part?" she asked.

"The fellow who holds the licence next to Nathan's – a man called Abe Whitehurst – has laid a formal complaint about the mine's boundaries. He's claiming the disputed boundary shows fraudulent documentation on Nathan's part." Silas sat back and brought his hands to his throat in a triangle. "I might add, Whitehurst's side is yielding nowhere near the gold that Nathan's is. Quite an incentive to dispute the boundary."

Posey smiled, and again Hawk Eye did not relax or return the gesture.

"Anything else?" she asked.

"Yes. One of Nathan's disgruntled employees, Cornelius Kneebone, has publicly criticised the way Nathan runs things. No real meat to it, but he could be dangerous if the other side got hold of him. He might be tempted to lie to get his revenge if he thought he could get something out of it."

Posey relaxed back in her chair. "And overall? Were you satisfied with what you picked up, the people you talked to?"

Silas rubbed his hands together, thinking.

He's so deliberate and prudent. Just what you need in a barrister.

"I talked to a lot more people than the ones I've mentioned," he said. "I might ask Jeavon to follow up on a couple of leads. But, yes. Overall, I believe we have an excellent case." He hesitated. "I'm just unsure if I will be able to proceed with it," he said, enunciating every word with care. "If Gideon Vane is selected to preside, I think it would be in your best interests to disassociate from me. I obviously will be perfectly willing to brief any new legal counsel."

Posey's stomach felt as if it had dropped to her knees. She half started up from her seat.

"You what? You can't… You can't desert us like this."

"Posey, I'm not deserting you. I am trying to explain that if Judge Vane is appointed to oversee the trial it would be best for you if I was a thousand miles from here."

He spoke slowly, patiently, as you might to a child, and it infuriated her.

"What is it with you and this new judge?" she cried. "Why won't you tell me what's going on? Don't you trust me?"

He leaned back. "It's not a matter of trust, Posey. There are things I can't talk about right now, that's all. That may change in the future. But not right now." He attempted a smile.

A fatherly smile, she thought, and it made her even more indignant. He might be the older of the two of them, but he could treat her like an adult. He always had before.

"I knew him in England, and we had a big disruption. That's all I can say."

"A disruption? Like a physical fight or something? Surely, it's not all that enduring. Why can't you fix it? Apologise or whatever? Forgive him?"

He sighed, but the air of paternal patience didn't slip.

"It's not that simple, Posey. I wish it were." He gathered up the papers on his desk, tidying them into a neat pile. "I want you to give some thought to who you'd like to brief to take over from me. If we're finished here, I'd better get on to my next appointment."

And it was at that moment Posey Barclay felt the entire weight of hearing "No" from Hawk Eye Williams land on her shoulders

Until now, she'd always had a tiny, secret hope that the door to a marriage between them might still be open. If she'd ever changed her mind, that is.

I've lost him.

As she rose and padded out, the enchanting Amelie was ushering in the next client, a harried middle-aged woman with two small children in tow.

I've lost him. And he's not coming back.

Thirteen

There were too many dogs loose in the streets, and Hyde Park could never compare with its namesake in London – sad, drivelled up, spot of desert that it was. But as Gideon Vane gazed around the candlelit table at Clifford and Cassandra Gilbert's imposing villa on Woolloomooloo Hill, he admitted Sydney had its attractions. Like this Gothic Revival mansion with towers and turrets set in a large garden, more like a castle than a house, and it had only been built thirty years ago! The house perched on the edge of the stunning harbour and through the windows he glimpsed the reflecting sparkle of light on water.

And there he was imagining he'd be coming to some convict settlement where they still lived in mud-brick huts. Well, that might be an exaggeration, but he had not pictured himself dining in surroundings that easily matched those he enjoyed at home.

At the oak dining table that seated sixteen he was enjoying the hospitality of newspaper proprietor Clifford Gilbert. The company sharing in the occasion included Clifford's sister Eudora, barrister and Queen's Counsel Hugo Davenport, and a bombastic American named Elias Astor who claimed to be part of the famous Astor family, one of the richest in New York. On white linen, they sipped a range of exquisite European wines from crystal glassware, and dined from an extensive menu, which included a first course of lobster mayonnaise, followed by main courses of roast duck and olives, and roast beef and beetroot. Dessert – which had just arrived – included Vienna creams, tipsy cake trifle, and Charlotte Parisienne.

Gideon turned to Eudora Gilbert on his right and acknowledged his surprise. "I say. You Australians certainly know how to live well. I admit I had no idea it was this good here." He gave a self-conscious chuckle and raised his glass in a private toast with his host's sister. "To Australia and Australians."

Eudora smiled and clinked glasses. She had lovely sparkling emerald eyes, along with copper-red hair that set them off to perfection. She'd maintained an animated, informed conversation through the long meal, obviously well drilled in what was expected of an upper-class girl.

No different to back home, really, he thought. *I don't know why I thought it would be.*

One of the upper ten thousand. That's how she'd laughingly referred to them. The Yanks used the same term because – well, they didn't have the real thing, did they? Gideon's chest warmed, and he didn't think it was just because of the alcohol he'd consumed.

There's nothing like a true-blue English lord. That should carry some weight around here.

"And, Eudora. How do you like to fill your days?"

"Me?" Her finely arced brows rose. The black-jet pendant at

her throat swung forward and she caught it with her left hand. She gestured to her mauve-and-black dress.

"Oh, forgive me," he said, resting his hand gently on her wrist. "I hadn't realised till just this minute. You're in mourning. I was so captivated by those beautiful eyes I hadn't got to your skirt."

As was the fashion, the later months of mourning often converted from all black to a lavender and black combination, and Eudora wore a lavender top with a black skirt.

He left a long gap for her to jump in to the conversation and she obliging did.

"I lost my mother, Clara, last summer. Everyone loved her. She was one of Sydney's most influential matrons and hostesses."

He sensed she was on the verge of tears. He placed his hand back over hers and squeezed a little more firmly. "I am so sorry to hear that," he said. "I lost my mother a few years ago, but the pain remains. I know exactly how you feel. They are irreplaceable, aren't they?"

"Oh, that's so true," she said with a sad laugh. "I'm very lucky to have Clifford and Cassandra. They look after me." She hesitated and gazed deep into his eyes. "Forgive me for getting personal at a first meeting, Lord Brook, but do you have brothers and sisters?"

"I do not," he said. "One sister died of yellow fever when she was very young. And another brother drowned, a few years back now. In the English Channel, travelling to France. So tragic. I'm the only one left."

The chinking of a teaspoon against crystal glassware broke their companionable silence.

"Attention, everybody." Clifford Gilbert was calling the group to order. "It's that time again. Men to the billiards room, women to the library."

"Ah. Just when we were enjoying ourselves. I like my brandy, I grant you. But I think I prefer the present company more."

Eudora's face blushed a pretty pink. "Careful, Your Grace," she said with a warm smile. "More compliments like that and I could become an utter nuisance."

"Never."

She giggled at his instant riposte and raised her index finger like a nursery room teacher. "Keep mindful of where we are, Your Grace, or we'll both be in trouble," she admonished.

They were both laughing as they rose to go their separate ways.

These Australian women. They're much more forward than the fawning English ones. It makes a gent's life so much easier.

Fourteen

"Hugo's not *that* bad, and he *is* an experienced lawyer. He'd probably be happy to take it on for Mother's sake. Have you even asked him?"

Petunia sat astride the straight-backed kitchen chair as if she were on a horse, and leaned towards Posey, her blonde locks falling around her face.

Does my sister think of anything but horses? Posey asked herself irritably.

Petunia was watching her through her fringe, with an open, inquiring look, waiting for her answer.

"No, I haven't asked Hugo. I don't trust him, you know that. And neither does Poppy," she said, suddenly feeling she needed her older twin by ten minutes to back her up.

"But is that entirely fair?" Petunia persisted. "He's devoted to Mother. You can see that. He's very generous to me, allowing me free use of his stables. And what has he ever done to suggest we shouldn't trust him?"

"I don't know," Posey wailed. "Everything is collapsing around me and I don't know what to think anymore. I never thought Hawk Eye would let us down either, but look what's happened? Who *can* we trust? I just don't know anymore…"

Petunia got up and came around to Posey's side of the breakfast table. She stood behind her sister and gently moulded her shoulders with her strong equestrian hands.

"It will be all alright, Posey. What's going on with Hawk Eye is bewildering, but it will all come out soon. And I'm sure he's still the knight in shining armour you think he is. There's just some complication we don't understand yet."

"I'm not looking for a knight in shining armour," said Posey irritably. "I'm not a damsel in distress. And if there's a complication, as you call it, then why can't he tell me about it? Two heads are always better than one."

"So says the girl who's determined never to marry," said Petunia with a laugh, as she stopped her massage and moved back to her original spot astride the chair.

"And Mother will be brassed off if she finds you sitting like that," Posey retaliated, though she had the grace to laugh too. "I don't know how many times she's told you it's unladylike. Starting when you were about five."

"What will I be brassed off about?" Arabella's voice was light and gay as she paused in the doorway and surveyed the room.

She'd recovered remarkably well from her fall, Posey observed. Her posture was straight and confident, and she was wearing one of her "mistress of all she surveyed" dresses. It was a dark-green-and-maroon brocade with apple-green satin sleeves puffed to the elbow and then narrowed down to fit snugly at her slim wrists. A deep green waistcoat that hugged the curve of her waist and hips reminded anyone who saw her she wasn't an old grannie yet.

"Oh, I see," said Arabella with a flitting smile. "Our equestrian is missing her horse. Well, just this once I'll pretend I haven't noticed. And, Posey? You're not to tell tales." Arabella's emerald eyes sparkled as they met Posey's darker ones. Her mother considered her for a few moments. "You're looking downcast, Posey. What's gone wrong today?"

Posey flicked a glance to Petunia and then drew herself up with a sigh. "Hawk Eye has gone all strange on us. He's talking about not being able to represent the family in the case anymore. He's going on about a potential conflict of interest if that new judge is selected for it. But he won't tell me why."

Arabella sank down at her usual place at the head of the table and glanced at Petunia. "Could you ask Mrs Crowe to bring some fresh coffee, pet," she said.

In one swooping movement, Petunia rose and started for the door.

"Oh, and some cookies, if she has any freshly baked." Arabella flung the request at Petunia's departing back. She turned back to Posey. "The new judge?" she asked. "I've been out of circulation for a few days. What new judge?"

"Gideon Vane," Posey replied. "The Earl of Worcester's son. He arrived a few days ago. He's got the honorary title of Lord Brook until his father dies and he takes over the entire estate. He's the new appointment on the Supreme Court. Hawk Eye's been acting strangely ever since he got here."

Her mother's mobile face settled into quiet thought. "The Earl of Worcester, you said? Percival Augustus Vane, you mean?"

Posey shrugged. "I've no idea what his father's name is. How do you know him?"

"I don't, really. My father couldn't stand him, so we never visited. But Mother knew his wife, Henrietta – she always called her Etta. They were absolutely best friends from school days, but after she married Percival Augustus, they could only see each other when the men were away, and that wasn't very often."

Another good reason to never marry, Posey thought mutinously.

"Really? What a strange coincidence that you should know them," she said.

"Well, as I say, I didn't know them well. Not really. Mother and Etta exchanged letters, but they grew apart as their families aged."

Petunia bounced back in, followed by Mrs Crowe and a tray of coffee and cookies.

"Wonderful," said Arabella. "Thank you so much." She relaxed back in her chair and sipped the hot brew Petunia poured for her. Then she refilled her and Posey's cups and they nibbled at Mrs C's freshly baked shortbread in silence.

There was a peaceful hiatus, each of them buried in their thoughts, sipping coffee.

Then Arabella spoke: "Me knowing the family is not so much of a coincidence," she said, her face dreamy and her voice sounding as if she was miles away. "You know how it is in England. The posh folk are all very tight. They track each other. But what seems odd is Gideon Vane turning up in Sydney right now."

Posey had been back to brooding on her most recent conversation with Hawk Eye, going over his words in her mind. She reluctantly turned her attention to her mother.

"Odd, Mother? How so?"

"The painting upstairs. *Angel Dreaming.* My mother got it from her good friend, Etta. The earl's wife."

The air whooshed out of Posey's chest so fast she was momentarily light-headed.

"The painting?" she said, her voice sounding strangely tinny and far away. "It came from the Earl of Worcester's estate?"

"Well, not exactly," Arabella said. "It belonged to Henrietta. It was her personal property. Percival had officially designated it that way because he commissioned the work for her as a thank-you for being such a wonderful mother to his children. I think he started planning it soon after Rosamunde was born. He was so thrilled to have a daughter after two sons. I mean, obviously he was grateful for the sons, but…" She arched her brow at Posey. "But you might be surprised to hear the earl was desperate to have a daughter. He'd got his two sons. The heir, and his backup, should bad fortune strike. But he adored his daughter from the day she was born. That's what Mother said, anyway."

Posey sat glued to her chair, as if stunned by a thunderbolt dropped from above. Her mouth opened and closed involuntarily. *I must look like one of those goldfish in a tank*, she thought.

"Are you saying…" she whispered tentatively. "Are you saying that the painting upstairs, the one we call Angel Eyes, is of Lord Brook's sister?"

Her mother's eyes widened to match her shock. "I… I suppose I am. Unless this man is an imposter. I can't remember what Etta's two sons were called. It might be another branch of the same family, I suppose. Maybe Percival died and someone else has inherited in the meantime. And this Vane is *his* son."

Her mother's eyes fluttered in confusion. She fidgeted in her chair. "But there is one way we might find out."

"Oh?" said Posey, her eyes fixed on Arabella with an intensity she'd rarely felt before. "And what is that?"

"The papers," Arabella said, sounding vague again. "The papers that came with the painting. I think there was a letter from the Countess Henrietta. Papers proving provenance." Her brow furrowed and her cheeks flushed in annoyance. "I can't recall the details. Something like that. It will all still be there, in my boxes upstairs. They might shed some light on things."

"Oh, my goodness, Mother," Posey cried, jumping up from her chair. "Why didn't you mention this before?"

Arabella rose in a more dignified fashion and held out her hand. "I didn't know it was important before," she said in a disgruntled tone. "And no one is rifling through my papers without me being present. Not even one of my daughters. Not while I'm still here on earth, anyway."

She held out her arm. "Escort me upstairs, and maybe we'll find something important."

Fifteen

Somewhere in this letter she would uncover what Hawk Eye was hiding from her. Posey knew it. Thirty minutes of panicky searching through Arabella's boxes followed, before she uncovered the missing letter. It seemed like an eternity.

"There it is." Arabella whooped with triumph, pointing at a yellowed envelope and then collapsing into sneezing. "That box is certainly dusty, but I knew it was there somewhere. I'd forgotten it was in that old chest of stuff from my Hong Kong days. I haven't opened that in years. I must have put it in there because it arrived soon after I got back from the East and I was still sorting things out."

She gazed into Posey's face with a sombre mouth. "I'd lost Robert and then found James. I was dumb-fogged. Most days I didn't know if I was coming or going." She settled on the edge of her bed and patted the space beside her. "Sit here, Posey, and read it out to me. My eyesight isn't as good as it was."

Posey shuffled down the side of the bed so she was close enough that her mother could read over her shoulder. She drew a big breath, pushed down the bubbling excitement rising within her, and began reading.

My dearest Louisa,

Your father, the Admiral, was kind enough to take this painting into his care when the pain of seeing it every day became too great. I know he plans to leave it to you when the time is right, and I want to reassure you that Percival and I couldn't imagine it in safer hands than yours, my dear friend.

You are one of the few people who understands the need for the utmost secrecy in where and how it is displayed. I love to think of it hanging where those who understand the travesty of what has occurred can feast on my darling's beauty and innocence, but you also know why it's not possible to allow it to be generally exhibited.

I implore you to keep it hidden from the world, for it carries a heavy burden of sorrow and secrets. In your keeping, may it find the peace and solace that has eluded our family.

Posey drew in a quick breath and slapped her hand over her mouth as she too broke into a sneezing fit. "This paper is certainly dusty," she said.

"It's been there for nearly twenty years, so it's not surprising," Arabella said with a raised brow.

Posey's mouth tipped up in one corner and she lifted the letter to continue.

May this painting serve as a symbol of the love and beauty Rosamunde brought into our lives for too short a time, and may you cherish it as we have.

Guard it well, and let no one uncover the secrets it holds, secrets that, for the sake of the family, must never be revealed.

Your loving friend always,
Henrietta, Countess of Worcester

Arabella cleared her throat. "My mother died soon after we reached Sydney, when I was fifteen," she said. "Father was hoping the Sydney climate would be good for her health, but it wasn't to be. The Admiral and Cordelia had never much approved of their marriage. That's why the painting came straight from Grandmother Cordelia to me."

Posey glanced up at Arabella from the musty-smelling parchment with trembling fingers. She let a long silence draw out between them before she asked in a scratchy voice, "Henrietta? Countess of Worcester? Spell it out for me, Mother. Is this Judge Gideon Vane part of the same clan?"

Arabella shrugged, as if it was of no consequence to her. "I don't know, Posey. Possibly. I didn't know the family myself. My mother, Louisa, never mentioned them when I was growing up."

Posey bit her lip, her distracted eyes focused on the painting, but seeing nothing that would give her the answers she wanted.

"If we are in possession of a controversial painting that this judge thinks belongs to his family, we'll be in even more trouble than we are now," she said.

Arabella shook her head. "Oh, he couldn't possibly think that. I mean, Etta's letter makes that clear." She hesitated and wriggled to get herself more comfortable on the edge of the bed. "Besides, there's a note from Cordelia, that she included in the bundle, somewhere as well. Explaining why she was sending it on to me."

"Oh," Posey exclaimed, hitting the side of her head with a blunt palm. "Why didn't you say before? Where is it?"

Arabella gazed at her in blank amusement, and then gestured to the dusty Hong Kong chest. "In there somewhere," she said. "With the rest. And you don't need to get overexcited."

Posey grabbed at the chest and pulled it closer to her feet. With jerky, impatient fingers, she sorted through the papers at the bottom and drew out another antique envelope, spotted with brown age marks, carrying her grandfather's crest. It was addressed to her mother.

The Hon. Arabella Pemberton
From Lady Cordelia Fairfax,
June 24, 1854

She glanced towards her mother and back to the paper as she began reading again.

My darling Arabella,

This is a treasure your grandfather and I acquired from Henrietta, the Countess of Worcester. She was one of your mother's dearest friends until unspeakable tragedy cost the life of her only daughter, the beautiful Rosamunde.

Etta withdrew from society as a result. Her life was never the same again, and this famed painting of sweet Rosamunde – once the focus of national celebration – was too painful for her to gaze upon in the days afterwards.

The painting was part of Etta's private estate, gifted to her by her husband, Percival Augustus Vane, sixth Earl of Worcester, and she wanted it to find a secure home far from prying eyes.

The story behind it is not mine to tell, but I pray you will understand the need for discretion and kindness and keep it safe from curious sightseers, for it holds secrets that must never be revealed.

Your mother's untimely death, and the difficulties of shipping to Australia, meant that we held onto it for her, planning to pass it on when the time was right. That time sadly never came, so here we are, passing it on to you, the next generation, to give it the care it deserves.

Your loving grandmother,
Cordelia

Posey sat back and placed the second letter on the bed on top of the first. "What a mess," she said. "These letters only go so far in explaining the significance of this painting. And that leaves us in a worse position than before."

"How do you mean?" Arabella asked, her brow creasing above her alert green eyes. "I don't understand."

"We're committed to secrecy about some other family's secret when we don't even know what it's all about," she said. "It puts us in an extremely awkward position. Do we tell Lord Brook, or Judge Vane, or whatever it is we call him about it, or do we keep it a secret? After all, we might be breaking Cordelia's insistence on secrecy by even revealing to him it's here."

Her mother's eyes widened with understanding. "Oh. I see what you're getting at."

"And we've already shown it to Silas and Hugo. I guess that qualifies as having already broken the promise."

Arabella gave a wave of her hand that was intended to indicate that was 'of no consequence.' "Hugo wouldn't betray a confidence," she said. "You made it clear to him, didn't you, that he's to tell no one?"

"Of course," said Posey. "But I'm afraid I don't have the same confidence in his discretion that you do. And what about Hawk Eye?"

"Oh, he's a model of circumspection," Arabella said stoutly. "He'd never say anything to anyone."

Posey found herself agreeing, but not for the same reasons.

"This doesn't get me any closer to understanding why Silas was rattled by the painting. And what the feud with Gideon Vane is all about."

Sixteen

The Saturday lunch party had ostensibly been arranged as an exclusive group to watch the Commodore's Cup Regatta, but Gideon knew it was really a covert way for Eudora to spend time with him again without her brother and sister-in-law as chaperones. Their mild flirtation the other evening had apparently been a mutual pleasure, and Eudora assembled an agreeable party to watch the friendly rivalry on the water between locally designed-and-built racing yachts and imported competition from America and England.

She'd sent the invitation to his hotel by messenger the previous day, and when he'd arrived, she'd explained that the racing between England and America a few years back, racing which had led to the birth of the America's Cup, had captured the Aussie imagination.

"The contest inspired our local sailors. Several big boats will race today, and the weather's perfect for good viewing, so I hope you enjoy it. The rivalries are already hot. The *Chance*, a schooner yacht which was the flagship of the Royal Thames Yacht Club until it came out here, and the *Xarifa*, an Australian-designed sailing yacht, will be racing.

"*Xarifa* has already beaten *Chance* once, so of course, all the locals think that proved local superiority. Bill Walker, who owns the *Chance*, will be keen to prove them wrong."

Already Gideon was feeling as if he was developing his own "set" in Sydney. Hugo Davenport and the American Elias Astor, who he'd met at her brother's house two nights before, were present, as well as two new guests, Dr Ambrose Blackwood, a prominent physician, and his brother Jasper.

Jasper, it seemed, was a former clergyman who worked as a tutor for wealthy Sydney families, Gideon understood mainly for young men requiring extra coaching to get into overseas universities. Jasper was currently staying with the Bishop of Sydney, Phillip Stanton, coaching one of his sons for Cambridge University entrance exams.

An eccentric older woman, Minerva Thorne, an old friend of Eudora's mother, completed the party. Gideon didn't know what to make of her. With an orange headband around long greying hair, and a braided tangerine bolero over a full green skirt, she struck him as more of a gypsy than a respectable matron.

Rather an odd companion for Eudora, he mused.

Wattlewood, Eudora's manor house overlooking the sea, was every bit as impressive as her brother's establishment. Gideon understood she was living in the family home because of her mother's recent death, and though that may not continue when she married, clearly the family had sterling credentials.

They'd enjoyed a delightful light lunch before moving to the terrace, binoculars in hand, to watch as a cannon sounded the start of racing.

"Are you a yachtsman, Lord Brook?" Dr Blackwood asked him genially, as they settled into rattan chairs around a mosaic-topped outdoor table.

"Not at all," Gideon admitted with a wry grin. "I confess I've never been on one. The hunt and hounds is my chosen sport."

"Ah. Then it will all be new to you. Sydneysiders are proud of their sailing prowess. I'm not sure if you are aware, but the Royal Sydney Club is the only one outside of England chartered by the Prince of Wales himself, granted permission to carry the blue ensign of the Royal Navy."

"Goodness. No, I wasn't aware of that."

"As the flagship of the Royal Club, *Chance* will fly the ensign today, I would fully expect."

Gideon found the light dazzling. It was hard to keep his eyes open. It was so bright. As for the national rivalry, the British were clearly superior, no matter how the race ended.

He turned his attention to Dr Blackwood. "What about you, Doctor? Are you a sailor?"

Blackwood grunted. "It might look glamorous, but it's a colossal waste of money, if you ask me."

Hugo leaned in. "Not grumbling about money, are you again, Ambrose?" He addressed Gideon directly. "Ambrose is one of the many who lost investments in a financial collapse last year. They're still fighting to reclaim some of it."

He looked thoughtful. "In fact, you might become involved. There's a big case pending, and they haven't appointed a judge to preside yet. Silas Williams is acting for the defence."

Gideon's body reacted as though he'd been branded with a

hot iron, but he fought to mask his surprise. Every muscle and sinew tensed as he said, "Williams...? Do I know him?"

He put on a good show of pausing to think.

"Ah yes, I think I recall him from the chamber's cocktail party. Is he the chap with the black eyepatch? We only met briefly."

Hugo nodded. "That's him. He's a darned fine attorney. He's acting for the Barclay family. James Barclay went bust last year, taking down a lot of other people with him."

Ambrose made a disgusted sound in his throat. "You're not wrong there. Half the town – well the ones who matter – was affected. And a lot of them think there's skullduggery there. It just doesn't fit."

Gideon's interest quickened. "Skullduggery? Why?"

Hugo intervened. "Now, Ambrose, you see that's wishful thinking." He faced Gideon and said, "Malcontents have tried to make a case, because everyone was so shocked. Barclay was a good man. No one expected his investment house to fail. But these things happen. He had a ne'er do well son-in-law he allowed too much freedom."

He turned back to Blackwood. "You know as well as I do, Ambrose, that Brock Bartle was found to have been the real bad egg. He was the one who put the son-in-law up to it. The investigation earlier this year proved it."

Ambrose Blackwood clenched his jaw, as if refusing to accept anything Hugo had said. "That might be so, but there are still unanswered questions, in my opinion. It will be a good thing to have the business aired in the courts. Who knows what we might discover?"

Ambrose turned to Gideon. "Barclay's got a stepson who's raking in the gold from his Ballarat mine, and some people think they should be able to get their hands on some of that as compensation. Maybe the old man had shares in the mine? Who knows?"

"So, where's James Barclay now?" Gideon asked.

"Dead," said Hugo. "Some say the collapse broke his heart. He died not long afterwards."

"And that woman I saw Williams with at the party?" Gideon affected disinterest, but he was turning somersaults inside. "Didn't he say her name was Barclay?" He hesitated and glanced out at the water for a few seconds. Once again, the bright light blinded him. He shut his eyes tightly for a moment and opened them again.

"Yes, he would have." Hugo again.

"So, she's James Barclay's daughter? The one Williams said was an articled law clerk?"

Hugo smiled indulgently. "The same. Posey Barclay. She's one smart young woman."

"Is there anything going on there?"

"You mean like a pending marriage?" Hugo smiled again. "If there was, I'd probably be one of the first to know. I'm an old friend of Arabella's, Posey's mother. Posey is set on remaining single. She's one of those… what do you call them? Suffragist types? Who think women get a rough deal?"

He cast his eyes out to the harbour and raised a pair of binoculars. "Let's say Silas would like there to be something going on, but Posey seems committed to remaining a spinster. She's hard set on her course." He pointed out in front of him and guffawed. "Rather like that whaler that's bearing down on *Chance* right now. Are they going to redirect and avoid a collision?"

All thoughts of the Barclay family, of Posey, and of the case, were forgotten in the excitement of the action on the water.

Except by Gideon.

What a gift! I can see it now. Everything I need to destroy him utterly.

Seventeen

"I'm in the devil of a jam, Jeavon. And I don't know how I'm going to get out of it." Silas sat with the former police superintendent sipping coffee on his friend's back verandah, while tame butcherbirds squabbled over the remains of last night's shepherd's pie dinner, laid out on the ground before them.

Hawk Eye and the old cop often shared these daytime breaks together, and since Jeavon's son Thomas had left for London with Poppy, they'd become even more frequent. Silas understood Jeavon missed Thomas because they were tight companions, and he'd feared his health might deteriorate because of his son's absence. However, he was glad to see the opposite seemed to have happened.

He'd pulled Jeavon into acting as an adviser on his cases, and the old police officer flourished with putting his expertise to fresh use. His knowledge of the criminal justice system, and his remarkable network of contacts amongst both the legal profession and Sydney's seedier underworld, had proven invaluable.

"Tell me about it, Silas. And don't leave out anything important."

Jeavon gazed at him across the pine tabletop, purpose-milled for outdoor use. If the weather allowed it, he spent a good part of his day outside, soaking up the peace of his subtropical backyard.

Don't leave out anything important.

The wily old badger senses I'm not telling him everything, Silas mused. *But how can I?*

He fixed Jeavon with a serious stare. "A statutory declaration, Jeavon. I can't tell you everything. You'll have to leave it at that. And I can't tell you why."

Jeavon raised a shaggy grey brow. "Can't? Or won't? Everything said here is treated as privileged information. And I'm not one to blab. You know that."

Silas nodded. "Totally right on both counts, Jeavon. But it's upsetting. Extremely so. Until I decide how much of it pertains to what is happening today, I prefer to let bygones be bygones. I don't want to dig up ancient personal history if I can avoid doing so."

He glanced back at the butcherbirds. One of them had stolen away most of the food and was defending his hoard from his competitors. Silas thought of how much they reminded him of himself and Gideon. Two determined individuals who could never back down from confronting each other.

"All that is relevant for today is that this new Supreme Court judge, Gideon Vane and I have a disastrous history. I don't want to go into specifics, just take it as understood. A violent event occurred between us. One with life-changing consequences. I came to Australia to get away from him, truth be known. I never thought I would have to see him again, and as far as I am concerned, that was heaven on earth."

He flicked Jeavon a wry smile. "I don't know if you've ever made a lifelong enemy, Jeavon? But if you have, you'd have just an inkling of how things are between Gideon and me."

"And you think this is going to affect your future work? If you have a case come up before him, I mean? "

"Exactly," said Silas. "In particular, the Barclay case. It will be decided by a judge, not a jury. And with all the influence and money weighted on the other side, there will be a lot of political pressure brought to bear."

Jeavon stared at him intently, nodding his head slowly, as if he was digesting Silas's words. "And if this Vane fellow sits on the bench for it, he'll do his best to make sure you lose?"

"Yes. We'd be starting out with the cards stacked against us. I can't put Posey under that sort of risk. And I can't explain to her why."

Jeavon jerked back in his chair, as if that last statement was unexpected. "And why, pray, is that? I'd have thought of all the women of my acquaintance, Posey Barclay is the most down to earth. More than any other I can think of, she handles difficult – shall we say, even unsavoury situations – with calm good sense. Look at the women she's assisted through the refuge. She's not a woman who reaches for her smelling salts at the first sign of trouble."

Silas jumped up, agitated at his friend's gentle reprimand. "Don't you think I know that, Jeavon? Perhaps better than anyone? But this is different."

Jeavon eyed him coolly. "In what way? I'm still in the dark as to why?"

"The specific circumstances don't matter; it's ancient history. But the results could be catastrophic for her case, and I can't risk that. I've got to stand down and allow someone else to handle it. If Vane is appointed, we'll lose. It's as simple as that."

"Silas… Silas. Sit down. You're making me nervous."

Silas was leaning forward with both hands on the edge of the table, as if needing support. He gradually relaxed and sat down again.

"I've never seen you in such a state," Jeavon said. "Tell me. If you are so sure of this, why can't you go to the chief justice and suggest there's a conflict of interest? Either officially or unofficially?"

"They'd never believe me," Silas replied. "And I don't want to drag the Barclays through any more scandal. It's best I quietly withdraw and they find someone else."

Jeavon sat for a long stretch in silence, watching the birds.

"Unless you explain this better, Posey will feel both bewildered and betrayed. You understand that?"

"Only too well," Silas whispered. "Believe me. I've gone over this until I feel as if I'm going crazy. But I can't see any other solution."

Eighteen

Queenie's Tea House in Old Mill Lane was humming like a beehive on a sunny day, with morning-tea customers making a quick stop for a cuppa before buzzing off to gather nectar elsewhere. It provided a favourite haunt for groups of friends – mainly women – who met for leisurely chats ranging from topics serious – like the recent cholera fatality in Sydney, the discovery of a 240-pound gold nugget at the base of a tree in Bulldog Gully, Victoria, and whose horse won at Randwick last week. All of it without malice, of course.

As Posey sat at a corner table scanning the clientele, she smiled at the parallels between human and animal kingdoms. She had her antennae up, like a female worker bee seeking food sources. The workers in the hive were all female. She knew that much.

Some of those slouched at nearby tables would definitely qualify as the drones, she thought to herself. And they weren't all men, though a goodly proportion of them were. They mulled over morning newspapers – provided free of charge by the feisty Irish owner Beca O'Hare – and sat over one cup of tea for longer than anyone could imagine.

Then there were the workers – by far the most numerous – carrying out a variety of tasks from signalling to the waitresses that a recently vacated table needed cleaning, to foraging for coffee and cake on behalf of table mates, and guarding their table from interlopers while they approached the counter to order.

Rattled like never before by the fast-changing events at Barclay Manor, Posey had called for help from her wide circle of women friends.

Some of them – like Isabelle McGregor, who Posey caught sight of this very minute pushing through the rotating glass door that jangled every time a customer entered or left – belonged in the upper society cabal, the so-called "upper ten thousand".

Isabelle searched the room, conspicuous in the new bright-red of her gown, the product of the synthetic dyes that were all the rage. Her keen intellect devoured the polemic of Mary Wollstonecraft and other woman's rights advocates, but Isabelle still liked to maintain herself in the height of fashion. She was the privately schooled, Australian-born daughter of a wealthy New South Wales pastoralist family, and before she'd married farmer and businessman Frank McGregor, she'd travelled widely in Europe.

But others of Posey's circle, like Jamaican widow Matilda Sinclair, knew how unforgiving life could be. Matilda's sugar-plantation-owner husband died leaving her penniless. She had moved to Sydney to be closer to her brother and opened a small bookstore selling progressive literature.

Women's physician and herbalist Amiria Chaudry, born of

a British father and an Indian mother, was a naval officer's widow who'd breached prejudice concerning both her birth and career ambitions. Amiria had learned her mother's and grandmother's traditional herbal medicine practices, as well as studying with other unregistered female practitioners of modern treatments.

Posey had called an emergency meet up of the Teacup Trust – their tongue-in-cheek name for their lighthearted accord – because without Poppy or Hawk Eye to debate with she didn't know where else to turn. She needed to clarify her thoughts by talking with people whose judgement she respected and these women were they. Not all the group could attend at short notice, but those who lived in the inner city, within reach of Gus the messenger boys' bicycle, and weren't tied up in other work or family obligations welcomed the excuse to pop out for morning tea.

Isabelle, Amiria and Matilda as well as Eleanor Fitzroy, wife of a prominent and wealthy businessman and mother of three, who volunteered in the same female refuge charity as Posey, were soon seated around the prized corner spot of the teahouse with their favourite hot beverage before them.

Amiria stirred her black Darjeeling brew, and Posey caught the fruity muscatel fragrance in the steam it gave off as her friend narrowed her large dark eyes and asked her a question without saying a word.

What's wrong?

Posey laughed and glanced around the table. "Okay…" she said with a drawl. "We're in a right fix – 'we' as in the Barclay family – and it's something I can't talk to Hawk Eye about, even though he's supposedly our lawyer and should be available."

"Supposedly?" Eleanor Fitzroy, one of the sharpest people Posey had ever met, raised her brows and the flat-brimmed pork-pie hat she wore with brown-velvet-ribbon trim bobbed on her blonde head. Like Isabelle, she liked to keep up with the trends and bonnets were so much yesterday's look. English born, she spoke in the rounded vowels of London's West End. "Now that's a loaded sentence to start the ball rolling. Why can't you discuss it with Hawk Eye? He's been away researching your case for the last month or so. I'd have thought he'd have a lot to report."

"So did I!" The exasperation recoiled in Posey's reply. "There's something going on between him and the new Supreme Court judge who's arrived."

"The Earl of Worcester's son? Lord Brook?" Isabelle had done a London season, as a twenty-something at Park Lane luncheons and Mayfair balls, and she'd put that time to good use. Although she'd been back home and married for several years, she still liked to keep up with West End gossip. "What's the problem?" She took a sip of her Earl Grey and pulled a face. She squeezed more lemon juice in from the wedge on the saucer and added half a teaspoon of sugar.

Posey waited until the move was completed and Isabelle sipped again and nodded appreciatively. "That's better," she said. "Earl Grey the English way."

"That's just it," Posey said, her voice again edged with frustration. "That's the problem. Silas won't tell me what's wrong. All he says is if Gideon Vane gets given the case, there's likely to be a conflict of interest and he won't be able to represent us. He says I need to find someone else to take it." She placed her palms flat down on the table as if to emphasise the point and gazed around the mute circle.

They all stared back.

"He won't tell you?" echoed Matilda after a long minute. She'd slipped into a drawn-out, deep Jamaican intonation on the word *won't*. She repeated it. "Won't? As in 'can't'? Or 'chooses not to'?"

Posey shook her head, her jaw clamped tight. "Who knows? Not me, that's for sure. I don't know enough to be able to judge."

Eleanor broke another long silence. "You have asked him? I mean, it's an obvious question, but what did he say?"

"He simply refuses to say. When he met Lord Brook at the Law Society welcome a few nights back, he wasn't his normal self. That's all I can tell you. I could sense he was furious. The anger was nearly boiling over from inside, though he suppressed it. And you all know Hawk Eye. He's usually so calm and contained. It was quite clear they'd met before. I'd guess they hate each other."

She took a deep breath and gazed around the group, meeting each of their eyes in turn. "They've got a history. Must have. But how? From where? So far as I know, Silas has been in Australia since he was about eighteen, and the new judge hadn't stepped foot here until a few days ago." She cast her expressive hands palms up, lost for an answer.

"It stands to reason then that the feud, if that's what it is, happened before Silas came here," suggested Isabella. "Most likely back in childhood."

"Do people hold on to hate that long?" Posey's question hinted at disbelief. "It's more than twenty years."

"Of course they do," chimed Isabella. "Look at the Irish. They're still bitter about things that happened back in Oliver Cromwell's time."

Eleanor nodded. "If Posey's right, whatever's between them is significant enough to create a lifelong breach," she said in a level tone. "So, the issue is, how do you find out what the cause of that breach might be if Hawk Eye won't say? Who else might know?"

Isabelle tipped the last drops of her tea down her throat before answering. "We'd have to assume Lord Brook knows too. But it wouldn't be sensible to ask him. You don't know what hornet's nest you might stir up."

"I totally agree," said Amiria. "If there's deep bitterness, you'd get a very skewed version, anyway. And it seems disloyal to Silas, even if he won't give you his version just now. Maybe the poor man is in shock. Give him a few days, and it might be different." Amiria's words trailed away as she studied Posey's scowling face. "You don't want to wait a few days?"

"I don't feel I can," said Posey. "Too much hangs in the balance. If he won't handle the trial, I have to find someone else quickly. And as you all know, that won't be easy. Hawk Eye is by far the best chance of winning we have."

"Who else might know something? Do you think he'd confide in Jeavon?" Eleanor again.

From their shared work at the refuge society, Eleanor knew former police superintendent Jeavon Yates had grown close to both Posey and Silas because of their shared commitment to equality and justice.

Posey nodded. "Jeavon is probably the most likely person he'd talk to," she admitted. "But if he's spoken in confidence, Jeavon wouldn't break it, even if it was going to help me. He's a stickler for keeping his word. That's what makes him so special."

"What about your new brother-in-law?" asked Isabelle. "He's in London and he's a journalist. He's expected to be nosey. Why don't you ask him to poke around? See if he can dig up anything at that end that might explain it?"

Eleanor joined in. "When you think about it, why would an English soon-to-be earl want to come to Australia, anyway? He's well past seeking youthful adventure. You'd think if he's about to come into his inheritance..." She left the thought dangling, like a tasty morsel. "Why would he walk away from that, even for a short time? Unless things had got hot for him at home?"

They let out a shared breath, a mutual sense of relief, of the surprise at an imminent discovery, of congratulation at their shared cleverness.

"You know, I believe you're onto something there, Eleanor." Mathilda had been silent until now, but she'd followed the conversation with eagle-eyed attention.

"You and your Mayfair mindset. Why would he find the convict colony – forgive the description, but you know what I mean – attractive? Through his eyes, that's probably all we are... It's certainly worth pursuing."

Isabelle purred. "You've got me intrigued now, Mathilda. I've invited him to my Friday salon tomorrow night, along with Hugo Davenport. I thought he was a boring old fart, to be honest, but maybe there's something a lot more interesting lurking there. Why don't you and Posey come along tomorrow night as well to find out? All of you, if you want to."

Isabelle's salons in her Woollahra home were one of Sydney's most sought after and celebrated social events. She brought together writers, artists, musicians, philanthropists, judges, politicians and rising stars in every sector of life in a scintillating mix of good food and conversation, peppered with occasional live performances from poets and musicians. Controversial subjects – like the place of women in society, or the rights of "emancipists", the former convicts, in the new world – were aired with vigorous logic and good humour. What better place to observe the man and draw some fresh conclusions?

Posey laughed out loud. "You're incorrigible, Isabelle. You know I'm not much for wider society, but this time I can see the point. Your salons are irresistible."

They spent the next while in general chatter about their lives, husbands, children, for those who had them, and the state of the world in general, before Amiria gave a little hand signal indicating she must leave.

"Have to get back to the shop," she said with a grin. "I'm not a lady of leisure, like some of you."

They took that as their sign to call their gathering to a close.

Posey stretched her hand out into the table, carefully avoiding bumping the china teacups, and the others followed her lead and clasped hands. They stayed like that in silence for a minute or two, squeezing fingers as a message of solidarity. Then they leaned into the circle and quietly repeated their slogan.

"Pens are mightier than pins."

And for good measure, they said it again, almost in a whisper.

"Pens are mightier than pins."

Nineteen

Cassandra Gilbert turned her back on the scene unfolding before them and rolled her eyes. "I wouldn't have believed it if I hadn't seen it with for myself," she muttered out of the corner of her delicately coloured mouth. "The new judge and Eudora? I know my sister-in-law has become rather obsessed about marrying before she turns thirty, but I never thought she'd display it so publicly."

Posey responded with a wry smile. "He's probably a 'good catch.' And she's been on her own since Clifford and you married, and then Clara died. It's probably understandable?"

The guests circling inside Isabelle's two-storied Jersey Road villa were fizzing with the excitement of being in one of the city's most desired and glamorous gatherings. Being invited was the stamp that they'd "made it". The black-tie waiters circling with fruit punch, champagne, and appetisers, the soothing strains of the string quartet, the fragrant flowers adorning the mantelpiece and buffet that infused the warm air, were all a reminder that they'd "arrived".

And if that wasn't enough, Madame Celeste, a celebrated actress who was appearing in a Royal Theatre production of

The Taming of the Shrew, was to give a solo performance – an excerpt from the play – as the evening's finale.

Posey clasped her glass of punch and drew her hands into the waist of the burnt-orange gown Arabella had insisted she wear with her coral drop earrings. Usually, she disavowed dressing up for others, but she'd felt the need to make an exception tonight, and she was glad she had. Her hair was drawn back in a neat chignon, a style which was growing in popularity, and she'd already received a slew of compliments on her appearance.

Cassandra tapped her arm. "Is he though?"

Posey's brow furrowed in puzzled lines. "Sorry. I was away with the fairies. Is he what?" She glanced behind her. "Lord Brook? We're still talking about him?"

Cassandra gave a musical laugh. "Of course we're talking about him. He's the most interesting thing to happen in Sydney this week, isn't he?"

Posey's mouth set in an amused line. "I guess."

Until this evening, Posey and Cassandra had not spoken much. Cassandra was a social virtuoso, the ideal wife for a newspaper baron like Clifford Gilbert, always reading the tides of fashion and popular opinion, and adjusting her behaviour and values to suit. She was rapidly ascending to general acclaim as the Queen Bee of Sydney society, a role Eudora desperately coveted.

Before the disastrous collapse of Barclay Investments, Posey's twin sister, Poppy, was engaged to be married to Clifford, but when the scandal broke, he dropped her. Within six months, he'd married Cassandra.

Posey thought not for the first time that the woman beside her was far more suited to the role than her intelligent, ambitious sister was, but she'd never aired that view.

"He's clearly making a play for Eudora. And she would adore the idea of marrying an English aristocrat. That would show Clarrie."

Clarrie O'Reilly had been Eudora's escort in recent months, and she was tirelessly working to get him down the aisle.

Posey shook her head. "Clarrie and Eudora really aren't suited," she said. "Clarrie is a lovely chap, but he's more interested in his horses than in women. Eudora breathes society. Clarrie couldn't care less."

The cultured tones of a deep male voice cut through their female intimacy. "A man who prefers horses to women? I couldn't help overhearing that remark, Miss Barclay."

Posey and Cassandra both turned in mild shock as Gideon Vane, heir to the Earl of Worcester, loomed into their social space. He made an exaggerated bow to each of them individually, with a brief "Miss Barclay" and "Mrs Gilbert" as an acknowledgment of their previous meetings, and then drilled them with an arrogant gaze.

"I hope you're not talking about your escort of the other night. What was his name again?" He made a study of combing his memory, his index finger on his jaw as he considered. "Was it Mr Williams? Yes. I believe that was it. Silas Williams."

Posey stiffened to her full height, tall for a woman, but even so she stared up into Gideon Vane's liquid-brown eyes.

"Mr Williams, Lord Brook?" she said with a hint of ice. "You can be assured he far prefers people to horses. But as for women, you'll have to ask him yourself."

She sensed Cassandra Gilbert's warm solidarity at her side, but did not dare look at her. She searched Vane's face, but it was blank of any expression except a sneering superiority.

"You've never met Mr Williams before, Lord Brook?" she asked with blatant directness. "I thought perhaps as you are both Englishmen in the law, you may have come across one another at some time in the past."

She left a calculated pause as he stared at her with assessing eyes. Had she detected a faint shock in them at her brazen question? She feigned a softening in her approach, a feminine waver, and then almost apologetically she said, "All I mean is, if you had, you'd know his partial blindness hinders his riding. So, no, horses do not play a big part in his life." She flashed a quick smile. "But of course if you haven't met before, you couldn't be expected to know that."

She detected another flicker behind the masked lids. Was it anger? Suspicion? Did he think Silas had told her something about their previous relationship?

"I see." Lord Brook gave the impression of being too stunned for words.

A new female voice sounded from her side. "Lord Brook, I'm so glad you've talked to Miss Barclay and Mrs Gilbert, but there are other people I want you to meet. I really must highjack you for more introductions."

Isabelle was there, looking every bit the commanding hostess in a purple gown with soft-grey sleeves and underskirts trimmed in a deeper violet. Her ears bore large silver discs with amethyst centres that shone against her corn-silk hair.

The judge obediently bowed and turned to follow her. "Delighted, my lady. Lead the way."

When he was out of earshot, Cassandra fixed Posey with sharp, knowing blue eyes.

"What was that all about? Do Lord Brook and Hawk Eye know one another?"

Posey's gaze roamed past Cassandra's shoulder. This new friend was far too perceptive to be safe.

She shrugged. "In confidence, right? Strictly in confidence? Hawk Eye's been acting strangely about him. I suspect they've met before. And if I'm right, it didn't end well."

Cassandra's eyes followed Vane's back. "That man is a snake," she said. "I don't like the idea of him hooking up with Eudora one bit, and I'm going to tell Clifford so." She turned back to Posey. "When he arrived here – with us tonight, I mean – I got the distinct impression he was trying to flirt with you. He's a sleaze. It's only because you were so cold that he didn't continue with that line about women and horses."

The corners of her brighter-than-natural lips dropped in contempt. "Come to think of it, why is he here apparently looking for a female companion, if not a wife, at all? Surely a man of his status should already have done the business. Secured the wife and sired the next generation. There's no mention of him being a widower."

Her sapphire eyes flashed. "I'm going to warn Clifford. Get him to get one of his lads to investigate. There's something that doesn't ring true about that fellow." She tapped Posey's elbow. "But come on. Let's help ourselves to the buffet before Madame Celeste does her turn."

One of the lads? Does she realise she was talking about Thomas? Poppy's husband?

Isabelle's words came back to her. *She* would get Thomas to look into Sydney's new Supreme Court judge. She didn't have to wait for Clifford Gilbert to order it.

Twenty

"Jeavon, I've got a confession to make. I've telegraphed Thomas and asked him for information on the new Supreme Court judge, Gideon Vane. I wanted to tell you first. In case he mentions it in his letters," Posey said. She took a sip of the icy lemon and barley water Jeavon's cook had prepared.

"Oh? And why did you feel it necessary to do that?"

They were enjoying a lazy Tuesday afternoon on Jeavon's deck, watching the quarrelling butcherbirds as usual. Now that she and Hawk Eye were distanced in their communications, Posey was more grateful than ever for the former policeman's wise advice and encyclopaedic knowledge of Sydney's criminal past.

Posey took another sip and sighed. "Because there's something going on Hawk Eye won't tell me about. He says if Vane gets appointed to our case, he'll have to declare a conflict of interest and step down. But he won't tell me why."

Jeavon frowned. "I see. And how do you think Thomas might help?"

"I didn't think of it myself. It was Cassandra Gilbert's idea. I was talking to her at Isabelle McGregor's Friday salon. She suggested there might be something dodgy about Vane coming out here. He's on the top of the pile in England. He's going to become an earl, presumably with pots of money and a castle, any day now. He could take his seat in parliament, enjoy all the trappings of being an English lord. Why would he want to come out to the colonies? Is he running away from something?"

"Uh-huh." Jeavon took another piece of cake from the plate on the table and chewed on it as he thought. "And if there *is* some scandal? What can you do about it?"

"It depends what it is," Posey said. "I've got to do something. I will not stand by and see our case go up in flames. Tell me. Do you know who Hawk Eye worked for when he first came to Sydney? I've never thought to ask before."

"It was a lawyer called Archibald Beaumont," Jeavon said. "An Englishman who came here via Ireland, I believe. Why do you ask?"

"Because Hawk Eye sounds like he's ready to give up on us. And I wondered if this person who hired him first, whoever he might be, might be able to tell me why Silas came to Australia. He might shed light on his secrets, since he isn't willing to talk about it."

Jeavon sighed. "So you're going to poke around behind Hawk Eye's back? And do you think that is a good idea?"

Posey sat in silence for a long moment.

"Oh, Jeavon, that's hard. He's left me with no other choice. He won't tell me himself. And the entire case rests on me getting a better understanding of what's really going on here."

"Well, that's a shame," said Jeavon, patting her hand. "Because Archibald died years ago. Even if he knew Hawk Eye's secrets, he won't be telling them. Not unless you get Minerva on the case." He grinned. "Bad joke. I know."

Minerva Thorne was a dedicated follower of the occult, who claimed to call up the spirits of the dead. She was also part of the group opposing the Barclay family.

Posey changed tack. "How did Hawk Eye know Archibald Beaumont? Was there any connection between them before he got here?"

Jeavon threw up his hands. "Honestly, I don't know." He hesitated. "But I know someone who would."

Posey's heart jerked, as if struck by a lightning bolt. It had been in recess, and now it sparked onto high alert.

"Oh? And who is that?"

"Archibald's wife, Margaret Beaumont. She's an artist who lives out of town. She's an elderly lady now, a social recluse since her husband died. They were as close as any couple could be. If Archibald knew, Margaret probably would, too. Though what her memory is like in old age is anyone's guess."

"So, where can I find her?"

"That you will have to discover for yourself. Ask around in the arts scene. Last I knew, she was living out on the coast north of Sydney in an artist's commune. But I doubt she'd still be there today."

Posey gathered her skirts together and rose to go, leaning over to place a light kiss on the top of Jeavon's head as she did. "If this helps me solve this mystery, the whole Barclay family will be eternally grateful."

Jeavon's smoky blue-grey eyes crinkled at the corners. "Just let me walk you down the aisle when you finally agree to marry the man. That's all I ask."

Posey threw him a look. "Hell will freeze over first."

Twenty-one

Posey drew up outside Margaret Beaumont's two-storied red-brick house close to the Lavender Bay wharf on the north side of the harbour and took a deep breath. Her neck was hot and sticky from the ten-minute walk from the ferry. Her pulse fluttered like a bird's wings in her throat. And her eyes swam from the blinding glare of sun on water.

Should she reconsider this invasion of an elderly artist's privacy, arriving unannounced in this quiet backwater to ask impertinent questions about long-ago events?

A few wealthy lawyers and merchants had built homes here, but it was still considered an out-of-the-way place to live. She obviously wasn't encouraging a lot of visitors.

And would Margaret Beaumont even remember the young lawyer who worked with her husband two decades ago?

Mathilda, the bookseller from her Teacup Trust circle, had supplied her with the address, because Mrs Beaumont was a keen subscriber to brochures and books on political and social issues. But it had been several years since Mathilda had seen the old lady in her store, she'd told her when she'd called on her in the shop yesterday.

"She sends her housekeeper to collect materials she may be interested in these days," she said. "Perhaps she's doesn't like to make the trip across the harbour too often. But she herself hasn't been in for quite a while. I know nothing about her current state of health."

Posey dawdled on the sandy street, surveying the Beaumont house. Mathilda had also told her the old lady was a celebrated water colourist, who'd made a name for herself with plein-air landscapes of sea coasts and bushland.

"Before she moved to Lavender Bay a few years ago, she used to have salon evenings for fellow artists," she said. "She loved to encourage women artists in particular."

Everything about the place, from its ceiling to floor dark-brown shuttered windows to the wrought-iron fretwork on the upper verandah, declared it the residence of colonial gentry. A paperbark tree shaded the front path, its distinctive white paper bark peeled in folds from the silvery trunk, but none of it messed up the border of pink floribunda roses that lined the front fence.

A sweet fragrance, a combination of English nobility and crisp Australian zest, pervaded the air and, somehow, the mixed heritage gave Posey the push she needed. She filled her lungs with it, willed the pulse in her throat to settle to a quieter beat, and strode up the path to the front door before she could change her mind.

A housekeeper in a crisp white tunic edged in lacey broderie anglaise answered within seconds. Her brow furrowed into a question as soon as she saw Posey.

"Can I help you?" she asked in a voice that carried a foreign lilt.

"I'm seeking a few minutes with Mrs Beaumont." The words came out in a breathy rush. She proffered the bundle of latest literature that Mathilda had prepared for her. "I have some articles Miss Matilda Sinclair, the owner of The Radical Reader bookshop, thought might be of interest."

The housekeeper regarded the brown-paper parcel and a shadow of doubt crossed her broad, suntanned face. Posey stepped back to allow her a little more room. She was a robust middle-aged woman with thick freckled forearms and beady, intelligent eyes. Posey thought her accent may have been Danish.

The woman took the package and stepped aside to allow Posey entry. "Come and sit in the hall while I check with the mistress," she said.

***

Archibald Beaumont's widow was the farthest thing she could imagine from the infirm. Posey sat in the artist's studio in front of a freshly poured cup of tea, and watched Margaret Beaumont paint, breathing in the malty aroma of the black Assam. The artist, firmly planted on sturdy legs in front of her easel, added delicate strokes to a forest water colour taking shape before her eyes.

Posey smiled to herself at her earlier anxiety. When she'd explained that Mathilda's gift included a selection of Harriet Martineau's columns from *London's Daily News*, as well as several of the latest issues of *Victoria* magazine, a mainstream women's journal offering a wide selection of news and opinion, Margaret's plump cheeks reddened with pleasure and her smoky eyes sparkled.

"Oh, my goodness, she shouldn't have," she cried, bringing her right hand to her face and leaving a streak of green paint under her right ear. "Harriet Martineau? Mathilda knows I admire her work. And she's so prolific!" She glanced at her brush hand, mottled with red and green paint. "I've got paint on my face, don't I?" she queried. A happy chuckle issued from her unlined throat. "Ah well. Occupational hazard." She turned back to her canvas. "Drink your tea while I finish this section. I want to get it done before the layers dry out too much."

She was a full-bodied woman, stocky, but not overweight, and she wielded her paint brush with the air of a conductor before a full philharmonic orchestra. She radiated a sense of being comfortable with her place in life and confident in her work. Everything about her, from the relaxed tilt of her finely moulded lips to her unwavering deep-grey eyes, promised a forgiving reception.

"Right. That's about all I can do now. Time for a break." She settled into an easy chair and tapped the side of the teapot. "I'll just get Billie to freshen this up and you can tell me why you're here."

Within minutes, she was back with the housekeeper and a jug of hot water.

"Mrs Bilsen, meet Posey Barclay. She's brought me a delicious offering from that bookshop I occasionally send you to."

'Billie' Bilsen gave her a cordial nod. "The mistress will enjoy them, I'm sure," she said.

"Now," Margaret said, settling in. "How can I help you?"

***

"Silas? Of course I remember Silas. Who could forget him?" Margaret gave her a warm smile. "I regret I haven't seen him since I moved across the harbour. But I certainly remember him. He's a handsome man despite the blind eye and the super serious demeanour," she said with a quick smile. "He's one of the few people I'd trust with my life."

"That's what I would have thought too," said Posey, a sense of relief invading her core. "But something odd has happened. He's letting me down, and I never thought he'd do that."

Margaret's groomed, dark brows furrowed. "Letting you down? That does not sound like Hawk Eye. My husband, Archibald, always said he'd endured more pain and tragedy before the age of ten than any child should. And he's come through it all with a resolute strength."

Posey edged forward in her seat. "I suppose you're referring to his eye? I've never wanted to ask him. And he's volunteered nothing more than a vague reference to a childhood accident. Do you know how he came to be blind?"

Mrs Beaumont shook her head. "That was all Archibald ever said as well. A 'childhood accident'. I got the impression they'd made an agreement to never discuss it, so I never asked."

She took a sip of her tea and hesitated, the cup halfway to her mouth. "My husband was a cousin of Silas's mother, but we were banished from the family circle because of controversial circumstances I don't wish to go into." She gazed steadily into Posey's face. "It all worked out for Hawk Eye, because he wanted to be anonymous. I suppose the eye patch gave him a certain notoriety he didn't enjoy. Archibald dealt with Silas's mother, Henrietta. He'd agreed he'd move to

Ireland and take Silas with him as his law clerk. Archibald set up a legal practice. Silas studied law at the university and worked for Archibald part time. They were both far from the prying eyes of the family and the Mayfair gossips, and they liked that."

She replaced the cup on her saucer and ran her tongue over her top lip. "By mutual agreement, we never discussed the past."

Posey dipped her head in courteous acceptance. Mrs Beaumont had just laid out the ground rules.

"And later they came to Australia together? Is that correct?"

Margaret Beaumont shook her head. "Archibald came out ahead of Hawk Eye. I believe Silas was finishing his final exams at the Queen's University, Belfast. He joined Archibald when he qualified, and I joined them both a few months later."

Posey saw that Margaret's eyes appeared suspiciously bright.

"Was that a welcome move?" she asked. "You've enjoyed Australia?"

A peal of laughter sounded from her, rather like the one she'd let fall at receiving Mathilda's books.

"Utterly welcome." She huffed. "You've no idea. Like getting out of jail."

"And what about Silas's family? Did Archibald ever mention them?"

Margaret shook her head, but could not meet Posey's eye. "We agreed we'd never look back. We all wanted to focus on the future." She wound her fingers together, as if contemplating. "The only thing I feel I can say – though I do not know why it should be relevant – is that I believe that many years ago Silas's family suffered a tragedy. His sister died when she was very young. I got the impression in traumatic circumstances. But I don't see how that could affect his life now. It's a long time ago."

Posey had a strange surge inside, a premonition, perhaps.

Is someone walking on your grave?

"There's a new Supreme Court judge just arrived. His name is Gideon Vane, the Earl of Worcester's son. Did your late husband ever mention him?"

Margaret Beaumont stiffened and fixed her with a strange stare. "The Earl of Worcester? No, I'm sorry. It doesn't ring any bells."

A charged silence filled the space between them.

And Posey's sixth sense told her that for the first time in this encounter, Margaret Beaumont had lied.

Twenty-two

Silas is different. He keeps his word. That's what I told myself.

Posey gazed out over Sydney Cove as her ferry sped back to Circular Quay from Lavender Bay, but she wasn't seeing the crested foam of the waves, or the seabirds circling in their wake, hoping for food scraps. She'd gone to Margaret Beaumont's studio with high hopes, but those last few moments, when her hostess had clearly lied… That had left a hard ball in her stomach. And it meant the key information about Silas's past – the very thing she'd hoped she might discover – was still a mystery.

She swallowed down on the disappointment that lodged in her gut like rocks. She sensed her disillusionment was due to far more than this one set of circumstances. It confirmed what she'd suspected for a long time: men couldn't be relied on; they always let you down.

It was the same with Father. I said to myself, "Dad's not like other men. He'll never let me down." And then look what happened.

She steadied herself, clasping one arm around the vertical strut of the open cabin roof. She swayed with the motion of sea and vessel, recalling the dreadful day when she'd found her father dead at his desk, his head folded into his ice-cold arms.

At first, she'd thought he'd fallen asleep. She'd stroked his arm, ever so gently to wake him up, and then when she realised something was wrong, she'd called his name, louder and louder, as she grasped he was never waking up again.

The hairs on his forearm were stiff and lifeless, his limbs strangely torpid, with no sense of life or warmth radiating from beneath the skin. If that wasn't enough of a clue, there was the carefully penned note, propped up on the ink bottle at his right elbow. The note she'd never shared with anybody.

James Barclay had been looking increasingly grey and exhausted in the months after the collapse of his investment company. And who could wonder? Willoughby Martens, someone he'd chosen to trust for the sake of his beloved daughter-in-law, had stolen life savings from dozens of investors. He'd embezzled a level of funds that destroyed the business, as well as people's dreams.

On top of that, soon after, the same darling daughter-in-law – their half-brother's wife, Charlotte – and his first grandson, Joshua, had drowned in a ferry grounding during a disastrous storm. Charlotte had been travelling up the coast, frantic to convince others Willoughby had been wrongly accused. She'd insisted her brother had not stolen the money.

Everywhere he looked, catastrophe surrounded James Barclay. It would be natural for his heart to give out under so much stress, and Dr Appleton had pronounced James's death to be a heart attack within minutes of attending him at the house.

Even now, when she thought of that day, her heart pounded so hard it felt as if it would jump out of her chest. If Dr

Appleton had seen that note, it might have been a different matter. Would he have been so quick to characterise a heart attack as the cause of death?

I couldn't put Mother through that as well. She's not strong enough to stand it.

She didn't need to dig out the note from her secret hiding place in her room to read it. She knew it by heart. The words that rang through her head so many times flooded back in.

To my beloved wife and daughters,

The strain of recent days has taken its toll. My heart aches, both figuratively and literally. I fear I may not have much time left. Please know that, whatever happens, I have always tried to do right by you all. Forgive me for any pain I've caused.

I fear I may not have much time left.

Had he sensed his time was running short? Or did he decide to hurry his own end?

I'll never know.

Posey's legs were hollow as she stepped down the gangplank and onto the quay.

I never want Mother to ask herself that question. Nor do I want anyone to say such an action is an admission of guilt. That we deserve to lose everything. It would drastically weaken our case if people thought James Barclay took his own life.

Oh, Father. I don't know for sure, but I feel so let down even thinking you might have done that.

Twenty-three

Silas stepped aside to allow his practice assistant Amelie to exit the office ahead of him. The late-afternoon winter sun that Friday was warm on his back as he locked the door of the villa at 86 Elizabeth Street. He and Amelie stood side by side and looked out on the passing traffic in companionable silence.

The week of Gideon's shock arrival had been the worst he'd experienced since his arrival in Australia nearly two decades ago. First, his shock confrontation with the painting he'd thought he would never see again. Then Gideon's bombshell arrival. And, finally, Posey's distress at his failure to explain himself.

This week had been quiet by comparison, and gave him a welcome opportunity to muster his courage and resources. The chief justice had apparently kept Lord Brook busy meeting new staff and learning the inside running of the court system, so he'd neither seen nor heard anything of him for the last few days. He was thankful for small mercies.

However, he still was in great doubt about whether he could continue with the Barclay case, and yet the idea of giving up on it made him sick to the stomach every time he thought of it.

He'd already devoted months of work to it, and he knew there wasn't any reputable lawyer in town who would take it up if he surrendered it. They'd all been intimidated by the powerful anti-Barclay cabal amongst the rich and famous who'd lost money in the collapse. Word had got around: *Take the case and you won't be getting any more work from us.* He'd be leaving her up the creek without a paddle if he withdrew.

He couldn't imagine a worse combination of circumstances, but he refused to consider they were anything but coincidental.

His thoughts wandered to another blind man in a famous play that had fascinated him as a young man: "As flies to wanton boys, are we to the gods. They kill us for their sport." Like Shakespeare in *King Lear*, he'd questioned if there was justice in the universe. He'd chosen to believe there was, and made it his life's work to prove it.

He was fighting hand to hand to keep faith in the course he'd set himself. With his face tilted up, his one good eye closed to the sun, he hoped for some rejuvenating warmth on his face. Instead, a familiar sensation of being hit by a massive wave of grief overwhelmed him, leaving him emotionally floundering. He was giddy. He fought to stay upright against the sudden dizziness.

Once again, life is challenging my cultivated optimism.

He gazed out onto Elizabeth Street, where the Friday-night traffic rumbled on. All manner of wheeled vehicles – from a showy four-wheeled barouche with its collapsible rear hood, to a humble two-wheeled practical gig, were bearing folk home to their end-of-the-week dinners.

As an English visitor had noted in a newspaper column,

Sydney's citizens preferred to ride rather than walk wherever they could. The heat, the dust, the dogs and perhaps the protection of female complexions from the searing sun were all part of the justification for why Sydneysiders, especially the women, did not walk anywhere. Whatever the cause, the city was in retreat, wheeling its way home with what seemed to be a communal sigh of relief. And he was restless to join in the escape.

The rattle of metal wheels drew his attention to a luxury coupe in shiny black enamel, which was grinding to a stop at the curb outside number 86.

He turned to his staffer. "Have a great weekend, Amelie," he said in kindly dismissal. "See you Monday."

She glanced up at him, her eyes bright with gratitude. "Oui, sur… On se voit lundi." Yes, sure. See you Monday. She dipped her head in tacit acceptance and moved down the path to the gate, her apricot floral skirts swinging around her ankles as she moved.

He glanced to the street, the lowering sun that shone directly in his face making it difficult to see the new arrival. Not someone for him, he was certain. He'd completed all their scheduled appointments for the week. He watched with lazy curiosity as Amelie set off down the path, while a footman hurried to open the door of the coupe on the pavement side and set up a stepping block to ease the way for disembarking passengers.

All he wanted to do now was drag himself wearily onto the Hunters Hill ferry and lose himself in the scent of sea air and green woods in the pastoral suburb up the Parramatta estuary he called home. This weekend he planned to isolate himself and work out what he was going to do about the mess he found himself in. Every time he attempted to think about it, he developed a burning pain behind his eyes that was exactly like the one he'd suffered when he was first blinded.

I suppose it's all in my head, he thought. *I'm finally going barmy-brained.*

He glanced past Amelie's retreating figure, and his heart turned to ice. A long-necked figure stood staring into the number 86 garden. His elongated head and protruding nose bobbed in and out in an awkward rhythm, a barely discernible emu-like dance. Silas didn't need a second glance to recognise Gideon Vane. And this wasn't any coincidence…

Gideon stood aside and swept off his hat in a bold compliment as Amelie scuttled past. Silas moved halfway down his office path to the street, blocking the judge's advancement, front door key in hand.

"What are you doing here?" he growled. "We're closed for the day. And, anyway, I'd have thought you'd have bigger fish to fry."

"Oh, I do, Mr Williams, I do," Vane replied, his eyes sliding over Silas to the shingle that hung on the wall behind him. He shouldered around him for a better view of the board and read aloud in the haughty intonation that was his hallmark. Always aware that as an oldest son and heir he'd be inheriting a title, he'd affected plummy upper-crust diction since childhood.

"Let justice be done though the heavens fall," he read slowly, dragging out the vowels. His eyes, with their familiar oily sheen, flicked back to Silas.

Snake's eyes. He was born with them.

"Still the defender of the defenceless," he scoffed. "How touching." His thin mouth curled in a sneer.

Silas stood with his arms hanging loose at his sides and said nothing.

Gideon made a studied play of looking around him, taking in the full view of the office and street. "My, my. I am surprised," he said after a long silence. "The current earl led me to believe you were long dead. I thought I was rid of you forever. And here you are, on the other side of the world, with what I'm told is a burgeoning legal practice. An office in the heart of the best part of town. A good name."

He poked into the grass along the cobbled path with the silver-topped Malacca cane he carried in his right hand. It was pared into a sharp silver-tipped point that sliced through the grass to the soil beneath. Again, how like an emu, Silas thought. One prodding the ground for food.

Gideon leaned on the cane with both hands and stared up at him. "And, of course, we mustn't forget the pretty little chit in the office. Who was she, by the way? She looks far too stylish for an old, half-blind lag like you."

Silas stepped back, increasing the distance between them, and gestured to the gate. "Be on your way, My Lord," he said. The words flew like metal shards. "You weren't invited here and I'm sure you have someone else to slay."

Gideon ignored him. "She's a lot better looking than that tired old man-hater you were with the other night. I congratulate you on that," he said. "She's a definite improvement. A bit young for you, though, isn't she?" He swung about again, as if familiarising himself with a property before moving in. "But I doubt she'd look at a cripple like you, anyway. Am I right?"

"What do you want, Gideon? Tell me why you've bothered to come here or get out."

"Some things never change, do they? Defender of the defenceless," he said derisively. He left a deliberate pause. "Except for your name, of course. That's different. Silas Williams? Where did he come from? And wouldn't the New South Wales Law Society like to know they have an imposter, a fraud, in their midst? How impressed do you think Sir Fred would be if he knew that? Have you even got a proper law degree?"

"Are you finished?" asked Silas.

"I haven't even begun," said Gideon Vane. "I suggest you let me into that law office of yours." His plummy voice leaned on the word "law" as if calling it into question. "I'm tired of standing out here in the sun" He patted his cheek. "Blue-blood English complexion, you know. I've got plenty to say yet, and you'd be a fool if you refuse to hear it. As a judge of the Supreme Court, I have the power to make or break you, and there's not a damn thing you can do about it."

Twenty-four

"Has it ever occurred to you, Gideon, that you have as much to lose as I do in revealing our relationship? Quite possibly more." Silas stared him down from behind his broad polished desk, a silver-topped black-ink bottle and quill in a tray before him, an immaculate array of yellow legal files lined up at his left elbow.

Gideon gazed back, doing his best to appear nonchalant. But the whole set up – the respectable Elizabeth Street premises, the pretty assistant, the well-organised files on a desk that revealed not a speck of dust or disorder – the scene irked him, every tiny detail of it. This scoundrel he'd detested all his life was doing pretty well for himself while he…? He didn't want to cast his mind back to the mess he'd left behind him. All he needed to ask himself was, "If your life was going as well as this, would you be starting all over again in a convict colony?"

He knew the answer to that question without having to ask it. He'd had the devil's own luck, that was the problem, while this bounder had enjoyed unspeakable good fortune. And he was still talking. He switched his attention back to the man in front of him.

"After all, if you whisper abroad that I am not who I say I am, you're taking a gamble, aren't you? You think I wouldn't retaliate to save my livelihood?"

They'd retreated to Silas's office after their brief confrontation on the front steps, both of them realising it didn't look good for the new judge and one of the city's most prominent lawyers to be seen arguing in public.

Gideon wanted to know how and when he'd become Silas Williams. And how was he to answer that? He wasn't born Silas Williams.

"And how are you going to prove anything, without revealing more than you would care to about how we came to know each other, anyway? Have you thought of that?"

Silas's voice was cutting. Gideon's throat surged with fury. He swallowed hard to mask it, but he was certain Silas noticed his Adam's apple straining.

"There are ways…" He forced his tongue around the public-school vowels, determined to beat this blackguard into submission. "I've only been in town a couple of weeks, and I've already discovered you've got plenty of enemies." He lifted his head to a dominating haughtiness. "Or perhaps it's more accurate to say your girlfriend and her family do. People have been lining up to tell tales."

"My girlfriend?" Silas sliced through the gaping distance between them. "Your intelligence is way off beam if you're thinking that's the case. She no longer works for the practice? You know that much?"

Gideon's lips formed in a sneer he couldn't control. "Oh, I'm well aware of that. I saw that pretty piece you've got there now, remember? I'd hate either of them to meet trouble on a dark night."

"Are you threatening us?"

Gideon threw back his head and laughed. "Of course not! I'm just saying. Wasn't it an ancient Chinese general who said, 'Keep you friends close; your enemies closer?' I only have to whisper in a few ears and it will be all over town." He allowed himself a mocking smile. "The thing you don't realise, *Benedict*, is that the losers are always delighted to bring down the winners. Especially when they've lost a lot of money." He sprawled his legs out in front of him, laying claim to more of the space between them.

"I could whisper in Eudora's ear that you look vaguely familiar. I'm sure I've seen you somewhere before… But I didn't think your name was Silas Williams when I saw you in the Inns of Court years ago. I could hint at something vaguely scandalous or improper that might explain the change of name. All innocently dropped over a wonderful lunch at the Café Francais in George Street."

He gave him a sardonic stare. "And if she didn't think of it herself, I could make the throwaway suggestion that her newspaper baron brother might be interested in the story."

Silas glared straight back, seemingly unmoved. "But could you risk that, Gideon? Once you set the hounds on the hare, you have very little control of where they might lead. You wouldn't want them to dig up too much, would you? Or you might regret you ever started the chase."

Gideon rose slowly, his limbs languid in the stuffy heat that, in the last few minutes, had left him light-headed. "It's easy enough for you to avoid any of this, *Silas.*" Irony laced the use of the name. "Just drop the Barclay case. Allow all those good citizens to get justice and recoup their losses. Do that and I'll have a constituency of grateful supporters for as long as I'm here."

He twirled the silver-topped cane between his fingers, and turned for the door, where he paused and looked back. "And you never know. The old man's going to croak any day now. I mightn't be here for that long. Then you'd be free to be Silas Williams for the rest of your life."

Twenty-five

Elias Astor met Gideon in the Petty's Hotel foyer, and his fat claret lips widened in a broad American grin. Or at least, that's how Gideon interpreted it. Gideon had never understood what life gave anyone to smile about. But the fellow stood several inches taller than his six feet, so he responded with a courteous sharp nod. No Englishman would smile like that at someone they barely knew. All the Americans he'd met – and there weren't that many – seemed to assume they'd be best friends within minutes of being introduced, and that just wasn't the English way. Or rather, not his way, Gideon corrected. The future Earl of Worcester didn't bow and scrape to anyone except the King (or in his case, the Queen) and the Archbishop of Canterbury.

Gideon knew Elias claimed to be an offshoot of the legendary Astor family. He'd name-dropped his intimacy with the current family head, William Backhouse Astor, rumoured to be the richest man in America, when they'd met at Eudora's home to watch the harbour races. Elias had been quick to tell him about all the days – or was it weeks – he'd spent on "Willie's" yacht in Florida. Gideon noted he diverted to talking about the Astors' shared boating interests whenever anyone pressed him too closely on his actual relationship to the family. Was he a first cousin? A third cousin? A fourth cousin twice removed? Nobody knew for sure.

But Gideon thought it didn't harm his plan to acclimatise himself to Sydney society by getting to know the Astor scion better. He didn't know how, but he might come in useful.

They followed a butler to the private meeting room, which had a leather-topped table with seating for four masculine armchairs with broad armrests in the same black, studded leather. They'd only be needing two of them. Decent quarters for business hospitality were still in short supply in the city, but the Petty's hallways were frequented by farming barons and European princes, so Elias had obviously judged it suitable for an English earl.

His host gestured to the menu displayed on a plinth in the middle of the table as they sat down.

"We can select whatever we wish from the main dining room and they'll deliver it here," Elias said. "That way, we can enjoy a private talk with no interruptions."

Gideon liked that idea. He liked it very much. The hotel dining room buzzed on a Saturday night, and he didn't want to be spotted by curious tourists. He preferred to tread carefully until he'd decided the tactics he'd implement to further his own interests. The less anyone else knew or guessed of his motives, the better.

"Very fine idea," he said. "I appreciate your discretion."

"It must be quite a challenge, aligning yourself in a new town like this. And one so different from London." His host glanced up as a waiter approached, keen to immediately meet their needs. "Do you drink wine?" Elias asked, and at Gideon's nod of assent, he turned to the waiter. "We'll have the Châteauneuf-du-Pape. One bottle to start," he said. He turned his attention back to Gideon. "It's a nice drop. The only decent wine they've got." He nodded to the menu. "What's your pleasure?"

The details taken care of, Gideon resumed the conversation.

"It's not so different from home," he said. "You understand Australia follows our English law? Based on our centuries old common law? So, the legal side is all rather familiar. It's just the people administering it who will be different." He paused as the server returned with remarkable speed and poured their wine. "And even the people aren't all that different. You've got heroes and villains everywhere."

He took a sip from his glass and held it up to the light. "Quite acceptable," he said. "The light brings out the colour nicely. A fine drop." He glanced over at Elias. "Now where was I? Oh, yes. I'm already learning who are the heroes and who are the villains." He paused, considering, giving his customary nod, and then gathered his thoughts.

"There are exceptions, of course. I've heard something of this Barclay case since I've arrived. That one sounds like it's going to test our mettle, and I've had hints from Sir Frederick he will appoint me to hear it. Strictly confidential, and all that, but I'd be interested to learn your take on that one."

Over their meals – baked fish with hollandaise sauce and asparagus for Elias, roast suckling pig with apple sauce and specialty potatoes for Gideon, Elias told him about the Barclay scandal.

"There's no doubt they got two of the perpetrators," Astor said. "A young chap named Willoughby Martens was the dupe who stole funds, but a much older, cunning fellow Brock Bartle put him up to it. They're both dead. But the good citizens who lost their savings don't believe that's the end of it. There seems to be evidence to suggest James Barclay was in business with his stepson, Nathan Russell, in a very profitable gold mine in Ballarat, and that asset has been hidden away. The Barclays claim it's Russell's enterprise, and that James had nothing to do with it."

He finished his glass and refilled them both. "We've found convincing evidence to the contrary. That's why this group, headed by Hugo Davenport, is suing them to claim profits from the mine. And that's not the only asset the Barclays are hiding, they believe."

Gideon frowned. "Hugo Davenport, you say?"

Elias glanced around uneasily. Apart from a couple of elderly gents away in the corner, there was no one else in the room. "Hugo is a driving force – but he's incognito," he said. "He can't afford to be seen taking sides, so others will front with the evidence when we get down to the actual business."

The waiter had returned with the dessert menu. "Dessert? Or port, whisky, brandy and cigars, gentlemen?"

They placed their orders, and Gideon continued. "I gather that fellow Silas Williams is acting for the family? Who's acting for Hugo's firm?"

"Darry Patterson, a less experienced lawyer, I believe, but Hugo will pull the strings."

"And how do you gauge their chances?"

"Whose? The claimants? Or the family?"

"Both, I suppose," said Gideon.

"Well, Your Honour." He grinned at his poor joke. "It depends on the judge. Silas Williams is a damned fine advocate, but even he can't beat a judge with his mind made up."

The two men locked eyes across the table. For a tense moment, neither said a word. Gideon's head danced like a flower on top of a long, thin stalk.

"It's imperative we see justice done," Elias continued. "For the individuals involved, and for the integrity of the law as well. And the integrity of Sydney's civic reputation. What is it they say? 'Justice must not just be done, but be seen to have been done?' We were hoping you might see your way clear to making sure that happens."

"We?" queried Gideon Vane. "Who's we?"

"Why, the anti-Barclay coalition. Can we rely on you? For a consideration, of course."

"The anti-Barclay coalition? Might I ask exactly who that group comprises? In the strictest of confidence, of course. You mentioned Hugo. Who else?"

Elias hesitated and then stuck out one hand, fingers spread wide, and counted them off. "Eudora Gilbert, the Blackwoods, Richard and Jeb Martins, Hugo Davenport, Minerva Thorne…"

He registered Gideon's frown. "She's a strange old bird, but she knows a lot of secrets," he said. "There are several others you might not have met yet, but I'd be happy to introduce you. Thaddeus Grey, one of the leading thespians in town – he's currently appearing in a play at the Opera House. Ezra

Fairburn, a former Royal Navy officer who operates a respectable ship chandler's on the waterfront. And Levi Blackburn, one of the city's doctors. There are many others, of course, but these are some of the more prominent ones."

Gideon paused. He brought his fingertips together in a pyramid shape in front of his face and stared down at his hands for several moments. Then he looked up and his mouth stretched into a thin line, the closest thing Elias had seen to a smile since they'd met.

"Leave it with me. I'll have to do further research, but I think that it's highly possible I can help. As you say, it's important to see our citizens are protected."

Twenty-six

Silas trudged wearily to the ferry after his encounter with Gideon, determined to retreat and rejuvenate in his peaceful Hunters Hill haven. Over the weekend, he'd revelled in the rural village, with its soft warm sea air and the mournful cry of the gulls on the Parramatta inlet, but he hadn't been able to shake off a deep sense of peril, either. His fear was as much for Posey as it was for himself, though he hardly dared admit it. That anxiety had brought him to Jeavon's back verandah once again.

"Jeavon, I've called in to record what happened on Friday night as I was leaving my Elizabeth Street premises. The new Supreme Court judge, Gideon Vane, accosted me. The only way I can protect Posey and the family is to withdraw from the case, and she'll hate me for it. And there's no guarantee he won't still go after her, even if I drop the case. I know his treachery too well."

He stood by the verandah railing for a few moments, watching the mother and baby bird below them in the yard. Then he turned his attention fully on his friend, scanning his amused broad face. "I'm not joking," he urged. "If anything happens to me, take what I'm about to say as a sworn statement."

Jeavon scanned his expression, his eyes narrowed. "Accosted by a Supreme Court judge, were you? 'Accosted' and 'judge' hardly fit easily in the same sentence."

Silas allowed himself to relax a little under his friend's genial eye.

"They do with this judge," he said, his lips lifting at the corners despite the anxiety that still racked him.

Jeavon drummed his fingers on the edge of the table, as if thinking things through before he spoke.

"Silas, you know as well as I do. I'm not in the police force anymore. I can't take sworn statements, no matter how earnestly you may desire to make them." The former police superintendent gestured to the other spare deck chair on his back porch. "Take your usual seat and unburden yourself. The birds and I will take close notice of all you say. But that's the best I can do."

"Maybe I should write it down and sign it?" Silas said, half-joking, but with a hopeful rise of the brow above his good eye.

Jeavon shrugged. "Let me hear what you've got to say and I'll give my informed comment," he said.

Silas related the conversation.

"He pretty much said as a Supreme Court judge that his word is law. He can spread scurrilous rumours about me, so the law society will start asking questions. And he made veiled threats against Posey and Amelie. Their personal safety, I mean. He said, 'I'd hate either of them to meet trouble on a dark night.' That's the part that bothered me the most."

The teasing humour that rested in Jeavon's eyes vanished, replaced by a steely resolve. "He said that? That's inexcusable."

Silence stretched between them.

"I have to ask, Silas. Why does he bear a grudge against you?"

Silas leaned towards the birds, his shoulders hunched into his chest. "It's ancient history, and too painful to go into," Silas said. "I've had nothing to do with him since I turned thirteen. That tells you how ancient."

"And yet he still wants to make you pay?"

Silas leaned back and flexed his shoulders to relax them. He sighed. "You know what they say. It takes all sorts." There was a resigned note in his voice.

Jeavon sighed. "I should warn you that Posey isn't taking your secrecy well. And if you insist on not telling her what's going on, she's going to poke around making her own investigations." He glanced over to Silas, a kindly glint in the deep grey eyes. "In fact, I wouldn't be surprised if she already has."

Silas bristled. "I wish she wouldn't. She'll just put herself in danger and make things a lot worse."

"Easy enough to say, but when you're making noises about giving up on the case, you can't blame her. Winning that case has become the focus for that family, and Poppy isn't here to throw her weight around and help."

"Who is she trying to see?" Silas asked.

"Margaret Beaumont, I believe."

"Margaret Beaumont? You didn't?" He stared at Jeavon, his face stony. "You told her about Margaret?" he queried, his voice rising. "Well, thanks a lot."

"She asked," Jeavon protested. "And I didn't tell her where to find her. She'll have to work that part out for herself."

Silas pinched his lips together in consternation. "Luckily for me, Margaret has secrets of her own. I don't think she knows much about my story, and she's not keen to divulge hers. I think I'm safe there."

"Would it matter all that much if you told Posey what's going on?" Jeavon asked, his voice gentle. "After all, how many times have I heard you say that 'Honesty is the best policy' when talking about your clients?"

"This is different," said Silas, and by the set of his jaw, Jeavon knew he would get no revelations from Silas today.

Twenty-seven

The church bells struck 1 pm, signalling lunch hour in a city with a passion for stopping for their midday meal, and the tables at the Café Restaurant on George Street, the vanguard of eating houses, were already fully occupied. Gideon Vane glanced around at his fellow patrons and marvelled at the carefree spirit of the place. The tables overflowed with businessmen in well-tailored charcoal suits, more casually dressed fellows in loose sports coats – the clerks and underlings, no doubt – and a few discreet couples like him and Eudora, charting the possibilities, all enveloped in a twitter of happy chatter, like starlings coming in to roost. The formally attired servers, looking like original garçon de café, in white shirts with stand-up collars and thigh-length black waistcoats, energetically circulated, dispensing drinking water from big glass jugs and greeting regulars with a cheery "Bonjour".

He spotted one scandalous table occupied entirely by women, dressed in the parrot colours of emerald green and scarlet so favoured by females in the Antipodes.

You'd never see that in London.

He didn't know whether to approve or disapprove of their

freedom, but he had to acknowledge: These colonials certainly know how to enjoy life. He scanned the table to see if Posey Barclay was present, but no. Surprising. That was just the sort of company he'd expect her to keep.

He glanced across the crisp white tablecloth to Eudora, clad in an entirely appropriate heavy brocade in muted green and mauve. Attractive but not showy. Of that, he definitely approved.

"Thank you for accepting this invitation, Eudora," he said, expressing his appreciation with a nod of his head. "One of the pleasures of coming to Sydney is meeting you."

He watched as a pleased pink flush spread up Eudora's neck to her cheeks.

Good. First run on the board. She likes compliments. Women are so easy to read.

"Thank you for inviting me," she chirped in response.

Just then, the maitre'd swooped in. A full-figured, genial-featured host wearing a blousy shirt belted at his waist bowed in greeting.

"Lord Brook! Monsieur Cheval at your service. May we welcome you to our fair city and offer you complimentary drinks? You are aware we can serve you iced beverages? A sherry cobbler, or mint julep, perhaps? Or peach lemonade for the lady?"

Monsieur Cheval, who'd obviously remembered Gideon from an earlier visit with Elias, displayed the faintest of Parisian accents and all of the democratic ebullience of his adopted country.

"Merci, monsieur." Gideon matched his enthusiastic host

by answering in French. "We will forego the drinks today, but I'm sure the lady would appreciate ice cream for dessert."

Cheval raised one brow and then bowed. "Certainement."

Gideon turned to Eudora, who was watching the exchange with an indulgent half smile. "We'll have their three-course lunch – soup, joints, and sweets. But our host has kindly offered us ice cream to complete our meal. J'espère qu'il sera à votre goût?" *Is that to your liking?*

She replied with a delighted smile and a dip of her head. "J'aimerais beaucoup ça, merci." *I'd like that very much, thank you.*

Her French was passably good.

He turned back to Monsieur Cheval. "Your usual three-course fare with the ice cream for dessert," Gideon said. Then added: "Oh, and on second thoughts, two of the iced peach lemonades."

Monsieur Cheval beamed, as if his good taste was vindicated, and hurried away.

"It's wonderful to be invited out," said Eudora. "I tire of the Chinese tearooms. They're the only place ladies can take refreshments without escorts."

Gideon cast a significant glance at the women's only table.

She gave a demure smile. "Respectable ladies," she corrected.

"I'm surprised at this place. The food is as good as in any in the Palais Royal or the Boulevards," he said.

She tipped her head coyly. "We've had French eating houses here for twenty years, and very good ones for the last ten. It was always a joke in Sydney that 'God sends meat, but the devil sends cooks'." She looked deep into his eyes, as if conveying important local intelligence.

She has gold flecks around her irises. I've never noticed them before, but the subtle green of her dress brings it out.

Eudora was chattering on.

When we're married, I'll have to let her know I'm not fond of female chatter.

"But Marcel, the chef here, has disproved that adage. And next door they offer billiards, chess, and a writing room. You name it. Strictly for gentlemen, of course." She made a little moue with her full pink lips.

"I see I could come to rely on you for the inside story," he said, his voice teasing, surprising himself with his levity. Until this moment, he hadn't realised how nice it was to escape the restraints of Pall Mall. "So, what's keeping ladies of your station entertained this week?"

He paused while a server delivered two peach lemonades to their table, the coral fizz tinkling in the iced glass. He leaned forward confidentially when the garçon departed.

"I'd appreciate hearing something entertaining after several concentrated days of dry legal talk."

Eudora smiled and matched his intimate tone. "Hugo's been a dear lately. He's popping in often. He understands how much I miss my dear mother, and that house is so big for one person!" She fluttered her dark lashes. "He often stays for a light supper. It's boring for cook only to serve me, so everyone is happy when he visits."

"And what's Hugo's latest gossip?" he said, keeping his voice light.

'Well," she said, teasingly drawing out the vowel. "There's

been ructions in the Barclay household about some old painting. Arabella has had it for years, but no one's taken much notice until now."

She drew her glass closer and took a long sip through the straw. She licked her lips. "Oh, this is delicious. A heavenly elixir." She smiled.

He took her lead and tested the brew.

"You're right. Scrumptious. But you were saying?"

"Let me see… Oh, yes, Hugo and the painting." As an aside, she added, "Hugo is very close to Arabella. He knew her before she went to Hong Kong and married her first husband."

"Oh, yes? She went to Hong Kong?"

Eudora nodded. "She was married to some taipan up there. She came back home when he died."

"And the painting?"

"It's of a young girl. An exquisite young girl they call Angel Eyes. There's some mystery involved and Arabella has got all upset about it."

"Upset? What about?"

The peach lemonade suddenly tasted sickly. His body was rejecting it. Going nauseous on him. He took a deep breath to regain control. He focused on gazing into Eudora's face, and not giving anything away.

Eudora shook her head. "Hugo didn't know exactly. Arabella is inclined to fall into slumps now and then these days. I suppose with everything that's happened with James…" She stopped talking abruptly and stared into his face. "Are you alright, Gideon? You look pale, suddenly."

He wiped his hand across his brow. "I'm fine. Stuffy in here, that's all." He allowed for a brief pause. "Did Hugo say what the painting looked like?"

"Only that it was exceptionally beautiful. It was supposed to be a big secret. Posey told him not to mention it to anyone, but of course he couldn't resist telling me. He knows I'm interested. Clifford was once engaged to Posey's twin, Poppy, you know. If it hadn't been for the financial disaster, I'd have a Barclay sister-in-law by now."

"Mmm," was all that Gideon could add, grateful that steaming bowls of pea-and-ham soup arrived at just that moment and he didn't need to do much more than compliment the food for quite some time.

Twenty-eight

Silas and Jeavon met Jeremiah Hawkins at Tattersall's Family Hotel in Pitt Street, a popular meeting place for men who liked to talk racing and place bets on the horses, and as the Cobb and Co coach terminus, a comfortable home away from home for out-of-towners. It offered agreeable lodgings for Nathan Russell's Ballarat mine manager, who was making the trip at Silas's request.

Hawkins had been away at his father's funeral when Silas had visited the mine a few weeks ago, and he'd only interviewed the deputy manager, who'd never met Nathan and did not know of the history of the company. Silas had left a request for Jeremiah to come to Sydney, plus money for his fare, with a fellow solicitor in Ballarat. Apart from commendatory reports from locals like the mines inspector, George Downey, and Mayor James McDowell, he knew nothing of the chap.

He and Jeavon settled themselves in the quiet end of the bar next to the "tin bar", the rendezvous point for sportsmen and punters.

"I don't know if our guest is a sporting man or not," Silas remarked as they took their stools. "I don't know much about him at all, except that he seems to be respected in his community as an excellent operator."

"A good place to start," Jeavon said, sipping his ale. "People are not generally wrong about those they've lived next to for a long time."

They both glanced up as a tall wiry man with a full beard approached Silas.

"Are you the lawyer? Mr Williams? Appearing on behalf of Mr Russell?"

Silas put down his beer on the bar and swung on his stool to face the stranger. "Indeed, I am," he said, thrusting out a hand. "What can I get you?"

Jeremiah shook his head. "I leave the rotgut to others," he said. "In my line of work. I need to keep a clear hear."

Silas raised one brow in salute. "Lemonade it will be. And thank you for coming."

"An expenses-paid trip to Sydney? A man would be a fool to turn that down." He grinned and gestured to the stool beside Silas. "Mind if I sit down?"

"Not at all, but before you do, let me introduce my friend, Jeavon Yates, a former Sydney police superintendent. I rely on Jeavon to keep me on the right track with my questions."

"Sounds like a formidable team," said Jeremiah. "Just as well I'm not the fanciful sort. I like to stick to the facts."

Jeavon smiled. "Then we'll get on just fine, Mr Hawkins."

Silas ordered Hawkins a lemonade, and they got down to talking about Nathan Russell, his mine, and the history of their relationship.

"I've been in the mines since I was a boy, back in Cornwall," said Jeremiah. "And Nathan was a young lad with no mining experience. So when we ended up on the goldfields together, it was natural I offered him advice from time to time, and he was smart enough – or silly enough – to take most of it."

"And you saw nothing of his stepfather, James Barclay, in Victoria?" Silas asked.

Hawkins shook his head. "Never came near. And he said little about the old man. He talked about his family – his wife Charlotte and the little son, and so forth – but he never mentioned his brother-in-law until they discovered the money was missing. That was when he asked me to step in and manage the mine for him.

"We were on pretty lean pickings in Ballarat at the time, so he went to San Francisco to find his older brother, John. I think he was hoping some big deal would jump out at him there, which would enable him to bail the family out of trouble. He was worried about the future for his three sisters." He gulped back the last of his lemonade.

"And as it turned out, he fell on his feet over there. What he learned here in Ballarat set him up to manage a mine in California. And now he's married to the gal that owns the mine as well. Funny how these things turn out."

"And did you ever hear him discuss the Victoria mine? I mean in terms of shares. Did he give his family shares? Or anyone else you know of?"

Jeremiah wriggled his bushy brows. "Well, yes," he said, staring at Silas in surprise.

"Oh? Who?"

Jeremiah pointed his index finger at his broad chest. "Me.

He offered me ten per cent before he left for America. It was ten percent of nothing at the time, but he didn't have any money to give me an advance or anything, and he didn't know how long he was going to be away. He offered me that share as an extra incentive to stay on when he couldn't pay it in wages."

He grinned. "And either through good luck or good management, it's paid off for both of us. We struck a new vein eight months after he went to America. It took another few months to get things going, but we've got a productive venture working now."

"Does anyone else know about your arrangement?" asked Jeavon.

Jeremiah shrugged. "I don't know if Nathan has told anyone. I haven't. As far as I'm concerned, the fewer people know about my business, the better."

"Very sensible," said Jeavon. "I imagine Mr Russell is very pleased with the way your management has turned out."

"I reckon," said Hawkins. "For all of us."

"You have a written contract with Mr Russell, I imagine?"

"Yes sir, I do."

"And since you've 'struck gold', as they say, have you ever had any unscheduled inspections, or strangers poking their nose around?" Jeavon asked. "Anyone trying to threaten you or bribe you?"

Jeremiah pulled back on his stool, frowning. "There have been some whingers. Cornelius Kneebone, the fellow who has the licence for the ground next to us, has complained the boundaries were not accurately drawn up. He's tried to grab our most productive dirt, but his complaints haven't got him anywhere. Nathan was working his licences years before Kneebone turned up."

A silence sat between them and then Silas said, "I'd like to see a copy of the agreement you have with Mr Russell, Jeremiah. You'd have no objection to that?"

"None at all," said Hawkins. "I've got it in a safe deposit box at my bank. I'm happy to have a notarised copy made for you."

"We'll pay the expenses, of course," said Silas.

Jeremiah hesitated. "So, this is all about some of James Barclay's creditors trying to get their hands on the Ballarat mine, is that it? They claim that somehow Nathan gave him a share too?"

"That's it exactly," said Jeavon. "They've been making wild claims in the papers, but they've not got a leg to stand on, so far as we can tell. We're just trying to ensure we know the full story." He paused, looking directly into Jeremiah Hawkin's face. "We fear they may stoop to presenting false documents, or bribing folk into swearing false. If anyone ever approaches you with some offer like that, we'd be grateful to hear of it."

Jeremiah half rose from his stool, his hands fisted at his sides. "I'd never…" he said, his voice strangled, throat tight.

Silas reached out a hand and touched his wrist. "Don't fright yourself, Mr Hawkins. I am completely satisfied in your integrity. We're just warning you, some people aren't as conscientious as you are. And as we now understand, you are the only other shareholder, so it's very much in your best interests to protect the mine from free loaders. It's in all our interests," he said.

"Take care here in Sydney. And if you feel under threat or

uncertain about anything, please send a boy for help immediately." He handed Jeremiah his and Jeavon's cards. "We're all in this together. I see no reason for anyone to go after you, but we can't be too careful."

Twenty-nine

Arabella leaned back in her chair and gave a satisfied sigh. "That was the nicest lunch I've had in ages. Since I had that nasty fall, anyway. I lost my appetite for a time there."

She smiled at her daughters, who gazed at her with fond, soft eyes.

"It's wonderful to see you recovering so well, Mother," Petunia said. "It's been remarkable, considering my fears when I found you."

The dirty plates on the Barclay House dining table displayed remnants of bread crumbs and Mulligatawny soup. A light spicy aroma of the soup's Madras curry powder and stewed apple, together with the yeasty fragrance of freshly baked bread rolls, lingered in the warm air.

Posey, who'd been holding back on questioning her mother for days, took it as her opening to begin a conversation she'd been aching for. Had her mother remembered anything more about the painting? Had she known anything about Silas's arrival in Australia? Did she know Margaret Beaumont?

"Perhaps if you're feeling well enough, we could talk about the painting?" she ventured, a hopeful note in her voice. "I went to see a woman named Margaret Beaumont a few days ago. She's been in Sydney for a long time, and knows a lot about the early days. She knew Silas when he first arrived."

She hesitated, unsure exactly how to continue, and looked directly into her mother's face. "I wondered... Do you recall ever meeting her?"

Arabella gazed back, eyes blank, a vague, dreamy expression on her face, as if her thoughts were being interrupted by someone from far away.

"Margaret Beaumont?" She repeated the name with rising uncertainty. "I don't recall anyone by that name. Should I? What's she got to do with anything?"

"I'm not sure... Her husband, Archibald Beaumont, was Silas's employer when he first arrived here. I just wondered..." She didn't want to spell out Silas's obvious disquiet over the painting.

"Archibald Beaumont, you say? I might have met them in passing, but I don't recall." Arabella's deep hazel eyes glazed over, sliding her back into her preoccupations. She stared into the middle distance for a few seconds and then commented, "Speaking of lawyers, Hugo is such a dear. He came by yesterday to see how I was, and he invited me to a reception for that new judge. Apparently, they're becoming quite good friends..." She took a sip of her rapidly cooling tea. "It's not so surprising, really. I mean, Hugo is one of the foremost lawyers in town."

"A reception? What reception?" Posey queried, her voice sharper than she intended.

"I believe it's for Lord Brook's induction. They're getting

him started on the job. It's obviously important for Hugo to be there. There will be drinks and speeches, I gather. Hugo says he'd like me to be there because of our future plans."

"Your future plans?" Posey and Petunia chorused, exchanging unsettled glances.

Posey made a 'you go first' gesture with her right hand.

"What plans are those, Mother?" Petunia asked in a voice that was far more tranquil and composed than Posey could have managed.

"Why to marry, of course," said Arabella. "It's clear that's what Hugo has in mind. He wouldn't be paying me all the attention he is without serious intentions. I thought you'd both see that."

"But Mother," Posey cried. "Father hasn't even been dead a year!"

"I realise that, Posey. Better than anyone. And we won't do anything about it until the full year anniversary has passed, don't worry. We're just preparing the ground." She gave a girlish giggle. "To be truthful, I think Hugo has carried a flame for me all these years."

"Are you sure you want this, Mother?" Petunia spoke up, pert and crisp. "Because I understand Hugo has a woman he's been giving attention to for many years… Gwen someone?" Petunia gazed at her mother with her large, innocent green eyes, as if she was suggesting something no more contentious than whether she preferred beef or chicken stew for dinner.

Posey's jaw gaped. Since when had her young sister, whose one passion in life was horses, become privy to the inner circle's darkest secrets?

Arabella was unfazed. "Oh, you probably mean Gwen Sterling." She let loose with a high-pitched chortle and gave an airy wave of her hand. "Gwen's his secretary, sweetheart. Hugo would never marry her. He's a top man in town and she's a clerk."

An awkward silence stretched out between them.

Then Petunia pitched a quiet question. "You're not thinking of announcing an engagement or anything, Mother?"

"Goodness me, no," said Arabella. "There's plenty of time for that. Let's get this bothersome court case over first."

That's a load off my mind, Posey thought. *Looking on the bright side, if we lose the case the engagement will probably never happen.*

"Mother, you say Hugo is friendly with Lord Brook? Do you think that's a good idea? For you to be so close to Hugo, I mean? Considering our coming court case and all…"

Arabella frowned. "Why on earth would that matter, Posey? Hugo isn't acting for us. He's not involved in any way."

Posey's jaw tightened in a stubborn cast. "But what about him getting access to our private matters? The painting, for starters. You pretty well ordered me to take Hugo to see that thing. What if he's gossiped about it to other people? People like Lord Brook…?"

"Oh, Posey, now you're just being silly. Why on earth would Hugo want to talk to Lord Brook about some old painting? I'm sure they have far more important things to discuss." She gathered herself up like the aristocratic beauty she once was.

And still is, Posey admitted, as she watched her mother stand with well-rehearsed grace.

"I'm sorry you seem reluctant to accept my news. But Hugo and I are well suited, and you'll just have to get used to the idea. By this time next year it's quite possible he'll be part of our family." She turned for the door with imperial poise. "And now, if you girls don't mind, I will take my afternoon nap. That soup has left me feeling deliciously full and sleepy."

Posey put her finger to her lips in a silencing gesture as she sensed Petunia was about to burst into a voluble comment. "Shh," she said. "Let's make sure she's upstairs before we say anything."

They stared at each other, lips twitching.

When they'd left a suitable gap, Petunia choked with laughter.

"Well, Posey. How does it feel to be beaten to the altar by your aging mother and Husband Number Three?"

They bent over and cackled until their eyes ran wet with tears.

"Did you have any idea this was in the wind?" asked Posey once they had straightened up. "I'm afraid I've been too preoccupied with my other stuff. And Hugo has been around like a kindly uncle for so many years. I didn't really think about it." She eyed her sister with new respect. "But *Gwen*? Where on earth did you hear about Gwen?"

Petunia smiled. "You forget I spend half the week at Hugo's track, and I see what's going on. One of the stable hands wants something from the house, or I'm getting a carafe of water or something. I chat with Gwen now and then. But it was Clarrie that mentioned it. He says Hugo has been stringing Gwen along for years. She's a combination of household manager and secretary; she practically runs his life. Probably knows all his secrets if he's got any. Hugo would be lost without her."

"I see," said Posey, putting her index finger to her lips in contemplation. "I wonder what she'll think about his impending engagement? Will she be willing to stay on and see another woman take over the household? Has she got any idea of Hugo's plans, I wonder?"

"I don't know," Petunia said. "But I suspect she won't be happy at being pushed off her perch when she finds out."

Thirty

When Jeavon answered his front door and stood back in greeting, he recognised immediately that Posey was in her typical 'bustling business' frame of mind. Her eyes darted to meet his with urgency, and she stepped into his hallway with quick driving steps.

"Jeavon," she said, waving a paper in her right hand he hadn't noticed she was carrying till this moment. "I've had a letter from Nathan about the mine. I wanted to share its contents with you immediately."

He closed the door and waved her in, ushering her down the hall to his back deck. She'd visited him frequently enough to know exactly where to go, and settled on one of the hard bench seats without any hesitation.

"I won't read it all to you, but I just had to share this with somebody, and I don't know where Hawk Eye is in all this. I don't feel right about talking with him, he's been acting so strangely." Her words cascaded like a waterfall she couldn't hold back, and she paused to take a fresh breath.

"He had the strangest look on his face last night at the swearing-in ceremony for the new judge. I didn't even get a chance to speak to him." A faraway veil clouded her face for a few seconds, as if she were thinking back to the previous evening. "He seemed both intimately involved, and yet distanced from it, all at the same time. Is that even possible? Sometimes he looked tortured, and at others he was stony cold. When he's like that, he doesn't even seem to be in the same room as the rest of us."

Jeavon cleared his throat. "You plainly spent a lot of time watching his reactions." It wasn't a question.

Posey's cheeks flushed a light pink. She glanced towards him and gave him a wry smile. "I admit it. I did. But I hope it wasn't obvious to anyone else. I was discreet."

Jeavon gave a short laugh. "As always, dear Posey. As always. How did the ceremony go?"

She sighed. "Just as you'd expect. Lots of speeches in praise of the villain… If Vane is the villain, which I truly believe he must be to be having this effect on Silas. It sounded like it would if someone is appointed because of who they know rather than what they know. The valedictory was short on any substantial accomplishments, apart from having the good fortune to be born into the nobility, educated at Eton, and having a baron recommend you.

"But the important thing for us — not that it's a surprise exactly — is that Sir Frederick announced right at the end that Judge Vane will preside on our case. When he announced that, Hawk Eye turned ash grey."

Jeavon leaned forward and picked up his pipe and a leather tobacco pouch that sat on the table beside him. They sat in a mutual silence, broken only by the twitter of birds in the garden as he packed the bowl and lit it.

He sat back in his chair and took a few satisfying puffs before turning to Posey and saying. "You're right on all counts, as usual, Posey. That's what we have to work with. Now tell me why you're so excited about Nathan's letter."

***

Posey gazed into Jeavon's worn face as he relaxed back, quietly waiting for her to respond, clouds of pale-blue smoke rising above his head.

He is a rock, this man. He'd never leave a girl a note saying he can't take any more.

Her temperature spiked at the unruly thought.

Not fair, one part of her fractious mind cried. *True, nevertheless*, another part echoed back.

"Oh, yes," she replied to Jeavon's query, the original impatient energy that had driven her to his door returning. "Nathan says that mine manager Hawk Eye didn't manage to talk to could be a very important part of our defence. The one who was away on family business?"

Jeavon's hand froze, his pipe halfway to his mouth. "The mine manager? Do you mean Jeremiah Hawkins?"

Posey nodded, though a sudden sense of doubt, of uncertainty, was enveloping her. "I… I think so."

"What exactly did Nathan say about him?"

"He said he was an excellent manager and an even better man in that he was reliable and a man of integrity. Nathan gave him a share in the mine as part of their deal when he left to go to America. He trusted him more than anyone he could think of to run the mine while he was away."

Jeavon had placed his still-smoking pipe on an ashtray next to his pouch and regarded her with deep sadness.

"That's a great shame," he said.

"A shame? Why? Surely it shows that Nathan made excellent decisions regarding the mine's management, and that it was in reliable hands? Mr Hawkins sounds like an ideal witness."

"He would have been, Posey, you're right again." Jeavon searched her face.

Posey's eyes narrowed into slits. "Would have been? What are you saying?"

"Mr Hawkins was beaten to death by larrikins behind his hotel in Pitt Street last night. At this stage, the police don't know who did it, or why."

Jeavon left a long silence.

"Convenient, isn't it?"

Thirty-one

The Dead House on the edge of Circular Quay where the bodies due for inquest were stored, was a source of irritation and dread to all who passed by. Small and insanitary – "nothing more than a room with a table in it" as one local observed in a Letter to the Editor – the pokey one-roomed cottage was incapable of accommodating more than two bodies at one time. Even with mine manager Jeremiah Hawkins' single corpse, it was uncomfortably crowded when the twelve members of the coroner's jury attempted to visit, as required by law, to view the victim's wounds.

The event had the air of a hastily arranged conclave, pulled together in urgency because the deceased person's physical decomposition dictated inquests were usually held within two days of a death. And the weekend was looming, when the jury members would not be available.

By an automatically adopted long tradition in English law, inquests were public occasions, more legal than medical, with any witnesses to the victim's death, plus friends, family and neighbours giving evidence. The medical evidence would be provided by the reporting medical officer, in this case Dr

Arthur Renwick, recognised as the forensic specialist of the day, giving his post-mortem findings.

The jurors satisfied their curiosity with a brief public viewing of Jeremiah's ravaged body in the Dead House, noting his viciously caved-in skull, the bruised eyes and fractured cheeks before the inquest into his death was adjourned across the road to the far more commodious surroundings of Observer Tavern. Tavern owners were required by law to make premises available for these hearings, and it wasn't the first time the sandy-haired coroner Henry Shiell, Dr Renwick, Jeavon and Silas had sat around the big oak table in a private bar with a crowd at an inquest.

But it was the first time they found themselves to be practically the only summoned witnesses, apart from the Tattersalls Hotel's front office manager, and a saloon cleaner who'd discovered Hawkins' body when he took rubbish to the refuse bins at the end of the night's business.

Silas, for one, was greatly relieved he didn't have to stand around in the malodorous Dead House, but he nevertheless regarded the proceedings with a deep inner dread. He couldn't shake the conviction that if he hadn't arranged Jeremiah's visit, the man would still be alive.

The coroner's office regularly booked the private bar for these meetings, and despite the new location, Silas detected the faintest whiff of the mortuary in the air – whether from their clothes as they'd processed past the body, or from the medical examiner's bag? Or was it his imagination? He didn't know, but it set him on edge.

The coroner had the bearing of a proper English civil

servant, with no hint of his Caribbean childhood as a plantation-owning slave-owner's son. He carried himself with stiff rectitude and regimented punctuality, famous for insisting proceedings start on time. Everyone knew Henry Shiell handed out prompt fines to jury men who reported late for duty.

When the twelfth member of the jury slipped in the back of the already hot, stuffy room at one minute past ten, he earned a reprimanding glare. The late arrival, puffing and red-faced, had a heavy jaw and deep-set eyes. He pulled a cab driver's cap from his flattened hair, dipped his head in apology and sank with a sigh of relief into the last empty chair around the table.

Shiell first called the cleaner, a shuffling white-bearded ancient called Tom, who confirmed the simple fact that he'd discovered a man's beaten body when he'd taken the saloon rubbish out an hour after closing. He'd told the manager, who'd called the constables.

The Tattersall's manager, Sam Sutton, was a lanky white-faced young fellow who peered nervously through wire-rimmed glasses. The second witness, he confirmed Mr Hawkins was an abstemious hotel guest who had not frequented the sports bar, with its raucous drinking and betting clientele.

"He preferred a quiet lemonade in the private bar," he said. "He never caused our barmaids any trouble. The only time I saw him meeting anyone was when he spoke to former police superintendent Yates and Mr Williams," he said, with a nod to Jeavon and the barrister beside him.

Shiell acknowledged Jeavon, who he'd worked with closely, with a friendly raised brow. "Thank you, Mr Sutton. You can step down. Former Superintendent? Can you replace him?"

Jeavon stood slowly, his six foot six frame and rangy torso seeming to cast the seated jurors in the shade.

"Thank you, sir. It's a sad day that sees me appearing before you again. I thought those days were over with my retirement."

"It is indeed a sad day, Former Superintendent, but I am confident of your integrity as a witness. Tell us how you knew Mr Hawkins."

Jeavon glanced at Silas. "My friend and colleague, Mr Silas Williams, needed Mr Hawkin's evidence in a case he is preparing. I believe he paid Jeremiah's expenses to come to Sydney to talk to him. We met him together in the Tattersall's bar a few nights ago."

He consulted a notepad he had brought from his jacket as he spoke. "Two nights ago, I believe it was. Mr Hawkins seemed in fine form that evening, with nothing he confided to us causing him any concern."

"And was the information he gave you satisfactory?" Henry Shiel's bushy brows rose in a question.

Jeavon glanced at Silas. "I believe it was as Mr Williams expected it to be, but he will attest to that better than me."

"And how long was Mr Hawkins planning to stay in Sydney?"

Jeavon hesitated. "Once again, probably best for Mr Williams to answer that. I believe that night he said he planned to prolong his stay a day or two to take in the sights. It was the first time he'd been to Sydney, I understand, and he joked it might also be the last. He came from Ballarat."

"His remark about 'might be the last'? Nothing sinister in that, I assume?"

Jeavon huffed through hands he'd raised to his mouth. "Nothing at all, Your Honour. It rather indicated he had his hands full with his work in Ballarat."

"Is there anything else you believe the inquest might want to know about him?"

Jeavon shook his head. "Just that he seemed to be a steady, credible and hard-working man with a sensible attitude. I can't imagine him falling into dangerous company, or picking a fight on the street. Not in a million years."

"Thank you, Former Superintendent. Mr Williams, could you rise and add to that account?"

"Certainly, sir." Silas stood. "I arranged for Mr Hawkins to come to Sydney because when I visited Melbourne and Ballarat recently, he was away on family business and I could not talk to him there. I feel somewhat responsible for his unfortunate death."

Henry Shiell regarded him with steady grey eyes. "I don't believe you should concern yourself in that regard, Mr Williams. The circumstances are indeed most unfortunate, but you're hardly to blame. Are you able to give us any details of the case you were working on?"

Silas looked at his feet and shuffled. "I'd rather not, Mr Shiell. I'd have to plead the protection of my client's privacy in that regard. All I can say is that it was very much in the line of duty. Nothing scandalous was discussed or revealed. Mr Hawkins was a willing witness to a coming case. That's really all I can say."

Shiell pursed his lips and frowned. "And how many times did you meet with Mr Hawkins?"

"Just that one time," Silas said. "With Jeavon present as an additional observer. There was nothing contentious or dubious about anything we discussed. At the end of our meeting, which probably took thirty to forty minutes, Jeremiah thanked us and said he was going to take advantage of his time here to look around. That's all there was to it."

Shiell's response – a courteous "Thank you, Mr Williams. You may stand down." – was drowned out by the sudden arrival of a broad-shouldered younger man who elbowed his way past the coroner's clerk standing guard at the door, shouting angrily as he charged in.

A woolly full-chinned beard obscured his face that, along with the working-class bowler hat that shaded his eyes, marked him as a man from the bush.

Wild-eyed, he swept off his hat, spouting oaths as he did. "Blood 'n' 'ounds. Strike me blind. By all that's blue."

The clerk ran around him and blocked his path a second time, but the man placed a muttony hand in the middle of the clerk's chest and barrelled past.

Henry Shiell rose to his feet and cried, "Stop right now, or the constable will arrest you."

A policeman in a light-blue jacket rose from one end of the table the jurors sat around.

The intruder stopped mid-stride and glared up at Shiell. "My own da, s'help me Bob. Dead as Julius Caesar. And I'm not even told."

A pall of silence fell, and every man in the room stared at the panting young man with bloodshot eyes who stood before them.

Shiell gestured to the constable to find an extra chair, which he quickly dragged from a dark corner and placed beside his own.

The coroner pointed to it and then back at the newcomer. "State your name and business."

"I am Digby Hawkins. I am the only son of Jeremiah Hawkins who lies dead somewhere here." He whipped his head around, as if searching. "No one has told me exactly where."

Shiell pointed again to the chair next to the constable.

"Sit down, please, Mr Hawkins."

Digby Hawkins took a big breath and shouted again, a torrent of confused anger. "I don't want to sit down. I want to know what happened. Who killed him? I want to murder the thieves that robbed him. I want to—"

The constable was beside him in two strides, seizing his elbow and wrenching his arm up his back. Digby Hawkins howled.

Henry Shiell thundered, still on his feet, "Silence, Mr Hawkins! Silence. Sit down, or I will have you arrested. We are about to hear from Doctor Renfrew, who will have at least some answers to your questions." He paused and glared. "Sit down now, or you'll be locked up for disturbing the peace."

The young man's weaselly black eyes darted around the room until they alighted on Silas. He raised the arm that was not in the constable's restraint and pointed. "That man there. The blind geezer. He's to blame for this."

"My final warning," thundered Shiell. "Be quiet and sit down."

Digby Hawkins hesitated for a few more seconds and then

allowed the constable to lead him to the empty chair. Silas surveyed the crowd and things settled down again. At the back of the room, he noticed Jasper Blackwood, standing close to a knot of newspapermen, all with their notebooks out, frantically writing.

What's he doing here, he wondered?

His gut contracted. Among the pen pushers he recognised the *Sydney Herald*'s man Lucien Cross, the scribe Thomas Yates had dismissed as the proprietor's lackey, and the source of many anti-Barclay stories in recent months.

He'd be staying for the medical examiner's evidence. No doubt about that. But then he'd be scurrying back to his den with his latest juicy scandal.

Silas could see tomorrow's headlines even as he turned his attention to Dr Arthur Renfrew.

Prominent Barrister Accused of Man's Death.

Thirty-two

Silas could have sworn the charnel house stench in the Observer Tavern grew stronger as they sat in tense silence, listening to Dr Renfrew's meticulously compiled evidence.

His attackers had horribly abused Jeremiah Hawkins, who'd suffered internal damage, including a split spleen and badly bruised kidneys. The evidence showed they'd kicked when he was down, perhaps already unconscious. He had multiple wounds around his head and face, indicating he'd been struck several times on the back of the head with a blunt object, as well as being successively punched about the face. His cheekbones were shattered and one eye ravaged.

"If he'd lived, he probably would have been blind in that eye," Dr Renfrew said. "It's highly likely, but impossible to confirm."

"Amidst so much damage, was it possible for you to determine the cause of death?" the coroner asked.

Dr Renfrew hesitated for a long minute. "I believe it was, sir, and it's almost certainly not what you think."

"Oh?" Henry Shiell's professional interest sparked in his intelligent eyes, and he smiled at his colleague. "Then out with it, doctor. How did Mr Jeremiah Hawkins die?"

"It was a professional job, Mr Shiell. An almost forensic stab wound with a narrow, very sharp stiletto blade, through his ribs, straight to his heart. He would have been dead before his body hit the ground."

A stunned silence fell over the room, the only sound the scratching of journalists' pencils on paper.

"I beg your pardon, Doctor? Did you say it was most likely the work of a hatchet man?"

"I did, sir. All the other damage – to his head, his face, his internal organs – was post mortem. Apparently for display. Or for reasons unknown. It would have taken at least two men to carry it out. One to hold the victim upright while the other dealt the blows to the body."

Renfrew paused for dramatic effect.

"I would stake my reputation on it. This death was not the work of drunken street larrikins. It was the work of a brutal killer."

Digby Hawkins let out an anguished cry and rose to his feet again before the constable could reach out and restrain him.

"I knew it! That Barclay mob… they couldn't let him live. The evidence he was going to give would have been too damaging. They had to get rid of him and make it look like a street attack."

"You've had your final warning," Shiell screamed in a most ungentlemanly manner. "Take him to the cells, Constable."

"You're arresting the wrong man," Digby yelled as he was dragged from the room, his heels snagging on the carpet as he was evicted.

He attempted to spin around and face Silas, but failed. His cries were muffled as the constable wrestled him to the door, but Silas still heard them.

"It's that man there. He's the one you should be arresting."

Thirty-three

Chief Justice Sir Frederick Dooley pushed his circular gold-framed spectacles down his nose and peered over them at the men sitting opposite him. Between them sat a squat, brown leather ottoman on which perched an elegant silver tray holding a silver coffeepot. Set in front of the three men present in the Government House drawing room were Staffordshire Minton porcelain coffee cups, the required provision for all of Queen Victoria's embassies and domiciles of her heads of state. They steamed with the earthy chocolate fragrance of freshly poured coffee.

Sir Frederick stretched his arm forward to pick up his cup, the signal for them all that this little get together had formally begun.

"You appear to be settling in most satisfactorily, Lord Brook. How are you enjoying your stay so far? Have you questions about your orientation?"

Gideon Vane inclined his head courteously to his superior and then dipped it again in deference to the gentleman sitting on his right, the supreme authority for Her Majesty's government in Botany Bay, the New South Wales Governor, the Earl of Belmore.

They were taking mid-morning coffee over a customary briefing with the governor before Gideon's official swearing in as a Supreme Court judge on Monday, and it was the new judge's first meeting with the top man. He knew him by reputation, of course, for his wise and calm handling of affairs after the disastrous assassination attempt on Queen Victoria's son, Prince Alfred, in a Sydney park in March.

Another troublesome, unhinged Irishman, Gideon thought.

The governor had been hosting the prince, who was also the Duke of Edinburgh, at the event, but luckily Belmore was some distance away when Henry James O'Farrell took his shot.

It became clear O'Farrell had planned to kill the governor, too. Everyone agreed the judicious way the Belmore handled the whole incident had prevented a rabid Fenian uprising.

He's another Irishman, naturally, so he knows the type. We're surrounded by them. What is it about this place that draws them?

Vane thrust aside the distracting thought and focused his attention on the colony's top men. He knew he had to impress these fellows if he was going to get ahead here.

"My needs have been more than taken care of, Your Honour. Thank you. Your man Morgan has been most helpful with administrative matters, and I have found some of my legal peers, like Mr Hugo Davenport, for example, most convivial. He's been a great help to me in getting to know more about the colony's society."

Dooley took a sip of coffee and patted his long white beard, as if checking for spills. "That is most pleasing, Lord Brook. I've found Morgan to be a most reliable servant of the Crown. And Mr Davenport is well established and valued, of course, after representing the law here for many years."

Lord Belmore inched forward in his seat, hinting at a coming question, and Gideon focused his attention on him. He was a tall, muscular man, with handsome features and a light sandy beard, and he sat upright in his chair, drilling Gideon with sharp eyes.

"What do you see as the most pressing legal issues facing the state at this time, Lord Brook? Have you had a chance yet to make an assessment?"

Here it is. The ideal opening.

"It's been clear to me I need to understand the importance of balancing the Crown's interests and local sensibilities. The independence of many of the settlers has already struck me." He gave the governor a quick smile. He hoped he'd conveyed he was speaking as one Eton old boy to another. "You've managed those sensitivities extremely well, if I might be so bold as to say, Lord Belmore."

The governor indicated his pleasure at the compliment with a genial nod.

"However..." Gideon allowed for a theatrical pause.

Belmore waved his hand encouragingly. "Spit it out, man. What do you have to say?"

"I have questions about the verification of the credentials of lawyers and judges in the colony... and whether that process is being carried out to your satisfaction?"

Sir Frederick's hands twitched in his lap. "Have you any reason for asking that question?" he inquired in a testy voice.

Gideon did his best to look mildly embarrassed. "Oh... it's nothing, really... Just that I've seen a fellow here I thought I recognised from home, but he's certainly operating here under a different name than he had in England. It made me wonder, that's all."

"This is someone appearing before the bench?" Sir Frederick asked.

"As I understand it," Gideon said in his mildest tone. "Of course, I haven't been here long enough to see for myself."

Sire Frederick cleared his throat. "So far as I know it, the proper checks are done on all the men appearing as barristers and solicitors. Who is this fellow?" he queried, his voice laced with scepticism.

"Oh, Sir Frederick, I could well be wrong. I'm not suggesting any wrongdoing. It just raised a few questions," Gideon back peddled.

"I quite understand," said the chief judge drily. "But who is it you are querying?"

Gideon sighed as if he was reluctant to answer and possibly get another man into trouble. "Silas Williams, Your Honour. If I am correct, I believe he vanished from the Inns of Court under rather a black cloud. I can't remember all the details."

"Silas Williams?" Sir Frederick's bushy white brows rose to his yellow-white hairline. "You couldn't have surprised me more. Lord Brook. Mr Williams has always conducted himself with the utmost integrity, so far as I am aware. But I can ensure you discreet inquiries are made."

"Oh, I don't want to cause any trouble, Sir Frederick."

"There won't be trouble if there is no cause," the chief judge said grumpily. "And if there is a cause, we'll be beholden to you for picking up on it." He glanced at the governor. "I had almost appointed Lord Brook to the Barclay case. It would be awkward if I appointed him and then Mr Williams turns out to be a dud. It might raise questions."

Lord Belmore cast a calculating eye to his colleague, his black irises a pinpoint of inquiry, and then on to Gideon. "And you, Lord Brook? If you knew this fellow before and have your suspicions about him, do they rule you out of taking the case? Would you feel the need to declare a conflict of interest?"

Gideon stiffened. "You mean would I feel the need to declare myself out of the running because of difficulties in making an objective decision? Definitely not. I think I can decide on the merits of a case without being influenced by rumour and innuendo."

"Excellent," Lord Belmore said. "In that case, we've nothing to fear."

"I understand the importance of judicial impartiality," Gideon said.

"Pleased to hear it," said Belmore. He paused and took another sip of coffee. "And tell me, Lord Brook. What exactly brought you to the Bay? A comfortable estate in Herefordshire. A seat in the House of Lords in your future? What attraction can there possibly be for you in Botany Bay?"

Not running away under any black clouds yourself, are you? There it is. The most direct challenge I've received here yet.

Gideon thrust his head forward in the on-the-point gesture he habitually resorted to. He found it comforting. More than any other gesture, he believed, it stamped his authority on a situation. "No black clouds? Or scandals? Is that what you are asking, Governor?" He forced his lips into a rictus smile he knew carried no genuine mirth or warmth. He stared into the governor's ice-blue eyes.

"Not at all," Belmore replied in a lazy, neutral drawl with just a hint of a rolled Irish accent. "A random inquiry. In deference to your interest in ensuring credentials, shall we say…"

"Sorry to disappoint you, My Lord, but nothing like that. Sir Frederick can confirm my standing was avowed by my colleague Baron Kingshorn, a foremost judge on the Court of the Queen's Bench."

Belmore turned to Sir Frederick with a light smile. "Very good. That satisfies one part of my question. But the other remains unanswered." He paused for effect, like the able politician he was.

"Oh? My apologies. What part was that?" Gideon's heart was racing.

"Why the colonies? Why Sydney in particular? It's a very long way from home."

Gideon let a long silence fall before answering.

"Let's just say I was looking for a change, Lord Belmore, and your fair land hasn't disappointed. Already, I've had surprises I never expected. About unimportant personal matters, I hasten to add. But it's already been worth the trip."

Belmore regarded him with a curious glint. "Glad to hear it, Lord Brook. When it comes to visitors, Australians hate to disappoint."

Thirty-four

Gwen Sterling sidled up to the stable doors and peered in to the dusty interior. Beams of sunlight fell across two rows of stalls, separated by an aisle covered in hay. In a stall halfway down, its rays struck the back of the black-coated stallion, adding extra shine.

A late afternoon silence hung heavy in the air, broken only by contented snuffles from the horses in their feed boxes and heavy grinding of muscled equine jaws. Eric, the stable boss, had given Hugo's expensive bloodstock their last feed of the day, and contentment settled over Navigator and Sweetheart, Hugo's leading stallion and mare, and their progeny, the carriers of her employer's dreams.

For all the years Gwen had known him, Hugo Davenport had been infatuated by thoroughbred horses. And gambling on them, more's the pity.

One he surely can't afford.

She peered into the shadowy depths, her eyes adjusting after the bright sunshine outside, and satisfied herself Hugo wasn't there, mooning over his latest acquisition in horse flesh. She stepped towards a closed door halfway up, fronted in two frosted-glass panels.

Not secure if his creditors come knocking, but that's his business.

She tapped lightly on the glass, and Hugo's familiar bass voice boomed in response.

"Come in!"

She turned the handle cautiously and peered around the door's edge.

"Oh, Gwennie. Come in, come in."

He looked up with a distracted cast in his eyes. She saw he was pouring over stud breeding charts, working out the lineage for his next foals, she supposed.

"Haven't you finished up by now? I'm eating alone tonight, you know that. I don't need you here. You can enjoy an early night," Hugo said.

She stepped into his office and pulled the door closed behind her. The air smelled of his familiar Cuban cigars and brandy, and she noticed he already had a crystal tumbler of amber liquid at his elbow.

"I know you're not going out," she said. "And I'm finished for the day, but I'm not ready to go home yet. We need to talk."

A flicker of irritation crossed his smooth, tanned face. His eyes were the clear deep-brown of Irish bog water, and they flashed at her demand. He was still a looker, though his jowls became more noticeable every passing year.

I guess that doesn't matter when you're a man with money and standing. Not like me.

"What's wrong?" he asked. "Aren't I paying you enough?"

"Probably not. Not with the secrets I know. But that's not what's bothering me."

"What are you talking about? What secrets?" Hugo raised

one bushy black brow so high it brushed the speckled grey forelock that fell over his face. Their eyes met in a long silence and he added, "Why don't you enlighten me?"

"I want to come to the swearing in on Monday night. I don't care if it's as your legal clerk or whatever. I just want to come. I'm sick of being left out. I do most of the work around here and I don't get any recognition. It's not all about the money." Once she'd taken a breath and got started, the words had flooded out. She closed her mouth to stop herself from saying anything further.

Hugo's face took on the familiar stoney cast she knew so well. The "not this again" veil. She could hear his jaws grinding his back teeth from where she stood.

"What little bee has got into your bonnet this time?" He expelled a long-suffering breath.

She took a step closer to his desk. "Hugo," she said, raising the volume to emphasise her point. "I *am* your clerk. I do more of the donkey work in your practice than you do. I'm not complaining. I want to be recognised, that's all. I'm sick of being ignored."

"Ignored?" The querulous brow hitched up again. "You're hardly overlooked. I spend more time in my day with you than with anybody." He hesitated and frowned. "Most days, anyway," he corrected. "What are you on about?"

"I'm invisible as far as society is concerned. Except for Jasper, no one knows I exist. And I'm sick of it." She took a few more steps into his office and leaned her back against the full rolled arm of the chair that fronted his desk. She needed to preserve the advantage of height, so she would not sit down.

I couldn't sit, anyway. I'm on fire inside. Now I've got started, it's hard to stop.

"I know you've already invited the widow. But an important man like you, you're allowed more than one guest. Jasper's going, and he's not even involved in the legal profession."

Hugo's face darkened at the mention of Jasper's name, as she knew it would.

I know everything about this man. More than he knows about himself.

"Jasper? Why is he going? And is that why you've got all stirred up?"

"No, it isn't," she replied, the words sizzling from her lips. "And he's going because he wants people who count to remember he's out there. It's the same for me."

"But… but you've got me. I know you're fabulous. Fantastic. The best fidus Achates any man could ever want."

"The best what?"

"Oh, it means 'trusty friend.' Don't worry yourself. It's from Virgil."

A prickle of irritation flooded her.

Here he is. Talking down to me. Patronising me again. I'm a lot more than a blinkin 'trusty friend.'

He half rose from his chair, as if suddenly realising he needed to make a fuss of her, flatter her, tell her again everything would be alright. Except she wasn't listening anymore.

"I do more for you than that Arabella ever could," she said.

He nodded in unison with her words. "I've told you many times I couldn't live without you. You're indispensable. But it's not a competition, Gwen. Arabella is a lifelong friend. You know that. And she's been through a terrible time…"

His good-guy charm offensive. Hands raised, palms turned skywards, the helpless-little-boy smile spreading across his fifty-something-year-old face…

She lifted her backside off the chair arm, and stood straight, her arms folded across her chest.

Oh, no… I've fallen for the Davenport charm one too many times.

"Jasper is going because Bishop Stanton says he can't do without him. He's indispensable, he says. Just like me." She let her weight fall forward onto the balls of her feet to lend her next statement extra gravity. "Make it happen, Hugo, or you might not like the results."

She started towards the door and then turned back to him in a theatrical pause. "I don't want to be mean, but Jasper doesn't observe social niceties. You know that. And he knows far too much of your history. If I say the word, he'll be spilling your secrets all over town. And I'm pretty sure… I *know*… neither of us wants that."

At the door she turned again and gazed at him, a picture of innocence. "I'll bring my gown for the induction on Monday and change here," she said. "So now you know. You're catering for two lady friends. Not just one. Understood?"

She didn't bother to wait for his reply. From the dumb look on his face, she suspected it would be a long time coming.

Thirty-five

Gideon Vane, Lord Brook to everyone except his closest allies, was bored with his own company. Late on Saturday afternoon, he wandered downstairs to the bar in the Petty Hotel basement, resigned to eavesdropping and people watching to while away an hour or two.

He was delighted when he spotted a familiar face perched on a stool at the majestic mahogany bar. He sauntered over and thrust out his hand.

"Mr Jasper Blackwood, if I am not mistaken," he said with a ready smile. "I'm pleased to meet you again. We barely had time to exchange words last time, did we?"

"Lord Brook." Jasper's face lit with pleasure. "Allow me to buy the visitor to our fair land an ale. Would that be to your taste? Or would you prefer Guinness?"

"Local ale would be just fine," said Gideon, pulling out the stool next to Jasper. "Do you come here often?"

They both laughed at the cliché, and Gideon relaxed. The barman quickly filled a mug and Jasper turned to him to clink cups for good luck.

"Here's to your induction on Monday," he cried. "I'm fortunate enough to be coming."

"Oh, really?" said Gideon. "I will know some faces there then. How did you wangle an invitation? And why would you want to?"

"The goodly Doctor Blackwood, my brother Ambrose, might have explained to you I tutor the sons of wealthy Sydneysiders? I'm schooling one of the Anglican bishop's sons at present. Bishop Stanton is in a wheelchair, and he's administering a blessing at the end of the formalities. I'm there as an attendant to see the bishop's every need is taken care of."

"Ah, I see," Gideon said, although really, he didn't. Surely the man had servants who could attend to this kind of thing?

Jasper glanced around him, as if he was sensitive to the idea of being overheard, and then he ducked his head closer to Gideon and said, "It serves my purposes, too."

"Your purposes? How?" Gideon replied, frowning.

"Well, it's obvious, isn't it? These jobs never last forever. If I do it well, the young lad will be off to some fancy university overseas and I'm back to square one. It helps in lining up new clients if they see me at a function like this, rubbing shoulders with the likes of you." He flashed Gideon a frank smile.

Gideon pointedly looked around them. "Can't spot any sons lurking here looking for a coach," he taunted. "So, I'm not sure how much use I am."

"Oh, don't worry," said Jasper, "everyone is curious about you, so I'll get lots of dinner invitations after this so they can ask me all their questions about what you're like and what sort of judge you will make. A lot of locals are sensitive about being under English law." He paused. "Especially the Irishmen, as you can quite imagine."

Gideon nodded. "And there are an awful lot of them. I'd noticed."

Over the next couple of hours, the pair chatted on. Blackwood explained he'd initially entered the church himself, but found the role of a clergyman too limiting.

"I was rather drawn to the dark side," he said with disarming candour. "I spent a lot of time in The Rocks." He paused and fixed Gideon with a challenging eye. "I learned a lot about human nature. Far more than in theological college."

"I can imagine you would," Gideon said, gesturing to his empty mug. "My turn to buy the next round."

The fellow behind the bar – Gideon was fast learning you called random chaps "blokes" in Australia – was dressed in formal black-and-white tails and behaved more like a butler than a bar attendant. Once he delivered fresh drinks, Gideon turned back to Jasper.

"So, is your current pupil likely to make it into the college of his choice? And if so, you'll then be looking for your next student? Is that how it works?"

"That's correct," said Jasper. "Edward Stanton is not likely to graduate with First-Class honours, but he'll get through. I enjoy the variety."

"And do you know yet who your next student will be?" Gideon asked.

Jasper shrugged. "I've a few ideas, but I haven't decided yet."

For reasons he couldn't fathom, Gideon found the subject fascinating. As an afterthought, he added, "I guess you get to know quite a lot about the faux pas and peccadilloes of our ruling class?"

Jasper grinned. "Sure do. And it can come in very handy, I can tell you."

Gideon bobbed his head lower and assumed a confidential tone. "Ever heard anything about the lawyer handling the Barclay case? Williams, is it?"

Jasper stared at him as though marbles were tumbling around in the tutor's head to form a recognisable new pattern.

"What?" Gideon said. "Did I say something wrong?"

Jasper shook his head. "I've never heard a word against Silas Williams. Not a word." He paused and took a long draught of his beer. "It was a different matter with the geezer he articled for, when he first arrived here, though. Archibald Beaumont."

Archibald Beaumont. A distant bell rang in Gideon's brain. *Where do I know that name from?*

"Archibald Beaumont? Never heard of him."

"What about his missus? Or his supposed missus. A gorgeous redhead named Margaret. At one time she was married to a famous painter, but he was old, and she was young." Jasper licked his lips, relishing the tale. "That rarely works, unless the old man plays dumb, and this one wasn't deaf and blind."

An enormous thump kicked into action in his chest, but Gideon tamped it down and tried to play nonchalant. "What was the painter's name?" he asked, though he thought he already knew the answer.,

Jasper stared at him for a long, assessing minute, and Gideon had to suppress a shiver. The fellow gave the impression he could see right through you.

"You already know that," Jasper said slowly, his eyes

flickering over Gideon's face. "Don't you?"

"What? I don't know what you're talking about."

Jasper averted his eyes to his mug, fiddling with the handle, then drawing stripes in the condensation on the outside with his index finger.

"Have it your own way," he finally said, looking up again. "His name was Sir Francis Grant. A very famous portrait painter of his time, he was. Rich too. But Margaret ran straight into the arms of another man. Imagine that."

As he spoke, he searched Gideon's face for a sign of recognition. Of acknowledgment. Then, like a dog emerging from a pond, he seemed to shake himself back to the present.

"Even after Sir Francis died, it was too hot for Margaret and Archibald in London society. I can understand that. They ran away for a new start. And now you've got me wondering." He let the words die away, leaving a hollow vacuum.

"Wondering what?" Gideon had to ask.

"It's obvious, isn't it? Your hints that all is not well with Silas Williams. You know something. And then I think about him coming here with runaways and I ask myself: What has Silas Williams got to run away from?" He swallowed the last of his ale and ran an affectionate finger down the mug, as if this session had made them friends. "And possibly... even more so... What is our new judge, Gideon Vane, running away from?"

Gideon erupted into derisive laughter. "Mr Blackwood! You can't be serious? I have my suspicions about Silas Williams, that's true. But me?" His voice was querulous. "All I can say is you're barking up the wrong tree there, that's for sure."

Thirty-six

"We were all laughing in there, but really, it's not funny." Eleanor Fitzroy, balancing a glass of ice-cold orange juice in one hand, swivelled to scan the surrounding playgoers, decked out in evening finery and furs, supping in the overheated theatre lounge. "It's a frivolous farce, for sure, but sadly, more of a tragedy than a comedy," Eleanor continued.

Her husband George, a broad-shouldered genial property developer, slipped his arm around her waist as she turned back to confront the group. "It's not intended to be taken seriously, Ellie," he soothed. "Just relax and enjoy it."

Around the huddled knot of friends and their black-tie-and-tailed escorts, circled the crème de la crème of Sydney society, out for the opening night of a revamped Covent Garden show poking fun at love and marriage. Under the green-and-gilt arches of the Prince of Wales Theatre in Castlereagh Street, they were waiting out the interval of *London Assurance*, a five-act, country-house runaway success by the hugely popular playwright Dion Boucicault.

Isabelle McGregor glanced over to Eleanor and grinned. "I don't know who the actress is who's playing Lady Gay Spanker, but she's a wag," she chortled. "But Fanny Darrell as Grace, is my favourite." She mimicked Fanny's cultured English accent. "'Love? I must have been inoculated in my infancy'. Grace is quite the virago."

Amiria chimed in. "Oh, that's your favourite line? Mine is 'Marriage matters are conducted nowadays in a most mercantile manner.'"

Matilda wasn't to be left behind. "How about 'Every London ballroom is a marriage mart' where 'young ladies are knocked down to the highest bidder?'"

The women of the Teacup Trust exchanged understanding smiles. Posey cast an uneasy sideways glance at Silas, who'd been unusually silent all evening. Open talk of marriage within his hearing always made her feel queasy, because she didn't want to embarrass him.

They hadn't seen each other since the strained conversation in his office, but she was primed up to question him about Margaret Beaumont. She was simply waiting for the right opportunity.

Silas had bought tickets to the Saturday premiere before their awkward conversation, or she doubted if he would have turned out. And as it was, everything about him – his silence, his tight body language and stern expression – shouted reserve and withdrawal. He was there in body, but not in spirit, and she was certain her Teacup friends noticed.

"How about you, Silas? Are you enjoying it?" Eleanor asked. "Do you think I'm taking a silly farce too seriously by objecting to its themes?"

He flashed her a wry smile. "Boucicault's men are hardly models to admire," he replied.

Posey could feel the strain he was under, trying to share the jocular spirit.

"Sir Harcourt, a vain aging fop aiming to marry a beautiful young heiress for her money? His supposedly studious son, Charles, who's a secretly dissolute man about town? Comical deception all round." He glanced around the circle with an apologetic grimace. "Not people you'd want to know."

A shadow of pain crossed his face. So fleeting, Posey suspected she might have been the only one to notice it.

"Women can get a very hard time in marriage and out of it. I get that, I see it at my work every day. But not all men are mongrels." His eyes darted from face to face, like a trapped rabbit.

He'd rather be anywhere but here, answering these questions, thought Posey.

He attempted a smile. "I appreciate why it's popular. I'll give Boucicault that."

The chimes rang for the end of the interval, and they went to regain their seats with what Posey could only interpret as a shared sigh of relief.

***

Later, during the carriage ride back to Barclay Square, they sat by side on the bench seat, their backs to the driver up front, staring into the silent night. The second half of *London Assurance* had not dissolved the cloud that hung between them, despite all the jolly japes and ballyhoo of the action on stage. Real life was staring them down, and no comedy of manners could dissipate the gloom.

Posey felt a sense of desperation rise within her.

Is this our future? We always had such great discussions. Now we can't talk at all?

Her throat blocked up, and she cleared her voice box. She felt as if every nerve in her body was set on alarm.

"Um, Hawk Eye," she ventured. "Could I ask you something?"

He cast her a wary, sidelong glance. "What is it?" His voice was abrupt, restrained.

"Do you remember Margaret Beaumont?"

They were separated by several safe inches, but she sensed his body stiffen at the question.

"Margaret Beaumont? Why are you asking about her?"

Posey swallowed hard. *He remembers. Of course he does. How could he forget if what Margaret had told her was true?*

"I… I went to see her," she confessed in a rush.

She heard him let go of an enormous sigh, followed by a long silence.

"And why did you do that? Can't you let bygones be bygones?"

"Hawk Eye… please… I can't live like this."

She turned to stare straight at him, but he gazed ahead, his expression mutinous.

"I want to help. I'm your friend. I don't want us to have secrets from each other." She gave a sickly laugh. "After all, you know all the Barclay family's dirty laundry. The entire world does."

The appealing tone in her voice apparently left him unmoved. He still refused to look her in the eye.

"There's no one I admire more than you. You were right about that silly play. There are good men, and you are one of the best. I know you to be a man of integrity…"

He swept his hair from his brow in a frantic gesture and turned to face her, his eyes blazing. "Stop it, Posey. Stop it. Right now. I can't live up to your expectations. Due to circumstances beyond my control, I can no longer represent the Barclay family. I am letting you down in the most base of ways. I will find someone to replace me, I promise you that, but that's the best I can do."

He glanced at her mouth, as if he couldn't help himself, as if even now he wanted to kiss her and pretend this conversation had never taken place. Instead, he took in a long, shuddering breath. "Please, I beg of you. Give up on me. Stop trying to dig this out. No more questioning of Margaret Beaumont, or anyone else. I am not the man of integrity you think I am."

And, as if some divine force directed his desperation, their carriage came to a stop outside Barclay Square.

Posey's heart cracked as she stared into his pleading face.

"I mean it," he said. "I'll find someone else to take the case. I'll brief them to the very best of my ability. I'm letting you down, I know that. But it is the best way I know to keep you safe."

Thirty-seven

"It's with great pleasure I welcome the Right Honourable Gideon Vane, Lord Brook, and heir apparent of the Earl of Worcester, to take up his seat on the bench of the Supreme Court of New South Wales, under the commission issued by the governor, Lord Belmore, this day of July 27, 1868."

Sir Frederick Dooley turned to the man sitting next to him, decked out, as he was, in a full-bottomed white wig that hung like woolly flaps on either side of his ears, tipping his shoulders. No ceremony was spared on a day like this, a red-letter day for the New South Wales Court when another Supreme Court judge was sworn in, and all the senior judges, including Sir Frederick and Gideon, were clad in hooded red-silk judicial gowns trimmed with white ermine fur, with full lace jabots at their throats.

Until recently, the Australians had not bothered with the formal attire of the English court system, but that had changed in the last decade, and now gowns and wigs were adopted by all but the most stalwart of rebels.

The chief justice and the newly sworn in judge beside him sat at the apex of the court's circular seating, looking down on barristers like Hugo and Silas, who sat on a lower tier wearing shorter white wigs and black gowns. The governor and other important guests like Rupert Bellamy, the recently elected president of the New South Wales Law Society, sat adjacent to them, while members of the public – the wives, partners and interested family members, sat further away again.

Dropping Poppy like a hot cake seems to have certainly worked in Rupert's favour, Posey observed to no one but herself.

For a moment she thought of her twin, happily married and with her journalist husband, Thomas, in London. She'd been thrown over by her fiancé, the newspaper magnate Clifford Gilbert, and then, within a few months, by Rupert too. Sure, Rupert was nothing more than a casual flirtation to Poppy, but the rejection still hurt. He had, however, been honest with her as to the reasons why he'd ended their association: clients who'd lost money in their father's business collapse weren't happy about him squiring Poppy around town. A connection with the Barclays was bad for business.

Posey's eyes flickered to where Hawk Eye sat alongside Hugo. Despite herself, she shivered. He always looked so imposing in his formal court garb. His lean, intelligent face with its dramatic black eye patch slashed across one cheek somehow suited the austere setting.

If there's one thing you can count on with Hawk Eye, it's his integrity, and I find that attractive in a man. Even though he's trying to back out of our case, I know there's a good reason. I just don't know what it is.

Sir Frederick unrolled a parchment scroll and placed it on the desk before him.

A scroll! For goodness' sakes, you'd think we were in the first century.

Posey flicked a sidelong glance to her mother on her right, and then to Hugo's secretary on her left. It had been most odd. Her mother had seemed to anticipate this evening was going to be some sort of watershed revelation – or at least a hint the society matrons wouldn't miss – that she was emerging from mourning. She and Hugo were announcing they were an "item". To underscore the point, she dressed in an olive-green gown trimmed with violet ribbon and a matching bonnet.

Hugo, however, had sent Gwen in his carriage to Barclay Manor with a note explaining he had official duties to perform tonight and he would join Arabella at the party afterwards.

Gwen, as you would expect in a secretary who'd stayed adoringly at Hugo's side for twenty years or more, had mousey-brown hair and a thin, tight mouth. She eyed the surrounding crowd with sharp black eyes, as if suspecting even in this respectable company someone might try to pull the wool over them.

She's no competition for our mother, that's for sure. I don't know where Clarrie got the idea she might be.

So far in proceedings, very little had happened. The chief justice had made a proclamation after everyone had filed in and got seated. Then a heavy yellow document, the governor's commission, appointing Gideon a judge, was passed to the court's principal clerk who sat in a row of desks in front of the two senior men, and he read it out in a loud clear voice.

"The governor, under his rights to appoint any qualified person, was appointing Gideon..." and so it went.

Then Gideon swore his allegiance to the Queen and the judicial system and signed an official form, also on old, yellowing paper.

And now, so far as Posey could see, the valedictory speeches were about to begin.

Sir Frederick rose, and in his clear baritone, which always carried a hint of an Irish lilt, he began. "Ladies and gentlemen, esteemed colleagues of the bench and bar, it is my distinct pleasure to introduce our newest addition to the Supreme Court of New South Wales, the Right Honourable Gideon Vane, Lord Brook.

"His Lordship comes to us with the highest recommendations from the mother country, bearing the weight of centuries of noble tradition and legal acumen. Lord Brook's pedigree speaks volumes of the calibre of justice we can expect from him. As the son of the esteemed Earl of Worcester, he has been steeped in the principles of honour and duty from his earliest days.

"His education at Eton College, that crucible of Britain's finest minds, has undoubtedly shaped him into the man of discernment and character he is today."

And so, the praise rolled on like a river. Posey snuck a look at Hawk Eye now and then. She watched as his complexion turned ever greyer as the accolades mounted.

I suppose it's hard to hear your enemy praised to the skies. Even if you're determined to be noble at all times, like Silas.

Sir Frederick thundered on. "I am told that during his time at Eton, Lord Brook demonstrated remarkable leadership as captain of the first eleven. His ability to make fair and swift decisions on the cricket pitch surely presages the judicious temperament he will bring to our courts. Such experiences in youth often lay the foundation for a lifetime of equitable judgment."

I wonder if they became enemies at Eton?

And instantly corrected herself.

He doesn't want you to ask any more questions.

And it's all idle wondering anyway.

He's decided. He's not representing us.

***

From where Silas sat, another monologue issued as the tributes droned on.

Not coming here tonight would have brought more comment than I can afford to face.

And coming here is equally impossible.

Silas's mind wandered back to a time and place he'd spent his life running away from.

Just last night, after the upsetting confrontation with Posey, he'd dug out a memento from deep in his cupboards, a keepsake he couldn't part with, but usually couldn't bear to look at. Rosamunde's paper dolls, with the wardrobe for the English kings and queens she'd been cutting out on the night she was murdered.

And as he sat on the hard wooden bench in his short woolly wig, his thoughts returned to the games she cherished. He thought of the china doll in Arabella's bedroom. When he looked at the thing, the round, glassy eyes with their knowing innocence stared straight into his soul.

Tell them. Tell them your long-buried secret.

No one will believe me. They'll think I'm a mad man.

Even more importantly, he'd go after Posey.

He'll go after anything I value…

Lost in memories, he came to and saw that Hugo was now standing and facing the new judge.

He must be speaking on behalf of his practice. Making sure he scores big with the new judge.

"We are fortunate indeed that Baron Kingshorn of the Court of the Queen's Bench has recommended Lord Brook to our shores." Hugo had a warm bass voice which carried well in the domed chamber. "The baron's reputation for identifying promising legal minds is well known, and his endorsement carries significant weight in legal circles throughout the Empire."

He glanced around and caught Silas's eye. For a second or two, Silas got the impression a guilty cloud crossed Hugo's face before then he looked away quickly.

Must be my imagination.

Hugo continued, it seemed to Silas, with even greater fervour. "Lord Brook's tenure in his father's prestigious law firm provided him with a wealth of practical experience in the intricacies of English law. We can only imagine the complex cases and weighty decisions he has been party to in those hallowed chambers."

He tucked his hands under his gown, and into his waistcoat pockets and struck a triumphant pose. "In welcoming Lord Brook to our bench, we not only gain a jurist but also strengthen the ties that bind our colony to the Crown. His presence here is a testament to the importance of New South Wales in the broader context of the Empire, and we look forward to the fresh perspective he will bring to our deliberations."

It felt like a natural conclusion to the occasion, and the audience seemed to relax. Papers rustled, people fidgeted, whispers filled the air.

But it wasn't the end. Not yet. Sir Frederick struck his desktop with his gavel.

"We are about to close, but I have one more important announcement. I know many of you have an interest in the ongoing proceedings of Martens and Bartle Versus Barclay Investments and the Barclay Family. As evidence of the court's commitment to see this business settled, I'm announcing our new judge will make it his business to speed up this case and settle for the many people who lost money in the Barclay Investment collapse. This will be Lord Brook's highest priority in the coming months."

Black dots danced before Silas's eyes.

***

Gideon sat beside the chief justice and basked in the praise that rolled over him like warm, anointing oil.

As the Psalm says, 'like the precious oil rolling down' – that is where the Lord bestows his blessing.

Australia has been a good move for me, he thought, as Hugh Davenport rose to say his piece. *It's such a change to be appreciated, instead of unfairly hounded.*

His eyes roved the gathering seated opposite the senior bench, from the common folk who sat farthest away to the bewigged barristers closest to him. His heart warmed as he spotted Eudora, who immediately stood out because of her broad-brimmed hat.

His eye then snagged on the fellow on the end of the second bench back with the black eye patch, and Gideon's pent-up joy deflated in a rush that left his fingertips tingling.

He flexed his right hand. *The fly in the ointment. There always has to be one.*

He jagged his glance away before Silas saw he was watching him.

He's the only man on earth who knows what I've done. Apart from Boodles, of course, but he'll be dead soon.

Boodles. Boodles has known since the day it happened, but he's never going to speak of it. I've no worries there.

He wished his doddery, bent over pater, his weak-kneed, trembling-handed, word- fading father, was seated here to see this ceremony unfolding before him.

He never made it to the Supreme Court as a judge. He never had a chief justice sing his praises.

The chief justice was announcing his appointment to the Barclay case. He glanced across at Silas and saw his head jerk up as the announcement was made. The other man's eyes sparked and he could feel his flare of anguish across the floor of the spacious wood-panelled chamber.

They speared into him, uncowed.

You think you've won.

The heat of his previous joy returned like a desert wind, but this time stoked by fury. Like receiving an arrow from heaven, or some other place akin to heaven, he knew what he had to do.

You're not going to survive this contest.

One way or another, I'm going to extinguish you. And then there'll be no man on earth who knows.

Boodles doesn't count.

Thirty-eight

"I can't believe it. I was so furious I marched straight down to the telegraph office and sent Thomas another request."

Arabella stared at Posey, her elegant brows raised in concern. "Oh, Posey. It's not appropriate for you to be sending telegraphs to Thomas. Don't you think he's got enough to do, answering to Clifford's demands? And he's supposed to be on his honeymoon…"

Mrs Crowe's beef roast with home-grown vegetables – turnips, potatoes and pumpkin, with silver beet and thick gravy – was going cold on their plates as Posey's voice grew ragged around the edges with her complaints about Jeremiah Hawkins' unremarked death and the glowing tributes to Gideon Vane in the morning's paper.

"Something's not right about that man," she concluded. "I know Hawk Eye. He wouldn't be acting oddly without a good reason. And Jeremiah? Beaten to death? That's not just bad luck. That's intentional."

Arabella put down her fork and pushed back in her chair. "That report wasn't really about the new judge. It was more about national pride in our development as a nation. And that's fair enough."

Petunia's deep-blue eyes flashed a quick plea to her mother. "Please don't. You'll only encourage her." She gazed fondly across the table at her sister. "You say, quite rightly, sis, that if he's got some conflict of interest in hearing a case involving Silas, then he should declare it. Isn't that correct?"

"Completely," Posey replied, finality ringing in every tone. "To acclaim his appointment, especially to that case, as some triumph in the 'gravitas and maturity' of the legal system is a bad joke."

Petunia put the fork loaded with beef and vegetables which was poised over her plate into her mouth, and chewed appreciatively, before continuing. "And what exactly do you expect Thomas to do about it from London, for goodness' sakes?"

"I've asked him to investigate the background to that painting upstairs in more detail. I can't help feeling it has something to do with this rift between Hawk Eye and the judge. Silas hasn't been his usual self ever since he saw it."

She glanced at her mother and said, "I've mentioned Margaret Beaumont too. She's an artist. She probably moved in art circles at the time. I'm certain she knows things she isn't telling us. Maybe she knows something more about the painting… You never know. Thomas might throw new light onto the whole thing."

"That judge is making himself at home as fast as a Melbourne Cup winner hits the straight, that's for sure," said Petunia. "From what Clarrie says, Eudora is already imagining herself as the next Lady Brook."

"Goodness me," said Arabella. "He's only been here five minutes."

"You know Eudora," said Petunia. "Desperate to get married. She's scared she's already on the shelf."

"How would Clarrie know, anyway?" asked Posey. "I thought he's on the outer?"

"Oh, he and Hugo drift over there for dinner sometimes. Both bachelors, you know, and Eudora enjoys male company."

"Hugo too? A gathering of the lost and lonely, is it?"

Petunia flashed Posey another of her appreciative quick grins and shrugged. "Hugo's like an uncle to her. He's there a lot."

Posey set down her fork with a clatter. "Well, I hope he hasn't told Eudora about the painting. That's the last thing we need. If Gideon gets a hint of it, he'll be over here demanding to see it. We don't want any more problems with the new judge than we've already got."

"It's surprising what Clarrie knows." Petunia flicked a glance towards Arabella. "He says Hugo's lost a lot of money on the horses over the years. I'd never have picked Hugo as a gambler, but there you are. And Gwen Morgan? Word around the race tracks is she's more than one of Hugo's employees."

Arabella choked on the mouthful she'd just placed daintily between her lips. When she recovered from a red-faced coughing fit, she glared at her youngest daughter, eyes flashing bright green with indignation.

"Petunia Barclay, I'm shocked. What are you doing even mentioning such things? Ladies *never* gossip," she said in her haughtiest tone. "I'm shocked you would listen to gutter talk like that. And about a man you've known to be nothing but kind and considerate your whole life."

Petunia glanced to Posey and shrugged. "It's what they say," she said, unrepentant.

The sisters shared a conspiratorial look. "There's no smoke without fire," they chanted, and then broke into giggles.

"Isn't that what you used to always say to us, Mother, when you suspected we'd been naughty? Petunia grinned. "When the biscuit tin was empty and there were crumbs left on the bench?"

Posey directed a long gaze at her mother. "You've got to admit, it seems strange that Hugo invited Gwen along last night," she said. "I've never seen her at those functions before." She turned to Petunia. "Is there something going on there?"

Petunia shrugged. "How should I know? I spend all my time out on the track or in the stables with the horses."

"You're sleeping over there more and more frequently," Posey objected. "Surely you see things."

Petunia screwed up her mouth in wordless disagreement. "I only stay over because Hugo has been so kind as to make the guest room available, but I keep to myself and the horses," Petunia said. "Clarrie's the one who knows what goes on."

"Clarrie?" Arabella's interest piqued. "I thought he was just the jockey."

"Just the jockey?" Petunia squealed. "Mother, do you know how condescending that sounds? He's won a lot of money for Hugo. Probably more than anyone else. He's a jolly fine jockey, but that's not all. Hugo takes a lot of notice of his advice on the horses, and on other things too, I suspect."

Arabella sniffed. "Well, he didn't win any favour with Eudora, that's for sure. And I don't blame her. He treated her too casually. If he's lost out there because of Gideon Vane, then it serves him right."

Thirty-nine

"Where are we going? Oh, do tell." Eudora's hands were clasped before her chest, her face alight with childlike anticipation. Tucked comfortably alongside Lord Brook in her speeding cabriolet, Eudora's eyes drifted from Gideon's rapt attention to the open front.

Her driver, Robert, was slowing down, making a careful turn onto the hill road leading up to the old fort, with its panoramic views over the harbour.

"Millers Point," she cried. "What's up here?"

"It's a surprise. One I'm certain you'll like very much." His gaze lingered on her flushed pink lips, and flicked to her sparkling marine-green eyes, mirroring the colour of the seas that surrounded this place. A wave of self-satisfaction washed over him.

He couldn't believe how well Sydney was turning out after the hellish time he'd had in London the last few months. Marrying a woman with a grasp of social niceties, the maturity to understand what was required for a man's professional and personal success – that was what he should have been angling for all along. Not wasting his valuable attention on some flighty chit who was like Christmas tinsel; flashy, but only good for a season. He'd had a lucky escape from Primrose Hetherington, when he came to think of it.

Now he had to secure Eudora's hand before he started work on the Barclay case in earnest.

As the copper dome of the new astronomical centre came into view, Eudora gave another excited gasp. "The observatory? Is that where you are taking me? How exciting!"

A gnarly Scotsman with a full beard and the shiny dome of a receding hairline awaited them as the cab drew up under a pearly night sky. George Robarts Smalley was the city's astronomer, and a friend of Jasper Blackwood's. Gideon stepped down with a grateful hand extended.

"So good of you to make time for a personal showing for us tonight. I'm grateful to Mr Blackwood for arranging it. May I present Miss Eudora Gilbert, daughter of the late John Sissons Gilbert, and sister of the esteemed publisher of the *Sydney Herald*."

Smalley clicked the heels of his shiny boots together and extended his hand. "Delighted to meet you, Miss Eudora. You are most welcome. I am firmly of the view a knowledge of science in ladies is not inconsistent with their natural refinement, or incompatible with their usefulness in domestic and social life." He smiled through luxuriant white whiskers and turned to lead them inside, pausing every few steps to add to his introductory speech as they strode into the domed tower, built over a compact sandstone-block lower floor.

"Fortunately, we've got a wonderfully clear sky tonight, and a new moon. Perfect for viewing the Magellanic Clouds and the Eta Carinae. There's another Transit of Mercury later this year, but I'm afraid you're a little premature in your visit to see that." He smiled wryly at his own humour and moved on.

"The Magellanic Clouds are dwarf galaxies, as you may know, and are only visible from the Southern Hemisphere, so it is a particular pleasure for a Scotsman to get an opportunity to view them." He bowed courteously towards Gideon. "I can assume the same could be said of you, My Lord. Have you ever seen the Magellanic Clouds before?"

"Quite right, I have not, and I am privileged to view them with such an expert to advise us," said Gideon, smiling.

Smalley resumed his walk and his lecture. "And the Eta Carinae? It's an extremely luminous star system, also visible primarily in this part of the world. It had a major outburst twenty years ago, but there's still activity to be seen there today."

Eudora glanced at Gideon with something closely resembling adoration. Her eyes danced with unspoken joy.

Gideon reached out and squeezed her hand. She squeezed back, and he didn't let go.

I've just hit another six. If the night goes as I hope, it will be a century.

Forty

The George Street Market was bustling with midweek shoppers as Posey and Sally took in the street scene outside the four big sheds, each devoted to different produce and wares. Today the place was busy, but the shoppers were humdrum regulars; housewives stocking up for weekend family meals, meeting their budgets with end-of-the-week bargains.

Saturday was the big day at George Street, when the shop girls and apprentices went shopping for trinkets and amusements on their day off, the day when the fortune tellers and wandering minstrels were sure to be there, working their patch.

In addition to the permanent produce stalls for fish, meat, vegetables and fruit, there was an entire section for wholesale goods – kitchen equipment, books, second-hand and newly sewn clothes. A range of itinerant sellers moved through the crowds. Corner carts offered butcher's red saveloy sausages, baker's pies and coffee, and English muffins and tea cakes. Fish mongers sold their fresh catch and rock oysters.

"The clothing is over there." Posey pointed to the shed closest to them. She glanced down to the pram Sally pushed, where her ten-month-old chubby-cheeked son, Robbie, lay tucked up asleep, his thumb in his mouth.

They were hunting for good-quality second-hand baby clothes or some soft material – a muslin or similar – to make a gown or two for Robbie and extras to sell or give away through the refuge.

The hawker's cries floated in the still afternoon air.

"Pie and coffee… Ladies, come and buy."

"Hot, hot, taties and mushy peasssss."

Many of the voices echoed with Cockney reminders from the Thames docks where their fathers and grandfathers came from, threaded with the 'Strine' of their new homeland.

Posey breathed in the mingled aromas of baked potatoes and Worcestershire sauce, candy floss and raw fish. Her shoulders relaxed as the sun struck her back and a strolling minstrel walked past, guitar across his chest, strumming a well-known folk song.

"It's nice to be out in the world," she said to Sally, who'd stopped to pull up the blanket covering Robbie. "To take in some sunshine and forget about our cares."

Sally smiled indulgently. "All right for some," she said in a jocular brogue, the bright warmth of her words taking any sting from them. She smiled from a face that would have been designated as unusually pretty, but for her half-closed right eye – a defect from birth – that gave her a deceptively sleepy appearance.

Posey grinned and pointed. "Let's head that way first. We can check out the produce to take home for tea after that."

***

Sally Donegal was one of the star residents of the ever-changing round of women currently housed at the Female Refuge Society, where Posey directed her energies to righting social wrongs, especially against vulnerable women. The centre took in women who'd been left penniless and homeless, many times forced into prostitution, and gave them a chance to set their lives aright. They worked as laundresses or needlewomen to help pay their expenses until they were re-employed, married, or returned to family.

Sydney had given many women in the new colony a tough ride, firstly female convicts who arrived with no family or protectors, and then with the large numbers of females brought out on assisted passages to level up the town's early gender imbalance of one woman to four men. Many young female immigrants, some no more than thirteen, arrived with no money and no family, desperate for work as domestic servants or similar to feed themselves. Inevitably, many of them had struggled and crashed, forced into prostitution or exploitive employment simply to survive.

Sally was a refugee from the Irish famine, a skilled needleworker who'd been impregnated in her new employment and then turned out on the streets. She'd found a haven at the refuge, where they'd allowed her to stay on after the birth of her son, recognising her potential as a leader and mentor for other young women facing similar experiences.

She fussed over the pram, pulling the blanket up over her baby's mouth and standing upright to face Posey with a frown on her face.

"Is something wrong?" Posey asked, catching her worried expression.

She shook her head. "I don't want him catching anything, that's all. You don't know what could be in the air in a place like this." She glanced around her, as if fearful of being stalked by measles, which had killed hundreds of children a year or two before.

"He'll be fine," Posey said. "We haven't had measles for a while now. Here. Let me take him and your hands will be free to look for clothes." She took over the pram and Sally walked ahead, glancing around her uneasily as she went.

They spent a contented thirty minutes browsing the clothing stalls, where Sally found two long white cotton smocks for Robbie and a half bolt of fine white cotton to make toddler tunics to sell. After a bargaining round that got them down to a price that satisfied Posey, they moved on slowly to the produce section, seeking ingredients for vegetable soup.

It was a lovely afternoon, and Posey knew she should revel in the freedom, but a shadow had fallen over them ever since Sally had mentioned measles, and she found herself, rather like Sally had, glancing around, as if seeking some unknown threat.

What is wrong with you?

She reasoned with herself that it was a beautiful day. There was no likelihood Sally would attempt to abscond as some of their boarders had done, and little Robbie was perfectly healthy and settled.

So when he stirred and began a fractious whine, it sparked off anxiety levels that were already set higher than normal. She paused in her pram pushing and leaned over the carrier, drawing back the blanket to see the babe's pink face.

"He's probably too hot," she said to Sally as an aside, still gazing down at rosebud pink lips, screwed in protest.

Before she knew what was happening, she felt a mighty hand thrust in her back, and she grabbed at the handles of the pram as both she and the infant shot forward several feet.

Before she could turn, she heard a roar and a rush of air behind her, and Sally's full length cannonaded into her, amidst a spume of dust, grass particles, and soil-laden spuds.

One hand still grasping the pram and keeping it upright, she turned sideways and grabbed Sally by the waist. Right on Sally's heels, a heavy wooden crate, still half full of potatoes, crashed from the stall holder's bench.

"What the heck!"

The rotund aproned hawker minding the stall spun around, as if searching for the cause of the collapse, and finding none, turned back to them, hands raised in a helpless gesture. He had the characteristic broad olive face, dark eyes and brows of an Italian street vendor, and he wrung his hands together in operatic distress. Then he hurried to their aid, pulling the box free of the back of Sally's legs and bowing and scraping in profuse apology.

"Missus, so sorry. I don't know how that happened, missus. So sorry." He grabbed up an empty flour bag from behind the bench and began filling it with good-sized spuds. "Please, take these as compensation. Per favore. A terrible accident. Mama mia… Piccolo bambino… piccolo bambino. Sta bene? Sta bene?"

Is the baby okay?

Robbie was roaring his disapproval, but Posey knew it was the healthy racket of sound lungs, more in fright than injury.

She pushed the pram fully clear of the mess of dirt and vegetables that lay around them.

"He's fine. Just frightened."

"Please. Take these."

A woman – almost certainly his wife – had appeared at his side and quietly taken the flour bag from him and began filling it with more produce. Not just potatoes, Posey saw, but also a large Chinese-grown cabbage, carrots and turnips.

She turned to check on Sally, who was staring into the crowd behind the stall owner, her face scored in fearful, haggard lines. Her lips were bared and a thin white line circled her mouth. Her attention seemed fixated on someone or something, though Posey couldn't see what was causing her such obvious distress.

Amongst the gawping full-bosomed woman shoppers, a nattily dressed man in his late thirties or early forties, clad in top hat and a loose-fitting dark lounge jacket and lighter-coloured pants turned away.

He's not the sort to upset potato carts…

She tugged at Sally's shoulder to attract her attention. "Sally, it's okay, the danger is over…"

Her companion came to her senses, and squeezed her eyes shut before opening them again, as if emerging from a bad dream. Sally picked up Robbie and put him over her shoulder to console him. Posey took the flour bag of vegetables from the stall holder with thanks and placed it in the pram.

"Let's go home," she whispered to Sally, who was moving slowly and patting the baby's back as his crying quietened.

They turned up the small lane that led them back to the

main street, Posey ahead, pushing the pram with the vegetables, and Sally following, carrying Robbie and whispering calming endearments as she strolled. Around them, shoppers surged on the narrow fairway as they walked in silence, not attempting to speak.

Halfway up, Posey halted and pulled off the lane onto a kerb. "Do you want to put him down again?" she asked.

Sally leaned over and put Robbie in the pram, this time propped up with cushions so he could see out, the vegetables lodged in the space left at his feet. He gave a wave of his little fist and a cackle of joy, grinning broadly as they set off up the incline again.

The lane crossed into another wider entry into George Street proper. Crowds stalled, milling around them, and as Posey stood on tiptoe to see what the holdup was, she saw the crossing was blocked by a horse and cart loaded with crates of greens – lettuces and cabbages, by the looks of it. The vendor was out ahead of his horse, tugging at the leading reins angrily, but the horse dug his hooves in, refusing to budge. The man unleashed a wicked rawhide whip and circled back to his stubborn mare, cracking the whip in the air like a circus master.

People crowded in from behind them, jostling for space. Robbie squealed in delight, as if all these folk were here to keep him entertained, but Posey's instincts whistled like a kettle boiling.

Before she could turn to Sally, someone jolted her abruptly from behind. Robbie's pram jumped out of her hands, leapt the kerb, and rolled away downhill, into the path of the blocked dray.

Posey lunged for the pram and came up with empty air. She screamed and leapt forward again, just as the vendor smashed the whip across the bay horse's back. The animal howled in protest and wrenched forward, tipping the cart sideways, and bringing down a cascade of wooden crates filled with produce.

With every fibre in her body screaming, Posey dove again. Launching herself in mid-air, she grabbed the pram handles and hung on for dear life. Hers, and the baby's.

For a long sickening minute they hung in space, crates shrieking as they splintered onto the tarmac around them. Batons of rough pine sliced through the air, one across Posey's shoulders. Another piece of debris slammed across the side of her face.

But, propelled by a force she barely recognised, she kept moving, streaking ahead of the horse and into the open space on the other side of mayhem.

Seconds later she was in a free zone, the catastrophe behind her. She slumped against a stone wall that edged the corner of George Street and gasped. Robbie was staring at her in amazement, as if he was ready to try that trick all over again.

Still holding the pram handles for dear life, she bent over from the waist and heaved to restore normal breathing. She stood like that for a long minute, struggling for air, and then a gentle hand touched her shoulder. Sally was beside her.

"How did you do that?" the young mother wheezed, her face alive with exultation. "You flew like an angel. How did you do it?"

Posey slowly raised her head and stood upright. Robbie gurgled. She turned to face Sally.

"I have no idea," she said. "St Nicholas must have been right at my elbow, that's for sure…"

Posey glanced over at the wreckage that lay strewn in the street behind them. The dray had careened on two wheels and slammed into the bay mare, which lay bloodied and thrashing in the street. Green matter and splintered wooden boxes lay all around it. The vendor was still howling with rage. And standing on a corner, slightly apart from the mobs, was a top-hatted man in a dark suit, staring at them and smirking.

Her stomach turned over. She grabbed Sally's arm. "Who's that man? That one there on the corner. I won't point. But you see him? In the dark suit?"

Sally raised her head. Her face drained of colour.

Posey stared. "Do you know him? Who is he?"

Sally shook her head, as if attempting to escape from a bad dream.

Posey was tempted to storm across the intersection and ask him who he was right there and then, but when she raised her eyes again, his back was disappearing into the crowd. Within seconds, he had gone.

She grabbed Sally by both shoulders and stared into terrified blue eyes. "You know him. Who is he?" Her voice was sharp and urgent.

But Sally just turned away from her, shaking her head. "He's nobody. Nobody at all."

Forty-one

Quong Tart's Chinese tearoom in George Street was buzzing with the latest gossip when the Teacup Trust assembled there for afternoon tea and a plate of Quong's fabled scones soon after the proposal was reportedly offered. As the Teacup Trust women sipped on fragrant imported tea, poured from an embossed teapot decorated in delicate pastel renderings of flowers, birds and butterflies, whispers from the surrounding tables reached their ears.

"Have you heard? Eudora Gilbert's engaged."

"Engaged? Who to?"

"That fancy Lord. The new judge. Another jimmygrant."

"Aren't Australian blokes good enough?"

The offer had been made last night, and if all the hot gossip was to be believed, accepted.

"Mrs Carstairs told the groom and he told…"

"I suppose she couldn't resist being an earl's wife."

The town – the female component of it anyway – was agog at the news.

"But he's only been here ten minutes."

The bosom pals of the Teacup Trust – along with Posey

there was Isabelle McGregor, Matilda Sinclair, Amiria Chaudry and Eleanor Fitzroy – had gathered to catch up on the latest news from Barclay Manor, but news of Eudora's reported engagement had dominated the conversation so far..

"They hardly know each other…"

"A lord was just too tempting…"

And as the sister of the woman who came close to being Eudora's sister-in-law, Posey was called on as an oracle.

"Poppy always said Eudora was desperate to get married. But not to just anyone." Posey flushed with guilt at being caught discussing Eudora behind her back.

"Good on her, if it's what she wants," said Amiria.

"As that play we went to a few days ago says, marriage is a mercenary business," quipped Eleanor. "I suppose if you looked at it that way, you could say both of them got a bargain."

"In what way?" asked Amiria.

"Why, he gets an experienced society hostess to head his household, and she gets a title and presumably a comfortable ride for life. She'll hardly be complaining if she's Lady Brook for the rest of her days. There aren't many Aussie blokes can offer her a title."

A pregnant silence greeted Eleanor's brutal frankness.

"I suppose you're right," tendered Posey, her voice diffident. "It does seem rather calculating."

Isabelle laughed. "Well spoken, from the dame who's turned down a perfectly good proposal from an ideal man because marriage is against her principles."

Posey had the grace to laugh, and her cheeks flushed a brighter pink. "Yes. Well, maybe if I'd accepted, he wouldn't be able to pull out like he has. He'd be so grafted into the Barclay clan he wouldn't be able to escape."

Isabelle laughed again. "There is that."

"I'm still hoping he'll change his mind." Posey glanced up and saw all her friends had their eyes fixed on her. "I know. You all think I'm with Alice in Wonderland. Perhaps I am."

She wrung her hands together. "The weirdest thing happened yesterday, at the George Street Market. I took one of our girls there to get baby clothes and we had a narrow escape. A runaway horse and cart nearly trampled us. And that was after we'd also come close to being bowled over by potato crates that crashed near us. We were lucky Sally's baby, Robbie, wasn't seriously hurt. We had him with us in the pram."

She'd schooled her voice to sound offhand, but her friends weren't taken in. They greeted her words in stunned silence.

"What?" said Matilda. "You had two close shaves in one afternoon?"

Posey nodded, aware a sheepish grin played on her lips. "That's right," she said with an embarrassed laugh. "We must have been careless, I guess?"

"I don't think you're ever careless, Posey," said Isabelle. "Unlucky? Perhaps…"

"It sounds like a most unlikely coincidence," protested Amiria. "Are you sure there isn't more to it?"

Posey scanned her friends' serious faces and shrugged. "Like what? I can't imagine it would be deliberate. What possible reason could anyone have to do that?"

"Something to do with Sally, maybe? It seems to me you were targeted," said Amiria angrily. "Accidents happen, I know.

Once, maybe. But you know the saying about lightning never striking twice in the same place."

Posey pressed her lips together. "There is something else," she said.

She hesitated. A heavy reluctance pressed down on her, as if voicing her doubts might make them real. A nervous bubble rose from deep inside her.

"Both times, a fashionable gentleman was hanging around on the edge of things. I noticed him because he looked rather out of place." She stopped, struck by a sudden thought. "Actually, it was as if he wanted us to see him when I think of it. He had on a smart dark jacket over lighter pants – you know the loose-suited look that's become the rage this last couple of years among city slickers? And he wore a top hat too. He stood out amongst all the vendors with their canvas aprons and the housewives looking for bargain meat for dinner. I got the feeling Sally knew him and was terrified of him. But when I asked her who he was, she said she didn't know."

Eleanor cleared her throat. "You've got to get Sally to talk," she said. "She might know something important without realising it."

"Speaking of things that might be important, did you see the report of the inquest into that man found dead behind Tattersall's? It was in the *Morning Gazette*," said Eleanor.

Posey froze. "That rag. We don't get the *Gazette*. What did it say?"

"The coroner entered a verdict of culpable homicide by person or persons unknown," said Eleanor.

"Homicide?" Posey yelped. "Jeavon was told he was beaten up by drunken larrikins…"

"Apparently not. The medical examiner ruled it was murder, and the coroner accepted his ruling."

Posey glanced around the table with wild eyes. "What's going on? I can't believe it. He was to be a key defence witness in our case. Now he's dead?"

Eleanor's lips flattened into a hard, thin line, and then she spoke. "You've got to tell Silas about the market business yesterday, Posey. You can't afford to write it off as a coincidence. Talk to Sally, and then to Silas and Jeavon, and do it this afternoon."

Forty-two

"Mr Hugo is here, Miss Posey." Mrs Crowe's ruddy face appeared around the corner of the library door a few minutes after Posey got home from Quong's tearooms.

She'd retreated to the library to rest and reflect after the bombshell news about Jeremiah Hawkins. When Jeavon had told her Hawkins was dead, she'd been shocked but resigned. It was awful bad luck, but sometimes that's just how life was. Now she had to figure in a deliberate attack. Not just random rowdiness, but a planned attack to take Hawkins out. There was something horribly personal about it, and it also had ramifications so far as the incidents in the markets yesterday.

It's far more likely than not it was deliberate, she thought. *Something's going on here. But to what purpose? To frighten us? Intimidate us into giving up?*

She was standing in the middle of the Red Sea when the waters had rolled back at Moses's command. And any moment now, those walls of water were going to collapse in on her, long before she'd made it to the other side.

I need to talk to Sally again. Find out who that man hanging around yesterday is. I suspect she knows his name.

Mrs Crowe was still standing at the library door, her face set in a query. "Can I show him in? Mr Hugo, I mean."

"He'll be here to see Mother, and she's doing some embroidery in the shade on the back deck. Show him through to her there," said Posey, fingering the glass of cold water she'd taken into the library with her.

Mrs Crowe frowned and shook her head. "He particularly asked for you," she said. "Not your mother." She hesitated and gave her lips an anxious lick. "He's got another gentleman with him." Geraldine Crowe shot her a meaningful glance.

"Someone else is here with him? Who is it?"

Mrs Crowe shifted her feet uneasily. "He didn't say, but I'm pretty certain it's that new judge," she said.

"Lord Brook?" Posey spoke the name in hushed tones. "Oh, please, no. I can't handle him right now."

Mrs Crowe hovered in the open doorway, her head bowed. Then she cleared her throat. "Miss Posey? Best you front up. It'll be worse if you ask me to turn him away."

Despite the churning anxiety in her gut, Posey laughed. "Darn it, Mrs Crowe, but you're right. We can always rely on you to stand firmly on a rock."

She rose from the armchair she'd slumped into and straightened her shoulders. "If Poppy was here, she'd be the one handling this, and she'd do it far better than me."

Mrs Crowe bit her lip. "Now that's nonsense, Miss Posey. You'll handle it differently, but equally as well, if not better. You're a young lady even an English judge can't take for granted."

***

Posey followed Mrs Crowe to the front door, consciously lifting her dragging feet to convince herself she was on top of the situation. When Geraldine Crowe opened the door and stood aside, Posey saw Hugo's cheeks were slick with sweat. He was dabbing under his jowly chins with an immaculate white handkerchief.

He's nervous. Not a good sign.

"Posey, my dear, sorry to call on you unannounced. So good of you to receive us." He slid a sickly grin her way and turned to his companion. "You know Lord Brook from our swearing-in occasion a couple of nights ago? Eudora mentioned the remarkable painting you have here to him, and the judge is keen to see it."

His words hit Posey like a punch in the gut. "Eudora? What has she got to do with it?" Her eyes bored into Hugo's shifty face.

You were sworn to secrecy. So how does Eudora even know about it?

That's what she wanted to say aloud, but she couldn't. She did her best to register her fury in her glare.

She puckered her brow and said in her blandest tone, "Painting? It's just an old family portrait. I can't imagine it will be of interest to Lord Brook." She flashed him her best hostess smile and said, "I'm sure your father, the earl, has a dozen paintings of finer quality than anything here."

Hugo intervened, turning to Gideon and saying, "My Lord, you have met Miss Posey Barclay, have you not?"

A silky smile crossed Vane's face. He extended his hand. "Of course, Miss Barclay. We've made our acquaintance on more than one occasion since I've been here, and I appreciate you receiving me today." A lizard-like tongue flicked out of his mouth and wet his lips. "Hugo has explained to me the discretion you've employed over this painting, and I respect that."

He cleared his throat in an almost theatrical gesture and creased his face in a commiserating mask. "But by some remarkable coincidence, from what Eudora said, it sounds surprisingly like a painting we once had at my family home, Worcester Park Lodge."

"Eudora?" Posey's voice was rasping and sceptical. "She hasn't seen it, so I have no idea why she's even talking about it." She glared rather obviously at Hugo. "Unless Hugo has broken a rather important confidence."

Hugo flexed his hands at his sides and smiled sheepishly. "I know you wanted it to be kept private, Posey. I apologise. I mentioned it to Eudora in passing. I didn't think there was any harm in it. And it would mean a great deal to the judge to see it. You must admit it's a striking coincidence."

Margaret Beaumont's words echoed in her mind, and Posey fought down a rising dread. Already she was certain this painting *had* once graced Worcester Park Lodge. Would Gideon Vane demand it back? And would they be forced to return it?

Posey pulled herself up to her full regal height and tipped her head to one side.

I have no choice, so I had better do it with grace.

"From what I hear, congratulations are in order, Lord Brook. I understand you and Eudora are engaged? We can't have any secrets between affianced couples, now can we?" As she stepped aside to welcome them in, her insides clenched at her hypocrisy.

I can't stand him, or the contract of marriage, and here I am congratulating him.

She led the way down the hall and paused at the foot of the stairs.

"I'll just check Mother is not in her room. I'll be back down immediately. Hugo might have explained, the work has never been on public display. Mother was charged with keeping it away from prying eyes." She flicked her gaze from Hugo to the judge and saw his face and eyes were bright with a strange, intense fervour. Again, the lizard-like tongue flicked out through the centre of his lips and back, as if catching flies.

"I understand, Miss Barclay. But don't be too long."

That sounds like a warning, she thought as she slipped silently upstairs.

She glanced into her mother's bedroom. Everything was immaculate. Perfectly cornered linen fitted the bed. Sweet-smelling jasmine filled a bud vase on the bedside table. The silver-backed mirror and hair brush sat on the dressing table next to the crystal perfume bottle topped with a satin-covered pump. Everything was in its proper place.

The painting, too, hanging there like a prayer, the doll still nestled beneath it. Her mother was obviously still on the back deck, possibly dozing off in the warm afternoon.

She returned and ushered the two men upstairs in silence, feeling no need to act as any sort of art docent. She stood aside in the hall and let them enter ahead of her, watching for their reactions as she did.

To her shock, as Gideon turned to face the wall, his faced drained of colour and his knees gave way. He gave an anguished cry and reached out to grab Hugo's shoulder. He doubled over, gasping, and clasping his midriff with his free hand.

"My Lord," Hugo cried, bolstering him up with his full grip. "Are you all right?"

The only sound was a deep rasping from Gideon's throat as he fought for breath. He slowly raised himself to full height again, his eyelids suspiciously shining under his dark lashes.

"I… I… don't believe it," he barked. He stared at the work for a long time, his eyes roving from top to bottom, lingering for endless moments on the figure of the young girl. The expression on his oddly repellent face was unreadable. His head bobbed, and his oily eyes seemed to pop out of their normal setting, as if he was unable to believe what he was viewing.

After a few increasingly uneasy minutes, Posey spoke to break the unnerving silence.

"The child is beautiful, isn't she? We were told her nickname was Angel Eyes."

Lord Brook's cheeks flushed a bright red, and his temples pulsed in a feverish beat. Wrong thing to say, she realised too late.

He's furious.

With his right arm, he swept an arc in the air before the work. "I do not know how you got your hands on this work, Miss Barclay." He spat the words out like poison. "But it is a valuable Vane heirloom, and part of the Earl of Worcester's estate. My estate. Or what will be my estate in a very short time." He shot her a venomous glare, and then went straight back to staring at the figure of Rosamunde, as if bewitched.

Posey had the weirdest sensation that the child stared back, dumbstruck but defiant, as if she did not welcome his gaze.

Angel Eyes does not want to go home with the upcoming earl.

His hands balled into fists, so that his knuckles turned white. Then he stepped closer and reached out to trace the artist's signature with one light index finger. "Sir Francis Grant," he announced to no one in particular. "One of the foremost portrait painters of the last generation, now dead. This piece is irreplaceable."

He turned to Posey, and his voice took on an accusing edge. He repeated his earlier statement. "How it came to be in the hands of your mother, Miss Barclay, is a mystery. But I can most certainly tell you I intend to claim it back. It belongs in my family, and whatever argy-bargy has brought it out here, I will pursue all the means at my disposal to settle it back in Worcester Park."

Forty-three

Silas's eyes bored into Posey's face. "He what?" Then, without a word, he jumped up from his desk and strode to the back window of his office, his head down, his hand tugging at the front lock of his hair. He stood like that for a long moment, with his back to them, as if pulling his hair might cause some inspirational brain wave.

After a few moments, he raised his head and stared out the window into 86 Elizabeth Street's back garden. Posey could see beyond his shoulder the fluorescent mauve blossom on the bare-branched jacaranda trees, swaying in a light breeze.

Silas swung around and stared, first at Posey and then Jeavon, his countenance a roiling, thunderous cloud.

"He demanded to see the painting, Hawk Eye," she protested. "I had no choice but to show him. And when he saw it he said, more or less, that come hell or high water, he would get it back. It was stolen property; meant to be part of the Earl of Worcester's estate."

Hawk Eye leaned both hands on the back of his chair, and the length of his body stiffened. Posey and Jeavon had arrived in Silas's office only minutes before, requesting an unscheduled interview. They were still both standing, interrupted by his outburst.

Posey had never seen him so angry. The bones in his cheek worked under his skin, clenching and unclenching.

"Over my dead body," he said through gritted teeth. "There's no way in the world I'm allowing that painting to go back to him."

In the stunned silence that followed his declaration, Posey and Jeavon stared back, dazed and uncertain.

How can he say that? Vane has made it clear. It's come from his family. Margaret confirmed it.

After a charged lull, Jeavon gestured to their chairs. "How about we all get seated and you explain why you feel so strongly about this, Silas? We're completely in the dark here."

When Silas remained staring blankly in front of him, Jeavon continued. "I've always known you as a supremely rational fellow, Silas, and logic would suggest that if the painting is from the Earl of Worcester's estate, then Vane, as the future heir, would appear to take precedence for its ownership. Unless you have some connection with it of which we are unaware…"

Silas's head jerked back, and he fixed Jeavon with a gimlet-eyed stare. "I've tried to protect him from himself, but this is just one step too far," he said. "I've no choice but to speak up."

"An excellent idea, Silas," Jeavon said. "Especially as part of our reason for coming over here was a rather weird attack on Posey and Sally at the market yesterday. I should say *attacks*. Two different incidents."

Silas's brow creased into a deep furrow. "Attacks? What attacks?"

Jeavon waved his hand at Silas's seat. "Why don't we all sit down? And before we get to what happened in the markets, we want to know why you think you have any right to stop Gideon Vane from getting his painting back."

231

Forty-four

Jeavon and Posey sat. After a moment's hesitation, Hawk Eye pulled back his chair and followed suit. Now that he'd decided to speak, his body seemed to decompress. He let out a long breath. His spine and shoulders relaxed, and as he gazed out from behind his steepled hands, the yellow flecks in his dark-brown iris glittered.

"When I came to Australia many years ago, I was escaping an unhappy past," he began, glancing from one to the other. "So much so, that I didn't want to use the name I'd been born with anymore – the name under which I lived the first fifteen years of my life. I changed it to something different, something only a few people – including my darling mother, who died before I came here – knew. I chose names related to my maternal side, in gratitude for the support my mother gave me growing up."

He smiled at Jeavon. "And, yes, before you ask, Former Police Superintendent, it was all done legally. I even went to the extent of getting a Royal Licence, in case it became an issue in my legal career."

He allowed a pause to fall upon the group. When no one else spoke, Posey cleared her throat.

"So, it sounds like you became Silas Williams when you began studying law? What was your name before that?"

Silas's body stiffened again. "Before I was Silas, I was Benedict. Benedict Vane."

She gaped at him, her mouth dropping open to show her perfectly even white teeth, and she wiped her hand across her face, as if expecting when she took it away again that the scene would have changed. She'd be in another room, talking about something else. Not having a conversation that challenged all her accepted reality.

When he remained silent yet again, she whispered hesitantly, "So… you're related to Gideon Vane…" Her sentence dropped off at the end, a statement rather than a question.

When he nodded, she repeated the statement with more force and certainty.

"You're related to Gideon Vane… so what? You're his cousin or something? So why all the secrecy? Why couldn't you say so at the beginning?"

Silas sighed. "Oh, my dear Miss Barclay. If only it had been that straightforward. Unfortunately, it's a great deal more complicated than that."

Jeavon interrupted, chuckling. "So out with it, Mr Vane. Stop sitting on the unhatched eggs…"

Silas sighed more heavily than last time. "Gideon Vane is my brother." He pulled back in his chair, as his revelation rebounded on his visitors like a shock wave.

Posey gasped and took a fierce grip on the arms of her chair, as if the world was threatening to tip her off it.

Jeavon sat forward, head raised, stone still, his hands clasped before him, a gentle kink of query between his brows.

"Benedict Vane was – is – the Earl of Worcester's second son," Silas said. He hesitated again, his face in deep shadows. "And Angel Eyes? Rosamunde in the painting? She was my adored younger sister."

He gazed back at his visitors, but neither spoke.

"Rosamunde was killed not long after *Angel Dreaming* was painted. Our family… my life… we never recovered. I've been forever cursed by what happened back then." He glanced away, deep in thought, and then turned back again. "And, to be fair, Gideon's life has been cursed as well, though in a different way."

Silence seemed like the only appropriate response, and none of them spoke for some time.

And then Posey ventured forth again.

"And Gideon? Was he one of the exclusive little group who knew about your new name?"

Silas shook his head. "No. I especially did not want Gideon to know about my change of identity. Or that I was in Australia. It's just been rotten luck that he's ended up out here." He added in an acid aside, "Or evidence that we really are cursed, you could say."

Posey got up to stand by him, stroking his back in an unprecedented, intimate gesture.

"This has nothing to do with curses, Silas. Please. No more talk of those." Her hand stilled and she looked into his eyes. "Now I understand why you say you can't take the case. But I'm still confused. When you realised the new judge was your brother, and he discovered one of Sydney's best lawyers was his long-lost brother, why didn't you just say so? Tell everyone, I mean? Have the public reconciliation?"

"Because what happened back then can never be forgiven or forgotten," said Silas. "I despise him, and he'd kill me tomorrow if he could get away with it. You don't understand what he's like, Posey. Stand in his way, and you're likely to end up dead. Like Jeremiah Hawkins."

Jeavon drew a loud breath. "I know you suspect him of being involved, Silas, but I still don't see why he'd need to be. What's he got to lose that's worth that kind of risk?"

Silas pulled his lips tight, intent on not saying any more.

We still aren't getting the full story, Posey thought.

After another long silence, Silas spoke in a measured voice. "I know this man. He's capable of the worst of human behaviour. And he's already made it clear to me he'll go to any lengths to see that I am run out of town, by fair means or foul."

Posey clutched her fists and cried out in protest, "So what? You're preparing to fold up your tent and leave?" Her voice was caustic.

Silas stared her down. "Posey, this has been a total bombshell in my life. I never expected to have to see him ever again. I've been in a quandary, as you know." He gazed at her, and then at Jeavon. "I was seriously considering starting anew somewhere else, yes. To try to limit the damage to others, like you," he admitted.

"But now? With the demand for the painting? With Jeremiah's death? And now this attack in the markets? I thought if I laid low and let him get on with being a Supreme Court judge, he'd leave me and those I care for alone. But it seems not. It sounds as if he's already overstepped the mark. First Jeremiah, and now this. Tell me about this business in the markets. What exactly occurred?"

Forty-five

The soft candlelight flattered her pale skin and lit up the auburn gold in her hair. Eudora ran her hands down the lines of the green-and-gold brocade dress that hugged her waistline, and smiled across the table at the English aristocrat who sat opposite her. Mrs Carstairs had excelled in her domestic and culinary arts tonight, setting up a small round dining table in front of the windows in one of Wattlewood's reception rooms with harbour views.

The windows were slightly ajar and a warm sea-salt breeze gave the big room a fresh airiness. Lights were coming on as dusk fell, giving the harbour a dreamlike quality and the busy water life – from ferry boats to tugs, leisure skiffs to commercial freighters – went about their business.

She'd been in a magic cocoon ever since she'd accepted Gideon Vane's proposal a few days ago. She hugged herself in bed at night, buzzing with the excitement of what was to come… the wedding she'd always dreamed of, the chance to fulfil the role she'd always imagined for herself as the leading society hostess in the prospering city. And maybe in a few years, the chance to extend that to London, to a titled estate, to

Mayfair balls… to who knew what glorious future? Her son, when he came, because of course he would come, would be the next Earl of Worcester, and she would be a dowager…

She looked up and smiled over the silver serving dishes to the man across the table and then bit her lip as she realised she'd drifted off into her brief fantasy while he had been saying something.

"My apologies, My Lord. I was woolgathering. You were saying?"

"Woolgathering?" He raised a wicked eyebrow. "Is that an Australian saying? I haven't heard it before."

She stuttered. "I don't believe so, no. It means day dreaming. I've got so much to dream about." She gazed at him adoringly. "Since I met you."

He gave her a quick smile and resumed where he'd left off. "I saw that painting you told me about today. The one at the Barclay house."

She immediately sensed this was important. "Indeed," she replied. "And what did you think? Was it as haunting as Uncle Hugo reported?"

Gideon Vane put both hands on the table, palms down, making an emphatic statement. "The cheek of them," he said, his bass tone rising with each word. "Like everything else about that blighted family, it's fraudulently obtained. Would you believe it's a valuable modern masterpiece, nationally celebrated when Sir Francis Grant completed it over twenty years ago in London? It's famous. Crowds went to see it at the National Portrait Gallery when it first opened.

"And they had it secretly hidden away in Mrs Barclay's

bedroom, so no one ever got to see it. Talk about devious. They must have known it would be dangerous to put it on general display."

"My word," said Eudora, picking up immediately on Lord Brook's rising indignation. "Are you sure? How do you know all this?"

He stopped his rant and stared at her. "How do I know? Because it belonged to my family. The child in the painting is my sister, Rosamunde. My mother put it into storage in a bank vault for safety and it was stolen. Just vanished. And now all these years later, it turns up here. It's an heirloom that rightfully belongs in the earl's estate. What will be *my* estate."

Eudora's already fair skin drained of its last colour. "Oh, my goodness, My Lord. What a scandal. I wouldn't have believed it! What are you going to do?"

He drew himself up to his full seated height, and his head jerked on his long neck like a bird seeking food. "I'm going to demand it back, of course. I can't believe the cheek of it. They have no right to it whatsoever."

Forty-six

Posey spent a busy morning assembling a file of all the paperwork supporting the provenance of *Angel Dreaming* and their rights to ownership of it. Silas had not given them any further details about his family history, but she was following his directions. They agreed they would not give in to the formal demand they knew would come for its return.

"You want to fight this, don't you?" Silas asked her as the meeting in his office broke up.

"I certainly do," Posey said. "We have an obligation to honour the request for it to be kept safely in our family that came from your mother. She didn't want Gideon to have it, or she would have left it to him."

"For good reasons, which I won't go into right now," said Silas. "Just believe me. If she thought Gideon was getting hold of it, she'd turn over in her grave."

Posey hesitated. "I had the weirdest feeling when he was there looking at it that Rosamunde did not want to go home with him. I rarely get superstitious, but this was so strong it was uncanny."

He froze at her words. "Posey, if I ever needed confirmation we're doing the right thing, it's those words. I'm certain you are right."

He'd also urged her to talk to Sally and learn more about the man loitering in the market. Who was he, and what was his motivation? Did she know him, or was he just a nuisance stalker who had nothing to do with any of them?

"It's important we identify him and work out why he was there," Silas said.

Posey didn't argue. She liked that he was fired up to act, and she still had secret hopes his fresh interest would ultimately extend to taking over the Barclay case again.

I'm not giving up hope, she told herself as she dug through the boxes at the bottom of her mother's wardrobe, looking for any further evidence she could find to support their claims on the painting.

"We're fighting to keep you here, Rosamunde," she whispered as she gazed once more at the image of the mysterious young girl. "I know you don't want to go with Gideon. I just know it deep down. Was he mean to you?"

Several hours later, she arrived at the Female Refuge Centre and trailed through the building, looking for Sally. She found her in the laundry, ironing sheets and pillow cases ready for delivery to clients the next day, while Robbie sat on a rug inside a play pen dropping wooden animals through the sides and then reaching through to recover them, happily gurgling gibberish to himself as he did.

"Sally! I haven't seen you since yesterday. Are you alright? Have you got over the fright of our narrow escape yet?"

Sally paused in her work and looked up, shivering as she did, although the day was warm. "Oh, Miss Posey. I still get the creeps when I think of it." She spoke with frankness, but her eyes were hooded.

Posey left a long silence, before asking in a gentle voice, "Did you know that man, Sally? Who is he?"

The young woman had momentarily placed the iron on a stone stand and had not yet taken it up again. Her eyes flickered. She threaded one hand through her light-brown curls and gave a nervous laugh. "Know him, Miss Posey? Of course not. I don't know any gentlemen. You know that."

"Look at me, Sally. Don't be frightened. Look at me."

Sensing her reluctance, Posey watched carefully as Sally raised her eyes and looked her directly in the eye.

"Where have you seen that man at the market before, Sally?"

The young woman stuttered, starting to deny any knowledge of him.

Posey stepped forward and gently took her right arm. "You have seen him before, Sally. I know it. Whereabouts?"

The girl gave a cry and wrenched her arm out of Posey's soft hold.

"At Bishopscourt. Bishop Phillip's house. I was employed there as a kitchen maid. He was tutoring one of the bishop's sons." Sally was shaking now, her body cringing, her hands wiping away hot tears.

"And what did he do to you?"

Sally had always refused to identify Robbie's father, and it had been assumed it was the oldest son in the house where she worked. Never in these situations was anyone ever brought to account. The girl was sacked and left to sink without trace, while life continued unchanged in the big house.

"Is he Robbie's father?"

Posey's question was barely audible above the baby's happy burbling. But once again, Sally flinched. She was holding her lips tightly together, as if afraid the name would escape her lips if she relaxed them.

"There's no shame in that, Sally. No one else need know. But it's important we clarify who he was and why he was there."

The sobbing girl raised her tear-slicked, red face and looked Posey straight in the eye. "He said if I told anyone he'd come after me. He said he'd take the baby away and make sure I got hurt."

"So, he forced himself on you? Is that what happened?"

Sally was sobbing too much to speak, but she nodded her head in mute confirmation.

"Do you think he was following you yesterday? Or was he following me?"

Sally huffed several breaths and her tears slowed. She shook her head, confused how to answer.

"Honestly, Miss Posey? He's never shown a blind bit of interest in me or Robbie since the night he forced himself on me. He doesn't care about either of us. And he knows I've got nothing. There's no point in threatening me or trying to blackmail me. He doesn't want a kid."

Her gorgeous brown eyes settled on her son, who was grizzling. "All I can think of is he was following you. And he wanted you to know it. He didn't hide. He wanted to frighten you. Maybe frighten both of us." She picked up the iron with renewed purpose. "I've got to get this job done before Robbie gets scratchy." She hesitated before putting it down on the white cotton slip.

Posey leaned down into the pen and picked up the restless baby. "His name, Sally. What's his name?"

Sally paused in her ironing and offered a resigned sigh. "Jasper Blackwood, miss. He's right uppish, he is. His brother is some famous scientist. He'd never look at the likes of me. It must have been you he was after. If you ask me, he was sending you a message. Letting you know he was onto you."

***

Later that day, as the afternoon sun dipped in the sky, sending orange reflections glittering on the deep-blue harbour, Posey strode up Elizabeth Street to deliver her file of papers on *Angel Dreaming* to Silas. She was lost in thought, counting off the items that she'd assembled to prove the work's provenance. Her fingers twitched as she went through them.

One: The Admiral's invoice showing he'd bought the painting from Percival and Henrietta.

Two: The Countess Henrietta's letter to Arabella's mother, Louisa, which had been retained in the family papers, even after Louisa's death, by Arabella's conscientious cousin.

Three: Cousin Christina's letter, explaining how she'd been charged with the special duty of delivering the treasured work to Arabella in Sydney.

Both make clear it was Henrietta's dying wish that the painting come to us.

Four: The bill of sale from the artist, Sir Francis Grant, showing the purchase was made on behalf of Henrietta's estate, not that of the earl.

Five: And a solicitor's letter accompanying a copy of Countess Henrietta's will, which made clear she held property separate from the earldom in her own right. Something Posey knew was very unusual and could only be set up with her husband's approval.

Six: A slip of a newspaper clipping, recording the death of Rosamunde Adeline Constance Vane, aged 5, on January 1, 1841, at Worcester Park. No cause of death recorded.

The documentary support is substantial. Surely, it's enough to satisfy questions.

She was waiting for a gap in the busy Elizabeth Street traffic to cross over to Silas's side of the road when a low-slung luxury landau rolled past, slowed to a crawl by the crowd of wheeled vehicles. The glossy black carriage walls set a striking contrast to the two snowy white horses that drew it. The retractable hood was down, and the late-afternoon sun sparkled on the pearly white of the men's cravats and the lady's gloves.

There was something familiar about the woman's auburn hair.

It's Eudora!

Posey stared, and saw she sat alongside a top-hatted Lord Brook, while opposite them sat two men, both fully bearded and also in top hats and evening wear.

And one of them brought her out in instant goose bumps.

It's the man from the markets.

What did Sally say his name was? Jasper… Jasper Blackwood.

She stared as they rolled on down Elizabeth Street. The third man – she recognised him too from the few social functions her mother had insisted she attend. It was Dr Alistair Blackwood, a well-known physician. She realised with a rush the two must be related.

They're probably brothers.

But Jasper Blackwood? In a landau with Eudora and Gideon? If I needed confirmation that the fellow was following me and not Sally yesterday, isn't this it?

A sudden lull in the crush of horses and vehicles gave her the opportunity she needed to cross over. She made for Hawk Eye's office with renewed purpose.

He's got to take the case up again now, she thought as she strode at an unladylike speed to catch him before he left for the day. *He's just got to.*

***

After she left Silas later that day, still struggling with his response, Posey caught a hack to the Exchange, an imposing four storey Corinthian columned sandstone building in Bridge Street, which was the centre of Sydney's communications. She sent Thomas another pleading telegraph.

> MY GOOD FRIEND THE SECOND SON IN DANGER STOP
>
> URGENT INVESTIGATION OF FAMILY HISTORY REQUIRED STOP
>
> PARTICULARLY RELATING TO ELDEST SON AND FAMOUS PAINTING STOP
>
> LOVE POSEY

That should be opaque enough to keep the Post Office spies in the dark, she thought as she hailed a cab to go home to Darlinghurst. *I hope Thomas has already started working on it.*

Forty-seven

The mid-morning knock on their brass lion head was tentative. Posey wouldn't have heard it if she hadn't been passing through the front of the hallway. On top of that, she wasn't aware Arabella was expecting any visitors. She certainly wasn't.

A jolt of anxiety lodged under her ribs at the thought it might be Gideon Vane again, returning with a bailiff to impound *Angel Dreaming*. Just to make sure, she tiptoed to the dining room and secretly peered out the window to check on who was there.

Her hand flew to the spot in her chest where a hard knob of fear still roosted.

Margaret Beaumont. It was Margaret Beaumont, the artist she'd visited a couple of weeks ago.

Why is she here now?

Geraldine Crowe came in to go to the front and answer.

"We've got an unexpected visitor, Geraldine. I'll see her into the library. Could you bring some tea and cookies to us in, say, ten minutes?"

Mrs Crowe gave one of her sunny smiles. "Certainly, Miss Posey. Today's morning tea has got another five minutes in the oven, so it's perfect timing."

Posey smiled. "And could you find Mother and ask her to join us? I think she might be upstairs in her bedroom. Tell her we've got a visitor she will be very pleased to meet." She took one stride towards the front door and hesitated. "Oh, and while you are up there, could you check Mother's room is tidy? We might want to visit there soon."

As Mrs Crowe left, Posey paused before the still-closed door, straightened up her dress and took two deep breaths. Then she stepped forward and pulled the door wide open.

The quicks of Margaret Beaumont's fingers still betrayed traces of the green, blue and red paints she'd applied in her recent works, but otherwise the septuagenarian artist was well turned out. She wore a sage-green dress with swirling embroidered red-flower designs, the colours picked up in a fine muslin shawl she draped across her chest. A chunky agate and silver necklace, matching agate drop earrings and finely tooled silver leather ankle boots completed her ensemble.

"Mrs Beaumont!" Posey smiled broadly. Genuine pleasure radiated from the greeting as Posey leaned forward to embrace the older woman.

Mrs Beaumont responded with a warm smile. "Miss Barclay! So good to see you again."

"This is a surprise. A wonderful one. I hoped Mother might meet you. Now she will."

A light tread coming up the hall behind her signalled Arabella's arrival.

Posey stepped aside. "Mother, meet Mrs Margaret Beaumont, one of our country's finest water colourists, and a close acquaintance of Mr Williams."

Margaret Beaumont stood her ground as Arabella approached. "I should have come sooner, Mrs Barclay. Better late than never, though, don't they say? I have much I would like to share with you." She paused and shot a meaningful glance from Arabella to Posey. "And, naturally, while I am here, I am very much hoping you will allow me to feast my eyes on this painting I'm hearing so much about. It's been thirty years since I last saw it. And from the deep whispers I hear in the art world, that lass needs our help."

***

Much later, after they'd taken Mrs Beaumont upstairs to see *Angel Dreaming* again, and she'd wept before Rosamunde's imploring eyes, they settled in the library to hear all she could recall of the work and its provenance.

"I was married to Sir Francis Grant," Mrs Beaumont confessed. "I was a young girl, an aspiring artist, married to one of the art world's acclaimed stars. When he courted me, he was always so encouraging about my work. I had visions of a partnership of gifted, creative souls, upholding one another in a glorious union that poor folk who weren't artists couldn't understand. People who didn't comprehend the power of the muse."

She sipped her tea. "Oh, what a fool I was, and what a tumble I took. I deserved it. I went from inhabiting the elysian fields of artistic endeavour to the prosaic world of housekeeping while Sir Francis went off like a knight in shining armour conquering dragons. I discovered how quickly things change when you have that ring on your finger." She gave them a quick, chagrin-filled smile.

"But I was there for much of the conception of your painting upstairs. After all, it was a portrait of a child. And the Earl of Worcester had especially commissioned it for his wife. Ironically, given my situation, this husband wanted the painting because he was so grateful to have a daughter after two sons. And it suited Sir Francis's purposes to take me along to the many sittings, to keep Rosamunde's mother, Lady Henrietta, out of Francis's hair. Effectively, that was my job.

"Lady Henrietta and I became quite close over those months when my husband was working on *Angel Dreaming*, and then fate took over. It was one of those paintings that captured the public imagination. Everyone was talking about it.

"I might add that not only was it commissioned by the earl specifically for his wife to thank her for having a daughter, but he stated in the documentation that it was being added to Countess Henrietta's personal trust, outside of the earl's own estate. So, she was fully within her rights to pass it on to whomsoever she pleased.

"I might be an old woman on my way out the door, but I keep myself informed. I've heard the whispers about some painting the new judge wants to get his hands on. I guessed instantly what that painting would be. And I am in a unique position to give evidence on it, if you so require."

Forty-eight

He's going to make as if none of it ever happened.

Silas gazed up at the riot of pink-and-white blossom arching over his head and breathed in the strong clove fragrance of white rhododendrons. The spring air throbbed with the humming of bees, their fast-beating tiny wings hard at work gathering in the new season's free-flowing nectar. As he stared, he momentarily lost himself in the glory of nature around him, and particularly this corner of Sydney's botanic gardens, with the spring walk plantings of azaleas and rhododendrons made in the last decade by its forward-looking director, Charles Moore.

The garden – located close to Silas's walk from his office to the Parramatta ferry he caught to reach his Hunters Hill country estate – provided a regular sanctuary for him from the harsher realities of life and law. He savoured the salt-edged crisp ocean air that wafted in from the harbour, enveloping visitors in a haven of calm that nudged right up against the city's bustling commercial centre. He couldn't see the Gothic towers of Government House from where he sat on a simple park bench, but the nexus of the state's administration – Parliament

House, the Mint, the Supreme Court and the General Exchange – home of the expanding telegraphic technology – lay only a few streets away.

Never had he felt a greater need for the peace of the gardens to calm his inner turmoil than now.

I'm about to lose everything I love. The life I've spent the last twenty years creating is collapsing around me. The catastrophe I have tried to escape since I was blinded at six years old has chased me down.

Silas did not think of himself as a religious man. He was a rationalist, a logician who excelled in assembling coherent legal strategies. But on that fateful day, he'd begged the God they talked about in church to save his sister; pleaded for her life until his throat grew raw and his voice ran out. But if there was a God up there somewhere, he hadn't listened.

Benedict, and then Silas, had lived his life from that day in his own strength. Proving to himself he didn't need the help of some fantasy deity. But Gideon's arrival in Sydney had drained him of his last reserves. If he ever needed proof God had it in for him, this was it. The worst catastrophe he could imagine, and so far-fetched he hadn't seen it coming. He was more likely to believe he could change a fly into an elephant than see Gideon Vane, the heir to the Earldom of Worcester, coming to Australia.

He rose from his bench and his contemplation of the great white rhododendron to continue his passage to the ferry. He always thought best when he was walking, anyway.

I've been telling myself I can do it again. Run away.

I thought it would be better for Posey if I did. With me gone, she might not attract Gideon's venom.

But Jeremiah's death. Posey being stalked by Jasper Blackwood. The demand for the painting. He won't let up until he's hounded me from the last patch of the earth I stand on.

For Posey, Jeremiah, for the Barclay family, for justice, and for all the other innocents he's going to go after. And, finally, for myself.

He's given me no choice.

It's time to fight back.

Forty-nine

High in the glittering southern sky, Captain Henry Augustus Graham watched threads of heavy cumulus cloud trail across the night sky, rimmed on their edges from the light of the bright waning moon. Driven by high atmosphere winds, they wreathed in and out like May dance ribbons, auguring a shower or two before dawn.

A strengthening sea breeze sprang up from the tidal waters of the Parramatta River, with just enough of a fresh edge and salty tang to rejuvenate a man with a full belly and drooping eyelids. What else to expect when he'd spent a couple of hours over a fine meal in the toasty atmosphere of the Garibaldi Inn, in a cheerful, crowded dining room smelling of garlic, warm red wine and cigar smoke?

As he climbed up to the driving bench of his uncanopied, workaday wagon ready to head home, Captain Graham gazed up in wonder at the dazzling river of light that was the Milky Way. He reached into the tray of his wagon to scratch his two rough-haired deerhounds behind the ears. He let his eyes rove the galaxies until he found the familiar hook of Scorpio, high in the west, with the big red star in its midst that mankind had known for thousands of years. It was one of the royal stars of Persia, his grandfather had told him. And here it was still, beaming down on him tonight. Locating that star always made him feel anchored and grounded. Yet again, he thanked his wandering star that his grandpapa had shipped out to Australia with the New South Wales Corps fifty years ago.

In tune with family tradition, Graham had taken up a military career, going back to the "homeland" to train and connect with a proud Scots heritage. Even his dogs came from a bloodline started by the first Graham to land here.

These days Captain Graham – no longer on active duty, but still "Captain" to all his friends – enjoyed a relaxed pastoral existence up the Parramatta River north of Hunters Hill village. He cultivated a remarkably productive garden, growing much of his own food and sharing his peaches, potatoes and pumpkins with a wide circle of friends, including the Italians who ran the Garibaldi Inn and warmly appreciated the basil, thyme, rosemary and oregano Captain Graham provided for their European-inspired dishes.

He'd delivered several large baskets of his latest produce there tonight, before he'd tucked into his meal. Now he planned to give Faust and Bianca, scrabbling around with their hefty paws on the tray of the wagon, an evening run before heading home.

They were sweet-tempered and placid creatures, bred for the speed and stamina required to hunt and kill stags. They'd proved suitable for hunting kangaroos and dingoes in their new homeland. Though loyal to a fault, they weren't known for their obedience. If they saw something they identified as a quarry, they were likely to attack first and answer the questions later. That was one reason Captain Graham let them run after dark, when few pedestrians or other dogs (or cats) were out.

He drove out of the tiny village and pulled up near a stand of bush on the harbour's edge. A perfect place for them to promenade. He called them down and they shot off the back of the wagon like shooting stars. All Graham could do was stand and gape.

***

Silas Williams had lingered in the botanic gardens longer than he intended, breathing in the fragrance of the trees and earth and turning over in his mind what his next steps should be. Then, when he finally got to the ferry buildings at the bottom of town, he narrowly missed one boat that was just leaving. After a considerable wait for the next ferry and a two-hour ride, he arrived home in total darkness. The full moon of a week ago was waning fast, but it was still bright enough for him to easily find his way home. The path to Ironbark Lodge was well known to him and the locals were always friendly.

The reassuring rhythm of the ferry's engines on his homeward journey had further lulled his anguish. He stepped off onto Ferry Landing in an end-of-week haze, still haunted by memories of Rosamunde and the violence they had both suffered at Gideon's hand, but less agitated than he had been. After trying to sidestep the ramifications of his childhood disaster his whole life, he'd finally realised he could neither run nor hide any longer.

His father, in particular, had been terrified by what public knowledge of Gideon's attack could do to the family name. Silas knew the earl feared the subsequent scandal would destroy his legal business as well as blacken their reputation beyond repair. He'd argued that it was in his interests too – *Benedict's* future interests – as much as anyone else's to keep it a secret. So the family made vague references to a "childhood accident" whenever anyone asked how he'd lost the sight in one eye, leaving the impression it was from a fall from a horse, or a tree, or by being struck by a branch or similar. The earl and his mother always kept the details vague and discouraged further questions.

Close to his front gate, Silas waved out to Captain Graham and the two handsome deerhounds he often saw bounding through the nearby park, straining to be freed from their leashes to play. Faust and Bianca, he called them. Silas smiled to himself yet again at the incongruity of the names. Bianca, the sweet innocent sister to bad tempered Kate in William Shakespeare's *The Taming of the Shrew*. And Faust, the misguided philosopher who made a pact with the devil, exchanging his soul for unlimited power and worldly pleasures. Bianca was docile, unless she was hunting for prey. And Faust? Again, a well-mannered critter. But it wasn't hard to imagine him sleeping at Lucifer's fireside.

Let off their leashes, the dogs rushed up, slobbering to greet him, and he patted the jagged grey hairline that ran down the spine of both. He understood deerhounds were especially receptive to human companionship.

"Bianca… How are you, girl? And you, big fellow Faust. Behaving yourselves?" He grinned at Captain Graham. "I must be mad, talking to your dogs like they're people."

"Believe it or not, they appreciate it." Graham chortled. "They're sensitive creatures, considering they're also the best kangaroo hunters around."

The two men shared a convivial silence, and then Silas pushed on, suddenly keen to get home and pour himself a brandy. His housekeeper would have left dinner out and he felt the sharp pangs of anticipation at the thought of a meal in his peaceful den. As he started up the path to his front door, the eerie shriek of the stone curlews broke the night's silence. The reclusive nocturnal birds were more commonly heard than seen.

Old folk said if you heard the call of the stone curlew three nights in a row, it prophesied death. Silas swallowed hard.

They're just birds foraging for insects, even if they sound like a woman being murdered.

Wee lo… wee lo… The plaintive screech echoed around the glade.

Silas stopped, ear cocked, all senses alert, and a dark flash streaked past right in front of his feet. He pulled at his eye patch, rubbing his good eye and attempting to adjust to the dim surroundings. He'd always found his depth of sight was the thing most compromised by the loss of one eye, and it was especially deficient at night. He lingered, uncertain of taking the next step forward. Was that streak the neighbour's cat being chased by foxes? Was it a rat, or a wild turkey, or a whole clutch of stone curlews, flushed out from under the hedge?

He glanced around him to locate the source of the disturbance. Some distance away, he heard dogs set up a baying call. Faust and Bianca, no doubt. Maybe the creature or creatures in flight had crossed their paths.

He huffed out a breath and re-started his journey.

You're just about home, and there's nothing to be afraid of.

But then he heard the snap of a branch behind him and swung around, uncertain again about what was going on. He was aware of another flash of something shiny – steel, probably – what the dickens was it? He impulsively ducked as something scythed the air overhead.

And then his world folded. His skull cracked open like an egg in a frying pan. A brief cry came from his mouth, and then he was toppling forward onto his knees. He saw and heard nothing more.

***

That night represented one of Captain Henry Augustus Graham's worst wild-turkey encounters. Wild turkeys? Or was it those stone curlews? A whole brood of them, it seemed, flashed onto the path where he and his dogs were fossicking. The dogs had been acting like typical hounds scenting their way along, noses to the ground, tails flag-waving in the air.

Until the birds broke cover.

In the dark it was impossible to tell if they were turkeys or something else, a fox even, but within seconds they were half running, half flying, as it they were pursuing the very devil himself. Their unseen quarry, probably panicked, did an abrupt reversal and started back the way they'd come, the dogs in hot pursuit. Graham raced behind them, struggling to keep them in sight.

It took him a few seconds to process the scene they'd stumbled onto.

A masked man, clothed all in black, had Silas by the heels and was dragging him roughly to a waiting wagon, partly obscured by overgrowth, parked near his gate. The barrister's eye patch had been dislodged and he was bleeding heavily from a head wound on the right side of his face. His head bobbed roughly along the ground.

In one bound, and it seemed with one mind, the dogs changed their target and direction, from pursuit of the birds to swarming the man holding Silas. Faust grabbed the attacker by the upper thigh, while sweet-tempered Bianca climbed on his back and attempted to jawbone the back of his neck.

The masked man screamed and dropped Silas's legs. Head down, covering his upper body with his arms, with Bianca still clinging to his back, he dashed howling for the small wagon waiting with a single horse and driver.

As he leapt on board, he shook the dog free and the driver whipped up a frenzy to push the horse into motion.

Growling, the canines circled back around, noses to the forest floor, making sure they'd cleared the place of enemies.

Good work, fellas. Captain Graham breathed the words to himself. He bent over Silas's bleeding, unconscious form. *Too bad it might all have been too late for Hawk Eye.*

But he didn't say that out loud either.

He pulled at his cotton shirt, ripping the buttons free and tearing the front panel into strips. He pushed the cotton firmly against Sila's head wound and observed an almost instant slowing in the bleeding. Then he gathered the solicitor's slack form gently up in his arms and transferred him to the bench seat of his wagon, lashing him in place with rope he kept there "just in case". With one hand on the reins and one holding his insensible friend stable, he began a slow journey back to Hunters Hill village and the doctor's house.

Fifty

Sydney Town and Country
August 1, 1868
A weekly journal read by everybody who is anybody; All the latest in royal doings, beautiful Australia, high society, sport, and the best political cartoons.

Christabel's Week

Much of the excitement swirling around town this last week centres on a certain English lord, heir apparent to an earldom, fresh on the scene to assume heavy responsibilities as a newly appointed judge to the New South Wales Supreme Court. The new My Lord Justice was sworn in at a ceremony presided over by Chief Justice Sir Frederick Dooley on Wednesday.

The assembled legal alumni made a dashing composition in their scarlet gowns edged with sparkling-white ermine. Sir Frederick delivered a speech designed to assure all who doubted an English import can administer Australian justice by citing glowing credentials proffered by none other than Baron Kingshorn, a foremost judge on the Court of the Queen's Bench.

*****

The new Lord Justice lost no time in signalling his pleasure at being in Sydney, announcing his engagement to Miss Eudora Gilbert, sister of newspaper magnate Clifford Gilbert, a short time after his arrival.

The handsome couple were recently spotted at a dinner given for them by Bishop Stanton. Lord Brook was the consummate polished Englishman in black tie and tails, Miss Eudora in a dark-green satin with a Watteau pleated back. The chiffon fichu she wore at the neck set off her porcelain complexion and her shining auburn hair to perfection. (And it might be added, was tastefully tailored to see out mourning for her mother Clara Gilbert, a beloved Sydney hostess.)

It can only be assumed the two had already made their acquaintance in the ballrooms of Mayfair and have warmly grasped the opportunity to reconnect.

***

Modistes throughout the city are all a twitter at the prospect of the coming wedding, but they may have to prepare to be disappointed. It is rumoured the couple plan to marry expeditiously within the next few weeks, although no date has yet been announced. Fashion followers will be sad, as the early date leaves little time for favoured guests to commission new gowns for the occasion.

***

Lord Brook was recently named as the judge who will preside over the long-awaited Barclay case, where city burghers and disappointed investors are taking a claim against the assets of

Mr James Barclay, whose investment house went down in flames in spectacular fashion last year, leaving many ruined investors. Some observers find it an interesting appointment considering His Lordship will have little knowledge of events leading up to this case, but Christabel is confident a man schooled at Eton and the Inns will rise brilliantly to the occasion.

***

Mr Silas Williams Q.C. will defend the Barclay family in the oncoming arguments, representing James's daughters, Miss Posey and Petunia Barclay, and their mother, Arabella, and Mrs Poppy Yates in the proceedings. (Poppy married Sydney Herald journalist Thomas Yates earlier this year and the pair are honeymooning in London.)

In a tantalising little cheep from a birdie on my shoulder, it seems the Barclay family owns a celebrated portrait that was once part of the earl's father's estate. The birdie could not tell me how it came to have migrated to the wall of a Darlinghurst manor, but it seems Lord Brook is not amused and may begin proceedings to claim it back as stolen property. Christabel is not sure how this little tussle may influence the outcome of the larger case between the Barclays and the NSW Supreme Court. I guess only time will tell.

Fifty-one

"I must caution you, Miss Barclay, that head injuries of this nature are notoriously unpredictable." Dr Joseph Thackery peered over the rims of his round wire glasses, and his mutton-whiskered face – what she could see of it under the hair – settled into a stern grimace.

He leaned over Silas's prone form and brushed an errant lock from his eyes with a kindly gesture. "It's fortunate the villain hit him on his blind side where there wasn't too much more damage he could do. If he'd hit the other side, he might have lost his sight altogether."

Posey drew in a sharp breath, and Thackery's sharp blue eyes softened.

"Ye can't tell me where I can find his next of kin, can ye, Miss Barclay? No one here seems to know anything about his family."

She drew up another ragged breath. "Next of kin, doctor? I'm afraid not. I believe he has distant family in England, but for as long as I've known him, he hasn't been in regular contact. Former Police Superintendent Jeavon Yates is one of his closest confidantes. He might be the person most like family that Silas has in Sydney."

The doctor puffed on his pipe. "Oh, aye, and I've already been in touch with Superintendent Yates, as I'm sure you'd know. He was very handy last night. Came as soon as the messenger arrived, helped us get entry to Mr Williams' house, and kept watch here overnight with the nurse. Just the sort of friend you need at a time like this."

The physician, a thirty-year veteran with ten years as a Royal Navy surgeon before he came ashore for general practice, took Silas's wrist between his thumb and forefinger and stood quietly, checking his pulse against a pocket watch. Silas's head sat straight on a small flat pillow, his face a ghostly white, and if she couldn't hear his soft, shallow breathing, she could imagine he was already dead.

Something deep inside her crumpled in a stabbing pain.

His eyes were closed, and the black patch removed. For the first time, Posey regarded his face unobscured by the piratical triangle. He looked so vulnerable without his patch, and her heart flooded with a warm affection. She scanned his features, the broad forehead over evenly arched dark eyebrows and knife sharp cheekbones. Even in this comatose state, his finely chiselled lips seemed to tilt in a faint, ironic smile.

He'd have been a gorgeous child. Nearly as beautiful as Rosamunde, in a boyish way.

She flushed at where her thoughts were taking her.

Any minute now, you'll be imagining his sons. Get a grip on yourself, Posey.

She glanced up and saw that the nurse Jeavon had brought in at short notice, and Silas's pretty office assistant Amelie were both watching her with unabashed curiosity. They stood some distance from the bed, having moved to allow Dr Thackery access.

They're wondering where I stand in all this. Especially beautiful Amelie.

The interloper. A wormy voice reared up and pinched at her guts.

Who – what – are you? You're not his wife. His paramour? Sister? We're doing perfectly fine for Mr Silas without you here.

She cleared her throat. "Thank you both for your care of Mr Williams. You've done a wonderful job."

She looked back down at the patient. Nothing had changed. Not a muscle moved. His eyes didn't shudder under the delicate, faintly veined lids. He remained insensible to words or touch.

Dr Thackery's voice was gruff when he spoke next. "While we hope for a full recovery, we must be prepared for the possibility of lasting effects on Mr Williams' mental or physical capabilities. The next twenty-four hours will be critical."

She knew that was true without the doctor having to spell it out. If Silas didn't regain consciousness within three days of the trauma, his chances of making a full recovery decreased.

"What can I do to help?" Posey asked. "It's awful seeing him like this."

Thackeray glanced at the two women standing aside. "Nurse Andrews and Miss Dubois are doing very well here, Miss Barclay. At present, I'm not sure we need extra help. However, if the situation continues for several days…" His voice faded and he cleared his throat.

"If that happens, then perhaps you could take a night shift to lighten their hours."

Heaven grant that won't be necessary, she thought. *Not that I don't want to do it, but I don't want him to stay in this state one minute longer than necessary for his healing.*

A bustling energy in the passage outside gave notice someone else had entered the house. They all looked expectantly as a bluff mountain man with a ruddy broad face and thinning grey hair to match his grey beard stomped in. He wore heavy leather walking boots and held two enormous dogs on chain leashes.

"Bianca! Faust! Sit."

At his command, both dogs sat on their haunches and surveyed the bed.

"You know who that is, don't you?" Captain Henry Augustus Graham made a brief ironic bow to the assembled gallery. "Morning, Doctor, Captain Graham at your service."

"Morning, Henry. You know Nurse Andrews from last night?" The doctor turned to Posey in explanation. "The nurse lives next door to the inn. She was willing to be called in on an emergency at short notice. And this is Miss Posey Barclay, a friend of Mr Williams, and Miss Amelie Dubois, his personal assistant."

Captain Graham nodded to the room. "I wanted to bring the dogs to say hello. I reckon without them, Mr Williams was heading for the next world."

"I agree with you, Captain. If he pulls through, I'm sure he'll be happy to buy them and you a fine supper." The doctor flashed a quick smile.

Posey, who'd been sitting in a chair at Silas's bedside, stood up and gestured to it. "Please, come and sit down. We're all so grateful you and the dogs were there to intervene." She linked her hands together in a nervous action.

"Tell me what happened, Captain Graham. I'd love to hear all the details. And I'm sure he will 'pull through', as Dr Thackery puts it. When he does, he'll certainly want to buy you all that well-deserved supper."

Fifty-two

Jeavon and Posey were about to set off for the wharf to catch the Parramatta ferry the next morning when Jeavon's housekeeper announced he had a visitor. She ushered in a weaselly faced fellow Jeavon instantly remembered seeing at the inquest for Mr Hawkins.

The young man who'd made a fuss. Jeremiah's son, Digby.

He shot Posey a warning look. *Let me handle this.*

She replied with furrowed brows. *Sure. I don't know who he is, anyway.*

Jeavon took a step forward and thrust out his hand. "Mr Hawkins. Jeavon Yates."

After an obvious moment of hesitation Digby shook his hand, though his lip curled in an arrogant curve.

Jeavon turned to Posey. "And Miss Posey Barclay."

Digby eyed her with a know-it-all sneer. "Barclay, aye? One of those Barclays whose been ripping off the good burghers, I bet."

Posey kept her twitching hands pinned to her sides. "You seem certain you know all about us, so who am I to dissuade you?" she said.

"Diss-what?"

Hawkins reminded Posey of a snake. He had narrow, cold eyes in a thin face, and he regularly ran his tongue along thin pale lips, a fang taking aim to strike. When he spoke, his already narrow eyes shrank to slits that opened just enough to show pinpoint black irises that glittered with venom.

Jeavon came straight to the point. "Miss Barclay and I were just leaving for an important meeting, Mr Hawkins. We've got a ferry to catch. I'm afraid we have little time for unexpected visitors. What is it you want with us?"

Digby stiffened. "I want to know what you're going to do to compensate me for losing my father. He'd still be alive if it wasn't for you rich coves."

"I beg your pardon," said Jeavon. "I believe the coroner found your father died due to culpable murder by persons unknown. We regarded Jeremiah very much as a friend. We are devastated at your loss." He paused. "Have you any idea who could have done it? Did he have any enemies?"

Digby shook his head and then stared again, licking his lips. "I'm thinking you paid someone to off him so he couldn't give evidence at this big trial that's coming up. That's what a lot of folks are saying, anyway."

"Folks? What folks would they be?"

Digby shrugged. "I dunno them all. Jasper Blackwood. That queer sheila, Minerva. The rich Yank who's related to someone over there with squillions. Some important people, it seems to me."

Posey's fists flexed, and she couldn't resist asking the question. "Jasper Blackwood? How do you know him?"

Digby twitched, annoyed at being challenged. "I got talking to him at the inquest, if you'd like to know. And he was most interested to meet me, seeing as I'm a shareholder in this mine they're all fighting over."

"A shareholder? How so?"

Digby bristled like a dog whose hackles rose at having his territory contested.

Invaded.

"On account of my dah of course. You don't know much, do ya? My father had a share in the Crossover Mine on account he did most of the work. And now he's dead, the share's mine." He glanced past Posey's shoulder, as if by being a woman, he didn't have to take her too seriously.

With a sly grin and a greedy glint in his dark-grey eyes, he spoke over her head to Jeavon. "Now I'm a shareholder, I want a say in that mine. And I won't be slaving in the dirt like my dah did. I'm no mutton head." He stared past Posey again, as if she wasn't present. "But that's not why I'm here. As I told you at the beginning, I reckon you owe me for my dad being offed. So how are ye going to settle that debt? You can pay me up front in cash, or increase my shareholding. What's it to be?" He shouldered Posey aside to get closer to Jeavon and folded his arms across his chest. He glared at the barrel-chested former superintendent as if he was bullying a barrow boy.

A heavy silence hung between them. Digby shuffled his feet, inching closer to Jeavon.

"Well, what's it to be? Cos if you're not ready to talk turkey, Mr Jasper Blackwood certainly is. He's got rich backers, and he's ready to do business. He says he knows I've got a wonderful tale to tell and they're prepared to pay for it."

Jeavon lifted a sceptical brow. "Oh? Rich backers, you say? Wouldn't be that rich American cove you mentioned earlier, would it?"

Digby smirked, and under his limp blond moustache, Posey glimpsed dirty brown teeth.

"How should I know? All I know is that I can spin them a yarn worth their money that will blow you out of the water. My Dah was a kind fool, always putting others before himself, thinking he had to give value in this world. Preaching on about treating others as we'd treat ourselves is a load of rubbish, if you ask me. How often do you see that work out well? Look where it got him. Seems to me in this world the rich just get richer and the rest of us can go starve. I'm not making the same mistakes he did."

Jeavon picked up his satchel and took a step towards the door. "Mr Hawkins, we were on our way out. All I can tell you is that we had nothing to do with your father's death. The very people you are talking about joining forces with are more likely than anyone to have killed him. They wanted him dead because he could speak with authority about the honourable way Nathan Russell did business. And they wanted to stop him from doing that at all costs. How does it feel to be siding with your dad's killer or killers?"

Digby roared with laughter, as if that was the funniest thing he'd heard in a while. "All I want is some good hot coin so I don't have to work again ever in my life. Truth is, my old man and I never got on. It's no skin off my nose if he kicked the bucket early. In fact, considering everything, it's turning out to be a real bonus."

Fifty-three

Posey and Jeavon finally rid themselves of the odious Digby Hawkins and headed up the river to Hunters Hill to find Silas's condition unchanged.

"There are some hopeful signs," Dr Thackery reported. "His wound does not seem to be infected. His temperature is only slightly above normal, showing he has no internal infection. And his breathing is still relaxed and steady. It's as if he's in a deep sleep."

His brows hooked in a worried question mark. "But we want to see him come back to consciousness, even if it's in brief lapses at first. I recommend we continue to have someone at his side at all times in case he wakes up."

Posey agreed to return later in the evening to relieve Nurse Andrews of the midnight shift. Between her and Amelie, Silas had received around the clock care, but now they were entering the third night of his unconscious state and they were worn out.

Mrs Crowe had fixed her Welsh rarebit for a late lunch, and the sunroom swooned with the smell of melted butter and cheese, and pinch of cayenne, ale and mustard, poured over hot buttered toast. Posey settled down to gorge the lot before jumping back on the Hunters Hill ferry when Petunia sauntered in, still wearing her riding habit, her hair windblown, her cheeks rosy from her day spent in the sun and fresh air.

"Yum!" She leaned over the pile of toast set in the middle of the table. "You don't need all of that, do you? Can I have some? I'm starving."

"Gwen's not making lunch today?" Posey retorted, mildly annoyed Petunia was elbowing in on her treat. "Ask Mrs C. to make some more for you."

Petunia flounced out and was back within two minutes.

"She's making another batch. Meantime, she says I can share yours. She'll have the next lot out in no time." She settled in her chair with the bright enthusiasm she seemed to bring to every task and asked, "How's Hawk Eye today? Any better?"

Posey shook her head, her mouth full of cheese and toast. She chewed and swallowed and said, "No better. But no worse either. He looks so peaceful. As if he's enjoying a long sleep." She sipped at her hot coffee and added, "I'm going up there later to take a midnight shift. The nurse and Amelie are exhausted, so I'm relieving them."

Petunia tossed her head and fingered her hair off her face. Neither of the girls noticed Arabella until she tiptoed in.

"My word. So nice to find you here together at the same time. It's a rare moment."

Petunia laughed. "Don't be silly, Mama. We're often here together. You're the one that's always out. Like last night. How did it go?"

Arabella melted into a wide smile. "Oh, Hugo is so sweet. I had a lovely time."

Posey looked up. "Where did you go? Sorry, with all this Silas stuff happening, I've been out of the picture."

"We went to dinner at Eudora's for a private engagement party. She's only just coming out of mourning, but they're not wasting any time. They're well into the wedding preparations. They haven't confirmed the date yet, but I think it's only weeks away." Arabella beamed and sat down at the head of the table, her usual place. "What are you eating?"

"Mrs Crowe's Welsh rarebit," the sisters chorused.

As if on cue, Geraldine Crowe appeared with a second plate of cheesy toast.

"I'm going out to nurse Hawk Eye tonight." Posey directed the remark to her mother.

"Oh, dear, do you think that's wise? I mean, you won't have a chaperone."

Posey gazed at her, a piece of toast suspended in midair. "I never have a chaperone, Mother, you know that."

"Oh, I know, but that's when you're really only with women. It's different when you're sitting at a man's bedside right through the night."

"A man, I might remind you, Mother, who is unconscious. He can't see, hear or speak. Honestly… Anyway, you can talk. What's this consorting with the enemy? Going to dinner with Gideon Vane?"

"Lord Brook was simply another guest. I hardly spoke to him. There was quite a crew there. Doctor Blackwood, the physician, and his brother. Jasper had a nasty leg injury. Minerva whispered he'd got a dog bite and Ambrose was worried he might get rabies."

"Rabies?" barked Posey. "We don't have rabies in Australia, do we? And anyway, how did he get a dog bite? The bishop doesn't keep dogs." Her heart was beating a frantic tom-tom.

Arabella trilled her characteristic pealing laugh. "Bishop Stanton doesn't have dogs, no, silly. And I don't know if it even was a dog bite. They seemed reluctant to talk about it. But you know how Minerva is. She always likes to be first with the gossip."

Petunia piped up. "I heard Gwen talking about it with the groom. She's getting very matey with Brownie. Brings him his morning tea most mornings. Apparently, Doctor Ambrose Blackwood worked in India and they have lots of rabies there, so he knows all about it and is extra cautious."

Her beautiful open face clouded over. "According to Clarrie, she probably would know, because Gwen and Jasper had a what do you call it – a tendre. Once upon a time. Until he dropped her for someone else."

Arabella waved her hands in the air in shock. "A tendre? Really, Petunia, where do you get these ideas from? That's not a topic for a young lady's discussion."

Petunia and Posey locked eyes and laughed.

"Mother, it's close to 1869 in Australia," said Petunia, reaching across the table for another piece of toast. "Soon it will be 1870, for goodness' sakes. The world is changing."

Fifty-four

One o'clock, and all's well.

The night watchman Jeavon had set to patrol the perimeter of Ironbark Lodge didn't utter such a cry, but he could have. The clump of his heavy boots as he patrolled the grounds, and the eerie mourning call of the stone curlews in the bush outside, were the only sounds that came to Posey's ears from her post beside Silas's bed.

She shifted in the olive-green velvet chair and leaned in for the umpteenth time that evening to check he was still breathing.

Yes. Still breathing, thank God. Now wake up!

She'd taken over from Nurse Andrew at 9 pm, and for the last four hours she'd hoped and prayed he would wake up and recognise her.

Hoped and prayed, and talked to him. She'd heard folk say that the last sense patients lost was their hearing, and she'd been determined to let Hawk Eye know she was there with him.

He lay motionless in a rosewood sleigh bed decorated in a subtle inlay fern and medallion pattern, his cream satin sheets a perfect complement to the delicate design. At its head stood an artist's easel with a beautifully wrought study of a woman in profile.

It is almost certainly his mother, Posey thought as she examined it. The shape of her eye sockets and brows had the same wide, intelligent cast.

She also resembles the daguerreotype in Mother's room, she thought with a sudden surge of excitement. I bet one of them is of her. And, come to think of it, the others will probably be Gideon and Silas.

When she'd been in the room the other night, she'd hardly noticed anything about it. Tonight, sitting here alone with only one lamp alight on a bedside table, she had time to store the details.

A landscape on one wall, a typical English country scene she suspected came from the estate where Hawk Eye grew up. And an item that would have been a mystery if she hadn't seen the Angel Eyes painting.

Propped up on a tripod was a finely detailed oil study of a strangely blank-eyed porcelain doll, bereft of eyebrows, in a lace ruche matinee jacket and a blue headband encrusted with sparkly beads.

"Oh, my goodness. You loved your family."

Because there it was, an elegant preparatory sketch of the doll Rosamunde nursed across her lap in the Grant portrait, preserved in a perfect miniature.

"Now I know more about it, I wonder what it cost you to come out here?" she said in a low voice, talking to herself. She leaned back over the sleeping figure and brushed her hand across his forehead. "Your temperature is normal. There's still no sign of infection, the doctor says. I'm praying you're taking your time to come around. That's all."

She fingered the *English Woman's Journal* article she'd brought to read during the long night, but her eyes dropped with weariness at the thought of attempting to read in the dim light.

I'll save learning more about the redundant woman for another day.

Redundant woman. She'd recently discovered the term from the fountain of new women's literature flowing from England. Women's presses were spurting to life, and with them an enlivening political discussion.

"I'm a redundant woman," she told the recumbent Silas. "Did you know that? I wasn't redundant when I was working for you as an articled clerk. But now I'm filling my days with charitable work, I'm considered redundant."

The debate had arisen a few years ago when a man – it had to have been a man, didn't it – William Rathbone Greg, had written a paper suggesting all women should be married to fulfil their natural destiny. And if there weren't enough men to go around in England, they should be exported to the colonies to provide wives for convicts, to make up the female deficit there.

A rising number of articulate women activists like Bessie Rayner Parkes and Barbara Bodichon in the *English Woman's Journal* had challenged the notion that marriage was the only acceptable path for women. They argued for better education for women, legal protection for their property, and opening up the professions – teaching nursing and clerical work – to them.

"Thank you, Bessie and Barbara," Posey whispered. "My thoughts entirely." She smiled grimly to herself and turned her eyes back to the man in the bed.

You're a good man. An honourable man. And I'm afraid I've rather taken you for granted.

"I know I said I wouldn't marry you, Hawk Eye," she said in a sotto voce voice. "But going on without you is unthinkable, too. Please don't die."

The long black eyelashes flickered. Hawk Eye released a long sigh and opened his eyes.

She leaned right over him, gazing at him, the blind eye closed, but the seeing one staring back at her.

His lips parted, but no sound emerged.

"Hawk Eye!" she whispered, exultant and urgent. "You're awake?"

He closed his eyes, and his mouth tipped up in a gentle, curving smile. "Posey," he said with a satisfied sigh. "I knew you'd come."

And then he fell back into his own world. Whether he was unconscious or just in a deep sleep, she didn't know, but a rising tide of joy inside her told her everything was going to be alright.

***

Towards dawn, Hawk Eye awoke again, and this time he didn't fall instantly back into the nether world. She gently propped him up with pillows and guided a glass of cold water to his lips.

"Mmm," he murmured. "I'd forgotten how good that tastes." He let his head flop back. "I suppose I'm expected to ask what happened?" he joked. His voice was thin and reedy.

"Just rest," she said. "You've been through an ordeal. There will be plenty of time for talking later."

He brought his right hand up to his head and felt for bandages. "Ah. My blind side. Just as well." He smiled again and she could see that even within these few minutes, the pink colour was returning to his cheeks.

"That's what the doctor said," Posey replied. She was gazing at him as if she was witnessing a miracle, and she felt she was.

"What? What's wrong? I haven't grown a second head or anything, have I?"

She reached out and touched his wrist lightly. "I'm just so glad you're alive. I thought I'd lost you forever." She quickly withdrew her hand and flushed red. "Not that I want to make this a drama."

She laughed at herself then and replaced her hand. "But it was a drama. Hawk Eye, you can't imagine how glad I am to have you back."

And this time, when he flipped his hand and held hers, she didn't withdraw it.

Fifty-five

Bishop Phillip Stanton pushed his chair back from the dining table with a satisfied sigh. He had the serious, genial expression of a seasoned cleric, and even when he dined at home with his family, he did not relinquish his ecclesiastical identity. The purple undershirt beneath his simple black jacket and the white clerical collar that circled his neck marked his status. He wore a large wrought-iron Celtic Cross on a chain round his neck. The glass of pure water at his elbow while the other adult diners – Lord Brook, the chief justice and Jasper Blackwood – had wine or spirits glasses in that position, showed him for the evangelical teetotaller he was.

Drunk on the Holy Spirit, not on wine. That's what the church taught.

The bishop's residence was a commanding Gothic Revival manor house in Darling Point, a suburb close to the commercial heart that boasted park-size gardens and wealthy manufacturer's mansions. The house had the classic steep pointed roof and arched windows of the Gothic era, and was built in solid sandstone blocks, presenting an austere face in keeping with its inhabitant's restrained, academic character.

A tall, scholarly man with slightly sloping shoulders, Bishop

Stanton earned respect for his genuine sobriety. The wags in the local pubs had even coined a nickname for the tallest beer glass offered in their establishments, calling it a "Bishop Stanton".

Gideon understood the cleric's wife died five years ago, but the housekeeper maintained a woman's touch in the furnishings and decorative elements on show, expressed in the bowls of flowers on the side tables and the highly polished candelabra that garnished the dining table.

The prelate wiped his mouth and gave his hands a final swipe on the linen diner's serviette before he nodded to his guests and two sons.

"I've got a Saint's Day early communion tomorrow, so I'll bid you chaps goodnight." He glanced down the table. His eldest son Edward, eighteen, was under Jasper's tutelage, following in his father's footsteps and preparing for entry to Jesus College, Cambridge University, to study theology. The younger one, Thomas, was at Sydney Grammar along with the sons of most of the town's professional men and wealthy merchants.

"Edward? Thomas? You'd better head off to bed, too. You both need to be fresh for your lessons tomorrow."

The boys rose without objection and left quietly, politely farewelling the other guests as they withdrew.

"I'll retire now, too, Phillip," interjected Sir Frederick Dooley. "Neither of us are spring chickens. After all these years, we're both old enough and wise enough to know when it's time to call it quits for the night. Please thank Mrs Pratchett for a delightful meal." He turned to Lord Brook and said, "Don't let that slow you down, My Lord. At your age, I'd have been doing the same thing."

Alerted by the sons' departure, Hobbs, the butler, slipped in behind the bishop's wheelchair and grasped the handles, ready to assist the Right Reverend to bed.

The bishop turned to the judge. "Lord Brook, please feel to enjoy your after-dinner brandy in the library with Mr Blackwood. Hobbs will see you out when you're ready to leave."

Jasper limped ahead of him down the hall to the library. Bright rugs – probably Persian – and tapestries in the medieval millefleur "thousand flowers" style, hung from the walls and softened the rigour of the classical fortress.

Jasper's posture noticeably relaxed as he bent over a clutch of crystal decanters set on a side table and positioned two balloon glasses beside them.

"Brandy or port?" he asked.

"Port, thank you," said Gideon.

A lingering fragrance of quality cigars suggested the cleric allowed himself one indulgence.

"And a cigar?" Jasper seemed to help himself from the Bishop's private stash.

"The bishop doesn't mind?"

"He's fine with it." Jasper laboured to dispense the drinks and smokes, and, once done, collapsed into a big chair with obvious relief.

Gideon stuck his neck forward in his habitual tic and asked, "I see you're limping. Is your leg still bothering you?"

Jasper made an irritated noise through his teeth. "Yes. It is," he replied, a sharp note sounding in the short sentence. "It was a nasty bite, so it's not surprising."

"But you haven't got rabies?" Gideon's voice was jovial.

Again Jasper bristled. "Ambrose has spent too much time in India. I haven't got rabies," he said.

"And you're sure he didn't see you close enough to recognise you? Him or that other fella with the dogs?"

Jasper let out an exasperated sigh. "Look, I had a black hood over my face. How can I tell? When you've got a bloody big deerhound fastened to your leg, you're not thinking about whether they find you good looking. You're trying to get away. Those things are bred to bring down stags and kangaroos, I'll have you know."

"Alright, alright. You don't need to get snitchy. I'm just checking. Trying to cover your tracks for you. It wouldn't look good for the bishop if you were identified."

Jasper's blood boiled. "It wouldn't be too good for you either. If they found out it was you that ordered it. That would put a definite kink in your nice new friendship with the bishop and the chief justice."

He grinned maliciously. "Sounds like one of those comedy melodramas, doesn't it? The Bishop and the Judge. All you need is a showgirl to complete the picture." He gazed at Gideon through slanted eyelashes. "I don't suppose Eudora Gilbert qualifies as the showgirl." He gave a sly grin.

"That's not funny," said Lord Brook, his tic pushing his head in and out again, like an emu searching for insects.

"Do you think I find this funny?" demanded Jasper, jabbing his bandaged leg with his forefinger. "I'm just reminding you you're involved." A sneaky glitter shone from his dark eyes. "I mean, I could go to confession with the goodly prelate. I could confess my sins. Ethics of confidence cover confessionals. Did you know?

"But you can bet he'd go sliding off to his best mate, Sir Frederick, and give him a quiet warning about what his new judge has been up to. Those two go back decades. Practically grew up together. Went to the same Cambridge college. They kind of came to the convict colony together. Stanton came out as bishop in 1855 and Dooley joined him in 1856."

"What are you talking about?" Gideon choked on his port. When he'd finished coughing, he glared. "You're not funny Jasper. Besides, old Stanton might be bound by confidence, but he wouldn't want you tutoring his sons anymore if he knew what you've been up to. You'd be out of a job."

Jasper shrugged. "I've only got another few months here anyway, before Teddy goes off to Cambridge. The bish wouldn't want me to go before his boy has sat his entrance exams. That would really leave them in the lurch."

Gideon stared. "So, what are you trying to say?"

"What I'm saying, old chum, is you're not as untouchable as you think. The Lord Almighty British toff doesn't go down so well in the colonies."

He paused and took a lazy pull on his brandy. "I'm still interested in why you've even deigned to come out here. I can't help thinking there's a story behind it you might not like Miss Eudora to hear. And her magnate brother Clifford even less so. I haven't begun enquiries yet, but I still could."

Gideon laughed, as if what he was suggesting was ludicrous, but even to his ears, the jocularity was unconvincing.

"I'm thinking my silence has to be worth something," said Jasper. "You've got a lot hanging on it. A consummated marriage to an heiress. You didn't find one of those back in the

Promised Land, did you? A prized position in Sydney society. The chance to take down one of your enemies… A lot hanging on it, I'd say."

He gazed at Gideon with undisguised contempt. "My silence should be worth – what? Two hundred and fifty quid? That's a bargain, if you ask me."

Fifty-six

They sat in bamboo deck chairs on Hawk Eye's Hunters Hill patio, watching a flock of rainbow lorikeets chatter in the ironbark eucalypts in the bush fringing his orchard, when Silas popped the question.

"So, when are you going to tell be about redundant women?"

In the three days since he'd "awakened" from his deep concussion, he'd made a rapid recovery, and now took half hour rambles twice a day. Nurse Andrews' ministrations were no longer required, and Amelie had returned to the city office to prepare for her boss's imminent return to work.

Hawk Eye shot Posey a sly grin, which broadened into a wide smile when he saw his question had flummoxed her. His usually composed companion gaped, jaw open, not disguising her surprise at the question.

"The redundant woman? Where did you get that from?"

He chuckled. "You tell me. I might have dreamed it. But I'm sure you told me about it during those grey hours when I was still in a deep daze."

Posey narrowed her brown eyes, the colour that reminded

him of a deep, still fresh water pool, but they were sparkling.

"You sly old fox. How long did you pretend to be out to it while you were listening in on everything I said?"

He made a face of innocence and smiled again. "It's interesting the things you can learn when no one knows you're listening."

Her face turned a light pink.

Raucous chattering from the trees disturbed their conversation and they turned to watch as a pair of nesting lorikeets drove off a magpie that had got too close. The brightly plumaged, blue-headed parrots were fiercely protective of their nests and food supplies.

"Did you know they're monogamous?" Hawk Eye asked, with another lazy smile.

She laughed. "Really? And how is that relevant?"

He shrugged. "It just interesting, that's all. I suppose I like to think some things last." He scanned the yard and his garden. "It's been great having this time to recuperate, but I must get back to work soon."

Yesterday he'd had notification from the court that the Barclay case would begin hearing in two weeks.

He turned to her again, this time his face serious. "But first, I want to hear about the redundant woman. I know it's important to you."

She laid out the arguments, and all the time she talked, his eyes never left her face.

"You'd never be redundant to me, Posey, whatever you do with your time. You know that?"

She nodded and flashed him a grateful smile. "I know,

Hawk Eye. There are very few men who'd understand about this, but I know you are one of them."

He turned away, and for several minutes they were both content to watch the birds settle back into their routine of shared feeding of the nestlings they could hear chirping from their hollow-branch home.

Then Posey said, "The trial, Silas. We haven't got around to discussing that yet. But you are going to act for us? You've decided to do it?"

He stared at her, his face resolute. "I tried to run away. But now he's come after me, I have no choice."

"And you won't go to Sir Frederick and expose him?"

He shook his head. "My father is still alive. It would kill him to have it all come out now. He's spent his whole life trying to bury it, ignore it, contest it ever happened." He looked away, his face suddenly set in painful lines.

"He's the oldest son. The legitimate heir. Father was determined to hush up the stain on a centuries-old name. He never publicly acknowledged the dreadful losses of that night, though I know it's ravaged him. He adored Rosamunde more than anyone."

He stared across the pavers, but Posey suspected he wasn't seeing anything before him. He was lost in time.

"I was a little boy who loved climbing trees and riding my pony and playing cricket. My loss of sight took all of that away. But worst of all, my darling Rosamunde. Gone forever before she'd even begun.

"And Gideon swaggered about unrepentant, protected by an accident of birth. Never facing up to the fact that he tore our family apart. He always made excuses, justified it as someone else's fault."

He shook his head. "I can feel my father reaching across the world, begging me not to besmirch the family name by revealing his secret – first of his heir's actions, and then his lifelong decision to cover it up.

"And what is it the Bible says? 'Vengeance is mine, says the Lord.' I long ago turned it all over to God's hands. It's for him to judge and repay."

"And the doll?" Posey asked. "It *is* Rosamunde's doll, isn't it? The one she held in the painting? Mother has the actual doll, but you have that beautiful oil study of it. I imagine Sir Francis did that as a model for the larger work?"

He nodded. "I took it with me when I left home. I knew I was never going back, and I wanted to remember her."

The lorikeets circled their hollow tree and, as Posey glanced up, she caught sight of a fledging, about to launch itself from the bole. It hesitated a moment and then it was airborne a few seconds before fluttering to the ground. It ran a few paces and took off in tentative flights across the grass, each time increasing the distance it remained in the air.

"Look," she cried, pointing as a second baby bird emerged and looked out on the world. "The babies! They're getting ready to fly!"

Silas shaded his face with his hand and glanced up as the second bird became airborne. He laughed. "Australia!" he said. "The place for new beginnings. It's been great for me and I'm not about to let my older brother change that. Let's get on with preparing your defence."

The words were barely out of his mouth than the former police officer Jeavon had employed to provide them with security came around the side of the house.

"Mr Williams, there's a messenger here for you from Sir Frederick Dooley, the chief justice. He's asking that you make an appointment to see him as soon as you've recovered enough to manage it. He says it's urgent."

Posey and Silas exchanged startled looks.

"It seems as if Sir Frederick has taken the initiative out of your hands," Posey said. "Maybe divine intervention?"

Silas grinned. "Only time will tell."

Fifty-seven

Supreme Court Judge Gideon Vane lay naked on his towel on a hot bench in the Turkish baths in Spring Street and fumed. Not because of the heat of his surroundings, which was perfectly delightful, but because the images that floated in his mind had him struggling to achieve the complete relaxation of body and soul the Turkish bath movement promised.

Those pictures included some of Silas swanning up Elizabeth Street as if he hadn't escaped death by a whisker six days ago.

And the Barclay chit – what was her name, Poppy? No, that was her twin. Posey? That's right, he knew it had something to do with flowers. Hanging off his arm and looking as if she didn't have a care in the world.

And behind them, trailed not one, but two burly bouncers. He'd obviously taken his close shave to heart and wasn't taking any second chances.

They had no business looking as if they were on the top of the world when their case was going to trial in two weeks. But that was so typical of his brother. Ever since he'd been born, he could rise to the top.

It was mid-afternoon, and a quiet time at the baths, with only one other bather in the chamber with him. He sat along the bench from him and had a towel over his head, so Gideon felt comfortable that his privacy wasn't compromised.

"Turkish" baths, they called them, but they were more like the Roman baths of ancient times. Hot, dry heat was pumped through a series of rooms, starting with warm, then going to hot – where he was – and then extra hot. After that the bather went through hot and cold showers and then a cold plunge pool.

The creator of these baths was an Englishman, Dr John Le Gay Brereton, a physician and homeopath who successfully sold them as a remedy for over twenty ailments including "Nervous Affections".

Maybe if I moved on to the hot room, these pesky thoughts would go away.

***

An hour later, Gideon Vane had progressed to the cool pool, and his limbs felt rubbery, all bendy and pleasantly spent. His mind, though? That was a different matter. Even with the soothing fragrance that permeated the place – a pervasive dusky Turkish rose, warm and mature, with hints of jasmine and musk – he couldn't free his mind of his nemesis. Lapped by the gentle motion of the cooling pool, his thoughts tortured him.

He's had it easy compared with me. He was always Mother's favourite, while I had to bear the cross of being the earl's heir.

When he'd arrived in Sydney and discovered the brother he thought drowned in a ferry accident years ago was still alive, he'd been dumbfounded. He'd considered it a continuation of the damned bad luck he'd endured from birth.

But he'd come around to thinking maybe the opposite was the case. Silas's survival represented the best fortune he'd ever had. It provided an opportunity to rid himself of his noxious sibling once and for all.

The fear that someone would discover he'd stabbed his little sister to death and blinded his brother had followed him his entire life. But once his father died – and that was going to be any time now – apart from Benedict, there'd be no one else alive who knew what happened on that star-crossed day.

I mean, what totally rotten luck! I didn't mean to do it!

They were both just so annoying! They got on my nerves from the day they were born.

Getting all Mother's attention when it should have been me. And then Rosamunde becoming the toast of the nation because of some sentimental picture.

It should have been me!

And after that awful accident, Mother never forgave me. And it was *an accident. I never meant to do it!*

***

Shampooed and massaged, and back in his Petty Hotel room with a strong brandy, Lord Brook reflected on his future. He was marrying an heiress in a couple of weeks. That had always been one of his ambitions.

He'd heard the Barclay's collapse had reduced Eudora's trust fund, but he'd be able to fix that from the Supreme Court bench. He should be able to organise a windfall for all the complainants before it ended.

He'd be the earl soon, with no hindrances. The thought of his present situation made his blood boil. His father had cut off any further emoluments because of that latest bother over Primrose.

It was just damn bad luck her father caught us before I'd consummated things.

All that remained between him and the total freedom to do what he liked was Benedict. Or, rather, Silas.

He glanced at the door as a heavy knock sounded.

"What is it now?" he called in a bored voice. "Can't a man enjoy some peace?"

The door opened a crack, and a broad-shouldered fellow poked an apologetic head around the door. It was Harrow. The disgraced former policeman Elias Astor had recommended as a suitable replacement for Jasper.

"Come in, Harrow. What is it?" He used his clipped "let's get it over with I'm a busy man" voice.

"Sir, just wanted to report to you, sir."

For a muscled powerhouse, Harrow's manner was grovelling.

If he had a forelock, he'd be tugging it, Vane thought.

"Tell me. What have you found?"

"I've followed the target all day, sir. He has bodyguards with him wherever he goes, and when he's at home they patrol the grounds. It would be dangerous to reach him in those circumstances, sir."

The fellow was almost cringing.

"So, what would you suggest?"

"The doxy might be an easier quarry, sir. She doesn't appear to have any guards on her house."

"Come back to me by tomorrow morning with a plan," Vane said. "And now, leave me in peace."

Why didn't I think of that? If I can't take him, I'll take his woman. See how he likes that.

Fifty-eight

Eudora gazed down into the trees outside Gideon's hotel balcony and wiggled her toes inside her shoes with contentment. Sunlight filtered through the green conifers, and she could see an untidy heap of straw near to the verandah's edge where a bird was building a nest. The city traffic rumbled on below, but from the third floor it felt like all the cares in the world were way below her elevated state.

The man she was engaged to wed, an English lord no less, had organised this special private lunch for just the two of them.

He's such a romantic, although you wouldn't think so.

She smiled to herself and took another sip from her champagne glass.

Champagne! In the middle of the day! Clifford would not approve.

Her newspaper baron brother took after their father in his Protestant work ethic. He enjoyed his pleasures, but never let them interfere with the important things. Business, family and church.

Gideon, it seemed, had a more laissez faire approach.

She turned to her fiancé, who was sprawled out with his long legs tucked under the wrought-iron table covered in a starched white cloth. Any minute now, the staff would arrive with their oyster soup.

"Tell me about your mother," Eudora queried, smiling, her eyes crinkled. "Were you close to her growing up?"

Gideon's eyes widened, as if surprised by the enquiry. "My mother? She died years ago."

"Yes. So you mentioned. I am sorry. But when you were younger? What childhood memories do you have?"

His expression shadowed into a vacant bleakness. He shook his head. "Nothing good. Raised by nannies and sent to boarding school at eight. A typical aristocratic family. Mothers consider they've done their job once they've given birth."

The cold distance in his words chilled her. She glanced out to see if the sun had gone behind a cloud, but the birds still chirped and the sun still shone.

"That's very sad," she said.

If they had children, would he expect the same for them?

"Don't you think?"

He stared at her, not answering.

"Is that the sort of childhood you want for your children?" she ventured.

It suddenly occurred to her she'd assumed they would have children, and she would want to raise them just as she was, with the constant, warm attention of their mother.

He smiled then, but she caught the dart of anguish in his eyes. He was playing at the conversation. Restoring the social balance. But he wasn't truly engaged.

"I'm happy for you to raise our children in exactly the way

you want to," he said. "I am counting on having children. A son, anyway. To inherit, you know. That's very important. My key role as an heir: keep the line going." He grinned again, but once more it lacked inner warmth.

She grimaced. "I very much hope I do not let you down in that regard, My Lord."

The serving man arrived with the soup, and for a short while, they ate in silence.

"Speaking of children," he said, a slight hesitation in his voice. "I know we haven't had time to speak of such things… and I hope I'm not embarrassing you… but I am eager to get things under way." His eyes searched her face, as if not sure of her reaction.

She was aware of her complexion warming under his gaze, and when he let the silence lengthen further, she spoke.

"We're both adults, My Lord. I'm long past being an ingenue. I'm honoured to be asked to be your wife and, God willing, the mother of your children."

He leaned forward in an urgent motion. "I know you're busy with the preparations, but do you think we might bring the date forward? Say two weeks? Could we wed next week? It doesn't have to be a grand affair, does it? We can have the big celebration when we have our first son."

Her stomach lurched. She was hardly out of mourning. She'd adapted to dark green, and grey and lavender as a compromise, but the thought of walking down the aisle so soon after her mother's cortege suddenly made her feel light-headed. The modiste had said the earliest she could have Eudora's wedding gown finished, encrusted as it was with tiny pearls, was the end of the month. Three weeks from now.

"You're utterly beautiful, whatever you wear," Gideon embroidered. "You don't need a fancy gown to light up a room."

"Why... Why... I suppose so," she said. "If it's that important to you."

"It is," he said. "You don't know how important."

More staff arrived to clear away their first course and deliver their second, and the conversation veered off to less confronting topics.

It was only much later, as Eudora prepared for bed, that she acknowledged the hard little knot that had formed in her stomach at lunch.

This marriage. It's a business arrangement for him. His task is producing an heir.

I guess that shouldn't shock me. But what is it that gives him joy?

Fifty-nine

Sir Frederick Dooley met Silas in full legal regalia, garbed up in the red gown and full wig he would wear in a Supreme Court hearing, and Silas understood instantly this would not be a relaxed chat between colleagues. It was a formal inquiry into alleged malpractice, and the chief justice was ensuring everything was done by the book.

They met five days after Silas received the first summons, and they'd exchanged several messages in the interim, so Silas knew exactly what he was facing. The chief justice wanted him to resubmit his credentials, because after two decades of practising law in the state, worrying allegations had been made against him.

"Nothing rock solid, you understand, old chap. Just a bothersome rumour that you are here under false pretences, that you aren't who you say you are. Mr Justice Vane has suggested we need to be more rigorous in the standards we apply."

His venerable face scrunched up in distaste at the idea. "It's only a formality. But with this big case coming up in a couple of weeks – the Barclay case I'm referring to, you are still representing the family, aren't you? – I thought it was best to check."

Silas stood before his grizzle-haired eminence and waited for the invitation to sit down. When it didn't come, the hands he'd clasped behind his back tensed in anticipation.

"Mr Justice Vane? Was he the one to bring the allegation?" he asked.

"No, no, not at all," said Sir Frederick, just a tad too quickly. "He merely suggested being more stringent would be a good idea and, as I say… with this case looming… I want to be certain we have no foul ups there. People claiming they didn't get a fair hearing, that kind of thing."

He hesitated and raised one straggly eyebrow. "The death of that fellow behind Tattersall's Hotel a couple of weeks ago. That's rather distressing. I gather he was going to be a key witness for you?"

Silas nodded. "Yes, he was, Your Honour. A most peculiar business. Might I ask, who told you that? That he was one of our witnesses, I mean."

The older man's brow furrowed. "I believe it might have been Doctor Blackwood. Ambrose Blackwood. How he knew, I do not know. Maybe he attended as the medical help?"

Silas would not be drawn. "I'm not sure, Sir Frederick. But I don't think so."

"Anyway. Sit down, Mr Williams. I'm sorry, I don't know what I'm thinking, keeping you standing. Would you like coffee?"

"No, thank you, sir. I've got rather a lot on with a big case looming and my unfortunate episode last week…"

"Yes. Another troubling thing. Have the police got any idea of who attacked you?"

"Not that I know of, Sir Frederick."

"Yes, yes, just one of those things…" He shifted in his chair uneasily and said, "Well now, to the subject at hand. Can you show me your legal credentials and swear that you are Silas Williams? That's all I need you to do."

Silas grounded his heels in the carpet and took a deep breath. He looked the chief justice straight in the eye.

"Sir Frederick, it is more complicated than that. I was not born Silas Williams. I changed my birth name by Royal Licence when I began my legal studies. My father is a well-known barrister in the homeland and I did not want to cause him any embarrassment by drawing attention to myself."

Sir Frederick's complexion changed to an intense red, and he bent over in a violent coughing fit.

"You changed your name? By God, man, why have you said nothing about it? All these years… and you've been using an alias? That is most irregular."

Silas bent down and drew his official papers out of his briefcase. His law degree, with the embossed seal of Queen's University Belfast, in his assumed name, Mr Silas Fitzroy Beaufort Williams. And the Royal Licence, also with an embossed seal, showing that he had changed his name from Benedict Cedric Fitzroy Vane to Silas Fitzroy Beaufort Williams. Without further comment, he handed them across to the law lord.

Sir Frederick adjusted his spectacles to read them, also without comment. But almost immediately he drew his head from the documents, his face turning an apoplectic purple.

"You were born Benedict Cedric Fitzroy Vane?" He spluttered over the words, as if his tongue were reluctant to pronounce them. "No relation of Gideon Vane, Lord Brook, I presume? A total coincidence?" He laced his words with furious irony.

Silas took another deep breath. "I'm Gideon's brother, Your Honour. The earl's second son."

Sir Frederick rose from his chair, towering over Silas like an Old Testament prophet. The only thing missing was his staff.

"Then why in the heavens above did no one tell me of this? I asked your brother about conflicts of interest and he declared none."

"You'll have to ask him about that, My Lord. In his defence, I can confirm he did not know I was in Sydney. My mother was the only one in the family to know of my whereabouts. The rest of the family believed me dead."

"And why, I pray, have you found this whole charade necessary? Wasn't being an earl's son enough?"

How to explain? Silas swallowed hard.

"We endured a tragedy in the family when I was a young boy, Sir Frederick. My father's way of coping was to pretend it had never happened. I found that very difficult, growing up. I didn't want it to shadow me my whole life. So, I suppose, like many others, I made a fresh start as far away from that sad history as I could. In my case, settling on the other side of the world.

"The names I chose reflect the maternal side of my family. My mother was Henrietta Beaufort Williams before she married my father. While she was alive, she always supported and acknowledged me, but after she died, there was nothing left for me in England but heartache."

He allowed for a long pause, and then said, "I have been careful to ensure I had the legal documentation required if ever a situation like this arose, which I expected it might. But as you well know, there is nothing illegal about changing your name. In fact, it's common among writers and artists. Just not so much among lawyers."

He shot Sir Frederick a wintery smile. "I was waiting for my brother to declare the relationship, Sir Frederick. I am sorry to say we are not close. Quite the opposite. We are sworn enemies. It was one of the most unwelcome events of my life when he turned up here. I had hoped never to see him again. But I have no control over his decisions and I don't want to cause any more grief."

Sir Frederick took a long time clearing his throat. "Fine words, Williams, but you've left me with a God-awful mess to clean up. Pardon the profanity, but this is one of those rare occasions when I feel it's justified."

Silas stood, preparing to vacate his seat. "Can I assume my answer satisfies you, Your Honour? You accept my credentials as legitimate? Can I continue to practise law in New South Wales?"

"You can, Mr Williams, but it most certainly will not be with your brother presiding."

And that was the best news Silas had heard in a very long time.

Sixty

Lord Brook sauntered into Sir Frederick Dooley's chambers in fine spirits. Everything was going along swimmingly: Eudora had agreed to an earlier ceremony; Harrow was working on the other problem. He was brimming with confidence that this invitation to take morning coffee with the chief justice was just one more piece of evidence that things were going his way. After all, he was the heir to a seat that dated back to the King Henry VIII. Sir Frederick, he'd discovered, was a merchant's son born in Bermuda. A merchant's son, for goodness' sakes. And Bermuda? Admittedly, Dooley's grandfather had come from an ancient Scottish line. He'd give him that. But they'd lost everything – lands and wealth – when the British beat them at Culloden.

"He's no doubt recognising how fortunate he is to have an English lord serving here. Someone who can add status and class to proceedings. It's only right he should acknowledge his betters."

But Dooley's countenance was cloudy as he invited Gideon to sit and the court staff served them coffee.

"Settling in alright, Vane?" the chief justice asked, his tone peremptory.

"Very well, thank you, sir," Gideon replied. "I believe you're aware Miss Gilbert and I are to wed soon? I'm delighted."

"Miss Eudora? Yes, yes, I had heard. Lass had a tough time losing her mother. She'd only just be out of mourning. But of course, you'd know that."

The observation stopped Gideon short.

Of course… She's been in mourning… She's mentioned her mother's death a few times, but it had slipped my mind… So much going on, it's hard to keep track.

Australian mourning practices were much less prescribed than they were in England, where children were expected to wear black for a parent for one year, but Eudora would want to be seen to do the right thing.

When did she say mother died? Barely a year ago, I vouch.

He adjusted the position of his feet nervously.

"We're both very keen to see the business done," he said. "We're not getting any younger."

The quip hung in the air and then fell flat, and Gideon flicked a glance into Dooley's whiskery face. A full head of white hair topped his head. An abundant white beard joined with silver whiskers down his cheeks.

Why has he got me here? He doesn't seem in a good mood.

"My Lord, I have asked you here today to clear up a matter that has come to my attention and caused me some anxiety," Dooley began.

"Oh? I'm confident if it relates to me, I will ease that in a dash. What's the issue that's concerning you?"

Dooley speared him with an eagle stare, his jaw set.

"Your brother," he said. "I want to know about your brother."

Sixty-one

"My brother?" Gideon stared, his heart in his mouth. "Which brother are you talking about, Sir Frederick?"

Dooley scowled and stared back down his nose as if he were addressing a stupid schoolboy. "Benedict, of course. Do you have more than one brother?"

In those few seconds, it seemed to Gideon as if all the blood was draining out of his head. Now the roar in his ears signalled it was rushing back in.

"Ah. Benedict…" He breathed the name in the great empty silence that yawned between them. He took a few moments to swallow air.

Sir Frederick spoke again, more sharply this time. "You might recall at one of our very first meetings the governor and I asked if you were aware of anything that might present a conflict of interest, and you replied that no, there was not. In light of this latest revelation, I have to ask you, My Lord, were you telling me the truth?"

Gideon stammered. "I-I-I was, Sir Frederick. At the time, I had no idea my brother was still alive, let alone here in Australia," he lied.

"Oh? And why was that?"

"We weren't a close family, My Lord. I went to boarding school at a very young age. Benedict left home to become an articled clerk for a distant cousin. We had word he'd drowned in a ferry overturning in the English Channel soon after. As far as I was concerned, he died long ago."

"I see." Sir Frederick's voice sounded a fraction mollified. "And when you discovered he was here? I presume you recognised him? With that eye patch, he's difficult to miss."

"Umm, when I discovered he was here… Well, I knew how much his privacy meant to him. If he'd gone to so much trouble to lead us to believe he was dead, I respected him not wanting to be found."

"And the case? The Barclay case? Didn't it occur to you at any time you were open to accusations of having a conflict of interest?"

Gideon sat stone still for a long minute, scrambling in his head for a plausible response. It came to him in another rescuing wave.

"It didn't seem relevant, My Lord. As I say, we were never close. We haven't communicated for over twenty years. I've always maintained a strict separation between my personal and professional lives. I didn't consider my family history relevant to my ability to preside over this case."

A sudden idea occurred to him, and he added, "If I had revealed our connection, it might have appeared that I was biased – either for or against Mr Williams and his clients. I wanted to ensure a fair trial for all parties involved."

Sir Frederick Dooley harrumphed in his seat and fixed him

with a steely glare. "In the interests of fairness, Lord Brook, I will not dismiss you on the spot, although I am sorely tempted. There is nothing I detest more than deceit, and I find your conduct lacking in the transparency I expect from servants of the Court, particularly at the highest level."

Gideon's stomach did a full revolution and landed with a thud that left him nauseous.

"Dismissal? Oh, no, Sir Frederick. I beg you. I apologise. I can see now how my actions might appear. But, believe me, I thought I was acting in the best interests of all concerned."

Dooley raised a sceptical, bushy white brow. If the whiteness had come from a load of ice, his expression couldn't have been more glacial.

"For now, I will delay the Barclay case while I make enquiries in London."

"Enquiries?" Gideon's voice rose in register. "What sort of enquiries? And why? I've explained what happened."

"You have given me one explanation, Lord Brook. But now that questions have arisen, I want to make a few checks I probably should have made at the beginning." He paused, and his heavy brow creased into a stormy frown. "By the way, Vane, how did that brother of yours lose his eye? I didn't like to ask, and he didn't say."

"I know nothing about that, Sir Frederick. As I say, we were never close."

Sixty-two

FROM THOMAS YATES:

CLIFFORD GILBERT
MANAGING EDITOR, SYDNEY HERALD
SYDNEY AUSTRALIA

URGENT STOP MAJOR STORY STOP
JUDGE GIDEON VANE IMPLICATED IN SERIOUS
SCANDALS STOP
CHILDHOOD INCIDENT INVOLVING SIBLINGS STO
RECENT ABDUCTION ATTEMPT OF SIXTEEN-
YEAR-OLD HEIRESS STOP
LEGAL PROCEEDINGS PENDING IN ENGLAND
STOP
FLED TO AUSTRALIA TO ESCAPE CHARGES STOP
SOURCES RELIABLE BUT UNCONFIRMED
OFFICIALLY STOP
AWARE OF PERSONAL CONNECTION TO YOUR
FAMILY STOP
ADVISE ON HOW TO PROCEED STOP
THOMAS YATES LONDON

Sixty-three

Her brother's leather riding jacket was shiny and wet with the misty rain that began falling on dusk and had got heavier as the night darkened. A slick of soaked hair stuck to his forehead, and he dashed it away with the back of his hand before he continued peeling off his riding gloves.

Through the open front door, she glimpsed the latest addition to his stables, the black mare, Ebony, being led away by a stable hand.

"Whatever is so urgent for you to ride over here in the rain after dark? You didn't even stop to get the coach loaded up? And you *never* call on me after ten o'clock." Eudora clutched Clifford's cold, wet arm. "What's happened? Please. Tell me no one's died."

He glanced up at her with stormy grey eyes that softened with affection as he gazed into her face. "No one's died, sis. Don't panic. No one's died," he reassured.

Eudora's housekeeper, Mrs Carstairs, had been preparing to turn in for the night, but she now came out into the hall and called, "Coffee or tea in the library, Miss Eudora?"

Eudora glanced at Clifford. "I think it will be coffee with

"

brandy for my brother, Mrs Carstairs, and I'll have a hot chocolate, thank you."

Clifford placed a comforting arm in the middle of her back and guided her down the hall to the library. Wattlewood was their childhood home, the place they had both grown up. When Clifford married Cassandra, he'd moved to a new home, leaving Eudora here with their mother, the formidable society matron Clara, who'd died months later. He knew Wattlewood as well as she did, and technically, as the estate's heir, he still owned it.

"Sit down, sis. What I've got to tell you will come as a shock, even though no one has died. Have you got your smelling salts? I don't want you fainting on me." He shot her a teasing grin. They both knew she'd inherited her mother's drive and determination. She wasn't the fainting sort.

She punched him playfully on the arm, grateful he was defusing the tension.

By unspoken agreement, they chatted on about family affairs until Mrs Carstairs brought the hot drinks. Cassandra had recently announced to the immediate family that she was "with child" and Eudora was unsure if Clifford would now want to move back into the family home. She knew someday it was inevitable.

Wattlewood. The place was surely too big for a single woman on her own.

As soon as Mrs Carstairs left them, Eudora turned to Clifford, her face tight with worry.

"So, tell me. Why the midnight visit? It must be something important."

Clifford sighed. "It's about your fiancé."

Eudora's heart lurched. "Lord Brook? Gideon? Has something happened to him?"

Clifford fished inside his jacket pocket and handed her a paper she instantly saw was a pale-yellow telegraph form, printed with the characteristic block-letter script.

"Here. Read this."

She opened the folded page with trembling fingers. The room fell silent as she read, the only sound the stairs creaking as Mrs Carstairs turned in for the night.

Eudora screwed her eyes shut and opened them again. She swallowed hard twice. Then she glanced up at Clifford with a weak smile.

"You know, sadly, I'm not too surprised. I had the strangest lunch with Gideon today. I admit, I came away from it with a feeling something was dreadfully wrong, but I couldn't figure out what. As we were talking, it came to me how very little I actually knew about him."

She gave a shaky laugh and turned to pick up her hot chocolate. She took a few sips and was silent for a further moment.

"But this? *Serious scandals? Abduction? Fleeing to escape charges?* How is it Sir Frederick didn't know about this? It's terrible. To say the least, embarrassing."

Clifford clasped his hands in front of his face and nodded. "I'm warning the chief justice first thing in the morning. All that fancy rhetoric from Baron Whatshisname and the playing fields of England at his swearing in! He's worse than the first convicts they sent out for stealing handkerchiefs when they were starving."

Despite herself, Eudora giggled. "Spoken like a true Aussie," she said. Then she grimaced. "It's awful to confess, but the proposition of marrying an English earl turned my head. I know I'm old enough to understand that marriage is a business, but Gideon seems to be *all* business. I had the awful feeling today he just wants a wife to beget a son and heir."

"A son and heir and an inheritance," Clifford said softly. "And you deserve much better than that."

"I do." She laughed and reached out and squeezed his arm. "What will you do about this? As a senior figure in our city, and as a newspaperman?"

Clifford took her hand between his and pressed it lovingly. "As a brother, I want to offer you all the support I can."

He hesitated then, and she got the impression he was weighing his next words. When he spoke, his voice was tentative.

"You won't want to go ahead with this now?" he asked.

Eudora shook her head vigorously. "Not in a million years."

"Then you'll have to do the tricky thing of breaking it off. I'd like you to do that tomorrow. We can hold the story for twenty-four or thirty-six hours, but longer than that, and I'm afraid someone else might beat us to it. In the meantime, I'll have a private session with Sir Frederick. Warn him what's coming."

Eudora took a great heaving breath and withdrew her hand from Clifford's. "What a mess."

"Do you want me to come with you when you see Vane?" Clifford asked.

She shook her head. "No, it's fine. It's going to be difficult, but, honestly? I'm relieved. The more I saw of the man, the less I liked the idea of spending the rest of my life with him."

Sixty-four

Posey was trailing up to bed, eyes drooping from weariness at sitting up late. She'd hoped Silas would have come by and reported on his interview with Sir Frederick, but he hadn't, and she was certain it was too late for him to visit now. But then the lion's head brass knocker thudded loudly in the night's silence. Mrs Crowe had already retired, so Posey reluctantly turned to answer it.

Maybe it's Hawk Eye, though why he's out this late goodness knows...

She opened the door a crack, keeping the safety chain attached, until she saw a telegraph employee in the pale-blue uniform and red cap, holding out the familiar envelope. She immediately unlocked the chain and opened the door wide.

"Rusty Biggins, isn't it?" she greeted the young man.

The kid – he was no more than seventeen – blushed. "Yes, Miss Barclay! Right first time!" he said, grinning broadly. He had a thatch of blond hair that hung over marine-blue-green eyes and a freckled nose that looked like it was permanently peeling. His extremely fair skin made the freckles stand out.

"Who is that for?" she asked, offering her hand to take the message.

The young man angled his long lanky arm back to himself and read out, "Miss Posey Barclay. That's you, innit, miss?" Rusty asked. He blushed. "I know your blonde sister is Petunia."

"That's right, Rusty. And good for you. Hang on a minute and I'll get something for you."

She dashed to the kitchen where she knew Arabella kept a rewards jar that rarely got emptied and drew out a coin.

"I'm hoping this will be good news, so you deserve a reward as the bearer of good tidings," she said on her return.

"Thanks so much, Miss Barclay. Have a good night."

And Rusty wobbled off down the path to the street, cycle wheels squeaking, his single bicycle light bobbed from side to side, flashing past trees, startling a night bird to cry out an alarm call and find another roost.

Posey stood for a long minute, breathing in the cool evening air, catching the fragrance of the scented night jessamine over the arbour at the side of the house.

So peaceful, she thought. *I wonder if this message is going to change all that?*

She shut the door behind her and walked to the kitchen to find a knife to slice open the envelope.

POSEY BARCLAY
SYDNEY AUSTRALIA

UNCOVERED SHOCKING GIDEON VANE SCANDAL
STOP
CHILDHOOD VIOLENCE AGAINST SIBLINGS

HUSHED UP STOP

RECENT ABDUCTION ATTEMPT OF YOUNG

HEIRESS STOP

FACING LEGAL PROCEEDINGS IN ENGLAND STOP

FLEEING TO AUSTRALIA STOP

MUST INFORM EDITOR STOP STORY TOO BIG TO

IGNORE STOP

ADVISE CAUTION AND DISCRETION STOP

THOMAS

She left out a long, slow breath.

Oh my goodness, Hawk Eye. It's too late tonight, but first thing tomorrow you have to see this.

Sixty-five

Eudora arranged to meet Gideon in the botanic gardens. She couldn't articulate why this seemed like a good idea, except that she was concerned he might fly off the handle if they were closeted in a room together, and she was pretty certain he would want to keep up a dignified front in public.

He has too much to lose if he doesn't.

She'd already guessed that appearances mattered more than anything else where he was concerned.

She wore the grey-and-lavender walking dress that was practically her uniform these days, and she hoped he'd notice. His failure to remember that she was still in mourning when he asked for an advancement of the wedding yesterday had brought home to her how little he considered her feelings. She doubted he saw her as anything other than a cipher in his bigger game.

Still, she was apprehensive about how he might react to the news that she was breaking their engagement.

Truth be told, Thomas's telegram had given her a way of getting off the hook. When she read that message last night, she discovered she'd already decided she didn't want to go ahead with it. The news it brought gave her the perfect excuse.

I suppose if you love someone, you'd stand by them. Believe in them. But I already know enough about this man to suspect Thomas's information is true.

And abducting a sixteen-year-old? That's beyond the pale. He's not a brainless lad infatuated by a pretty girl. He's a calculating fortune hunter.

She shivered and looked up to see Lord Brook making his way up the path to the fountain where they'd agree to meet.

She stood as he approached and smiled in greeting. "Lord Brook! Let's take a walk through the spring garden. The azaleas are at their peak right now. It will be all over by this time next week."

Like our engagement.

He took her hand and gazed into her eyes. "You're looking truly beautiful today," he said and smiled.

This time, though, she noticed his deep-brown eyes didn't light up. They remained flat and hard.

Has he always been like this and I didn't notice? I was too busy convincing myself I'd caught a lord.

"You flatterer," she said through smiling lips. The phrase was light, but carried a sardonic edge.

"What a lovely morning," Gideon observed as he tucked her arm into his and set off down the path at a leisurely stroll. "I must admit, Sydney's weather is beguiling after London's frequent rain. I don't think it's rained once since I got here."

"It rained last night," Eudora said jauntily. "Clifford came to visit, and he got quite wet."

Gideon frowned. "He didn't take the carriage? How odd of him."

"He was in a hurry. There was something he thought I should know."

Gideon hesitated mid-stride. "Oh? What was so important it couldn't wait till morning? Not bad news, I hope?"

Eudora stalled and turned to face him.

"I'm afraid it was. He'd had a telegram from his London correspondent with disquieting news."

She searched his face and watched as his eyes flickered with alarm before he regained his usual sangfroid composure.

"From London, you say?" His brow furrowed. "Why ever would something in London upset you here?"

"Because it relates to you, Lord Brook. You and your recent *liaison*, shall we call it? With a sixteen-year-old heiress?"

Vane let her arm drop from his and drew in a sharp breath.

"That old crock!" he cried. "I'm suing her father for defamation over that unfortunate business. The chit set her sights on me and did her level best to set me up in a compromising situation. I had to use all my wiles to escape."

Eudora took a step back, further increasing the distance between them.

"That's not quite how we heard the story. As I understand it, the events that occurred were far more damaging than that."

Gideon's dark eyes glowed with fury. "You can't believe that? Do you really think I'd compromise myself over some flighty female?"

"If she was rich enough, yes, unfortunately I can."

Gideon's eyes glittered dangerously, and Eudora shivered.

"If you were a man, I'd call you out for that," he hissed.

His lips curled in a cruel bow, and in that second she could believe him capable of killing anyone who stood in his way.

"Then perhaps it's just as well we outlawed duelling in Sydney years ago," she quipped. "It certainly isn't something a Supreme Court judge could engage in and get away with."

He put his hands on his hips and glared. "What's this about, Eudora? You're not taking some wild story from a totally unreliable female seriously, are you? You won't find anything better than what I'm offering, that's for sure."

Eudora glanced around her quickly, suddenly conscious of whether they had attracted an audience, but the surrounding paths were deserted. She turned herself forwards. "Please, let's keep walking. I don't want to attract unwelcome attention."

He hesitated for a few seconds and then fell into step beside her, but this time he did not recapture her arm.

"So, perhaps you can tell me what exactly is it you are offering, Lord Brook? I think I realised yesterday when we broached the subject of children, that we'd hardly given the subject of our match deep attention. Why do you wish to marry? And, more specifically, why do you wish to marry me?"

His face yawned disbelief, and for a few seconds she thought he was going to refuse to answer such an obvious question.

Then he cleared his throat and said, "Why? It's what people like us do, of course. We've both left our run a bit late, if you ask me. And that's far more serious for a woman than it is for a man." He gave her a sly smile. "You're in danger of missing the boat altogether, Eudora. It's as plain as the nose on your face that I'm likely to be your last best chance. By your next birthday – what is it, thirty? – you'll be a fully verified spinster. You know as well as I do, men don't take a second look at old horses or old women."

Eudora halted in mid-stride and stared. He failed to pick up her mood.

"Whereas an English earl? I could have a glass eye and the biddies will still come running."

Eudora gripped the handle of her parasol and twirled it dangerously.

"Oh." Her shoulders shook with anger. "What an insufferable snob you are, Lord Brook. I'd say the rich young heiress had a fortunate escape."

She stepped back and opened her parasol. She twirled it over her shoulder.

"As have I, Lord Brook. A very lucky escape. Please consider any arrangement we might have agreed to cancelled. From this moment. I find the prospect of a prosperous spinsterhood far more appealing than marriage to someone who doesn't care one jot about me."

She made a move to march off, but turned to share one more thought. "I wish you the best with all the biddies who come running."

She gave him a quick scan, up and down, and smiled. Then she strode off towards the garden's new summerhouse, leaving him speechless.

Sixty-six

It began like a glorious rite to spring, this dream that turned into a nightmare. A girl in a red dress who could have been Sally's twin, she was so like her, except that Sally's hair was a deep brown and this girl had a wave of flaxen locks that flowed down her back like a river of sunshine. Her light-blue eyes sparkled as she twirled beside a grove of pussy willows, the bare branches with their velvet white-and-yellow furry buds signalling winter was over and a season of growth and fruitfulness was coming.

The young woman – she couldn't have been more than sixteen – spun in a joyous gyre, her hands raised above her head, like a worshipper honouring a deity, her face turned to the rays of sun that penetrated the trees.

And then, without warning, the atmosphere changed. The benign sunshine faded, and the branches thrashed with a wind that blew with increasing strength. The force stripped the bare branches of new buds; bird's nests tumbled from higher up; and a mourning cry rose from deep within somewhere or someone. Was it within the forest? Or from within the maiden? Posey couldn't tell.

As the wind rose, she suddenly noticed a small child, about the same age as Robbie, deposited in a woven basket at the foot of one of the biggest trees. As she stared in horror, the tree bent over in the wind, leaning further and further towards the ground. An unseen force – no longer a rogue wind, but some malign power – had taken control and was uprooting the tree, bringing it down on the baby.

Posey struggled to run to the child; an invisible power holding her in place. The harder she fought, the more she felt the restraint bear down on her.

And then with a cry she broke free, and found herself breathless, and soaked with sweat in bed. Her hair was a tangled mess, and she'd dug the fingernails of one hand so tightly into fists she's punctured her palm, which was bleeding.

"What's going on? I never have bad dreams." She panted out the words, merely for her own benefit, she knew, but she felt compelled to state it. Then she fell back and lay there, breathing hard, waiting for her pulse to return to normal.

An instant later, she jolted upright. Thomas's telegram. Her promise to herself to inform Jeavon and Silas as soon as she could today.

She slipped from between her twisted sheets, but even as her feet hit the floor, she was fragile and trembling. She dressed in her most simple day dress, a walking-length full-skirted cotton gown in pale-green fabric, the skirt's edge garlanded with a print of yellow daffodils.

Heralding spring. Just like my dream.

She tiptoed downstairs and went to the managerial desk in the library they'd always referred to as "Father's Desk". *With him not here anymore, we'll have to change that name*, she thought as she flopped down and penned two notes, the first to Hawk Eye, with the telegram enclosed.

Dear Hawk Eye,

This message arrived from Thomas late last night. I enclose it as I know you will grasp much better than I do what it means and what we need to do about it.

With fondest thoughts,
Posey

The second, to Jeavon, read simply:

Jeavon: Thomas replied to our queries with startling news via telegraph last night. Silas has the details. Contact him urgently.

She placed each in an envelope addressed to the recipient and slipped out the back door to make her way to the stables, where she knew their stable man and driver would be feeding their sole horse and preparing for the day. Arabella, for one, often went visiting with very little warning, and he liked to be prepared for all possibilities. She'd just reached the stable door when she heard the main gate creak on its hinges and a skinny boy with a shock of startlingly black hair tripped up their path heading for the front door. She stepped out of the shadows of the garden and he started like a frightened rabbit.

"Oh, miss, you gave me a right fright, you did," he said.

"Sorry to get your dander up, Billy." She'd seen the messenger boy around about the city. "What are you doing out so early?"

He pulled a crumpled paper from his pocket. "I got a message for you, miss. The dude wot gave it to me said it's urgent."

He handed her the paper, which had been roughly folded in two ways. She opened up each corner. Someone had scrawled a message in pencil, in block letters.

Obviously doesn't want to be identified.

She scanned it in five seconds.

IF YOU WANT TO SEE SALLY ALIVE, COME IMMEDIATELY. BRING NO ONE WITH YOU OR SHE'S DEAD. BILLY WILL TELL YOU WHERE.

She stared at the kid, who appeared unaware of the note's threatening contents. He stood, scuffing his heels on the gravel path, staring around the garden.

"You've been told where I need to go to, have you, Billy?" she said, her voice unnervingly calm.

I don't want to frighten him so he runs off.

He nodded. "The geezer said you'd give me a shilling for delivering it and telling you where to go next." He gazed at her with expectant eyes.

"Right," she said. "Wait here a minute." She sprinted to the money jar in the kitchen for the second time in a few hours and fished out a couple of shillings. One for now, one for later. And then she rushed back, hoping his tip would tempt the kid enough to stick around.

She kept one shilling in the pocket of her skirt, and passed him the other. "Great," she said with the best smile she could manage. "So, where are we going?"

"Oh, I ain't coming, miss. The gent said you're to go to an address down at the wharves. The old wool store on Finger Wharf. That's what 'e said."

"I see. The old wool store? Who's there? Do you know?"

He shrugged. "Nothing much at all, so far as I know. Just a jumble of old buildings nobody wants anymore. Seemed weird to me, but I'm just doing what I'm told."

"I see, Billy. Just wait here for a moment, will you, and there'll be another payment for you."

She dashed back inside and added an extra line in each of the notes she'd already prepared. And then she completed what she'd set out to do, slipping to the stables where Robert was feeding the horse its morning hay.

"I've got messages for you, Robert. To be delivered to Mr Silas Williams and Former Police Superintendent Jeavon Yates." She prayed Silas would be at his town house, not out at Hunters Hill.

She stood at Robert's elbow as he fed hay into a feed box. "If Mr Williams is not at Elizabeth Street, take both of the messages to Mr Yates. They're urgent, and I don't want any delay."

Then she returned to Billy.

"Billy, you've finished all your chores for the gent who sent you here, have you? What are you doing now?"

"He ain't exactly a gent, but yes, I done all he asked."

"Not exactly a gent? Is that right? What did he look like?"

"Big fella, looks like the law."

"Oh, I see. Did you know him?"

A cloud obscured the little chap's artless gaze. "Um… I used to. Not so much lately."

"Oh? Why is that?"

"Well, he used to work for that copper up the hill from The Rocks. Until he got the chop. He was a mean critter when he worked for the blues. And he's even nastier now. You won't tell him I said anything, will you, miss? He'll have my guts for garters if you do."

She nodded reassuringly. "I won't say a word." She pulled the second shilling from her pocket. "I've got one more thing for you to do this morning. Promise me you'll do it?"

His bright-brown eyes lit up at the second shilling. He worked one grubby hand out of his pocket and stuck it out.

"Not yet," said Posey. "I've one more note for you to deliver and then you can take it." She tripped back inside and wrote Jeavon a second note for the morning.

If Billy brings this to you, Sally's been kidnapped. We're at the old wool store on Finger Wharf. Hurry.

She went back outside. "Now, Billy, listen carefully. I want you to go to the women's refuge in Bridge Street and ask for Sally. Insist it's important. Say Miss Posey wants to know. Miss Posey says it's important. And if they tell you she's not there, run like the wind to the old copper's house and give him this note. You know where he lives?"

She repeated the address twice, speaking slowly.

"I know where he lives, miss. Ya don't have to tell me twice."

"Good. Now run. If you go fast enough, the old copper might give you something nice at the other end."

As Billy disappeared out the gate, Robert rumbled out onto the street, ready to begin his run.

I wonder which of them will get there first. And I wonder if I'll be alive to find out.

Sixty-seven

Posey stood on the path at Barclay Manor and listened as the sound of the coach wheels gradually faded into the distance. To an onlooker, she might have been daydreaming. She had a faraway look in her eyes, and although she gazed out over the garden, she was not seeing the archway with its waterfall of white roses coming into bloom, or the hawk that soared overhead watching for a rat for breakfast. Her mind was racing, preparing for the ordeal she knew loomed ahead.

She turned back to the house and tiptoed upstairs, praying at every footfall she wouldn't awaken either her mother or Mrs Crowe. Once in her room, she swapped the spring dress she'd donned fifteen minutes ago for a pair of moleskin men's trousers, a white shirt, and a padded waistcoat with a series of useful inner pockets. Into one of these she stuffed the pocket pistol Jeavon had schooled her in using after she began working at the women's refuge.

Occasionally she had to deal with irate men – pimps who'd lost one of their "girls" or a possessive husband who resented being deprived of his punching-bag wife. She'd only had to produce it on two occasions and found it remarkably persuasive in helping a recalcitrant male to move on. She'd thought on more than one occasion it must be rather like mustering cattle. If they're determined to get their own way, desperate measures may be called for.

And if ever there were desperate measures, it sounds like they may be needed today.

She pulled a boyish cap down hard over her face, gave herself a quick check in the mirror, and exited the house. Within minutes she was in Darlinghurst's principal thoroughfare and hailing a hansom cab, glad to see it was a dusty and battered vehicle that had seen better days.

As anonymous as I can be. That's what the game is.

She directed him first to the women's refuge, keen to confirm for herself that Sally was really missing. She knew the girl would not abscond like some of their inmates did; she was too grateful for the lodgings for herself and her son to jeopardise the arrangement.

Posey slipped into the sleeping quarters using her staff key and checked Sally's room. There was no sign she'd run off, and the knapsack she used when she took Robbie out, where she fitted a spare nappy and rusks for him to nibble when he got hungry, lay on her bed. If she'd gone out on her own, she'd have definitely taken that. And Robbie's favourite toy truck. It too, lay on the carpet near his playpen.

She tracked to the front office where the night manager, Nellie, monitored things and casually asked, "You haven't seen Sally, have you?"

Nellie gazed back with big granite-coloured possum's eyes that folded into wearily lined sockets. Her usually tanned complexion was grey with fatigue.

"Haven't seen her since about eight o'clock last night, luv," she said, her Cockney inflection strong. "She didn't come by for a night cocoa. For herself or the bairn. Odd, that."

"Keep an eye out for her, and if you see or hear anything, send word to Jeavon Yates," Posey said.

Nellie's wiry, greying brows shot up to her frizzy hairline. "Is she in trouble?"

Posey nodded. "I suspect so, but it's too early to raise the alarm yet."

Nellie's brow creased into a deep frown, but the older woman's hunched shoulders relaxed. "Is that why you're dressed like a pirate?"

Posey welcomed the chance to laugh. "It is. And it's not so ridiculous where I'm going."

"Be careful."

***

The boy. They've taken the boy too.

Her heart raced at the thought. They probably took him because they saw Sally would not budge without him. But what would they do with him once they were out of here?

Panic swept over her, and she jumped back in her waiting cab.

"The waterfront, please. A few streets away from the abandoned old wool store on Finger Wharf."

Warehouses circled the quay area, giving commercial shipping access to berths in the city's heart, and as wool had grown an increasingly important export in recent years, the number of commercial berths had increased exponentially.

As they neared the water, she tapped on the cab roof and the driver drew to a halt.

"Let me out here. This will do fine," she said, handing him her fare. "I'm paying you to stay here for the next thirty minutes. If I don't return by then, you're free to go. If you dun me, I've got your details."

The driver scowled, but pocketed her coin. "Yes, ma'am. There's no one much about wanting a cab this early, anyway."

Her head down to avoid attracting attention, Posey did a circuit of the block where the wool store was located. The wharf side was busier than the rest of town, already bustling with pedestrians, and she could move freely without attracting attention. But the building she was seeking was further down the wharf and, because it was no longer in use, the only sight of human activity in this section was an old man who lent on a bollard, sucking on his pipe and watching the waves.

Is he a lookout? Should I fear him?

She decided not. She paused on the quay, looking out to the water, as if she were an idle sightseer, and then swung in a half circle, gazing up at the sky, equally nonchalant. But in the turn, she fixed her eyes on the wool store. The place had the look of a guardhouse, built of solid blocks punctuated by a series of narrow arched windows reinforced with steel. Two forlorn tattered flags hung limply from the top of the two square towers on either side of a wide front entrance, a remnant of days when this place would have hummed with activity.

They stood watch on an entry designed to provide room for wide wagons stacked three or four wool bales high to load and unload. The lines of narrow arched windows also ran along a narrow upper storey, and steel grilles reinforced them too.

At first glance, the heavy wooden doors that opened onto the wharf appeared closed, but when Posey looked more closely, she saw one of them was slightly ajar. Steel rail tracks embedded into the planked wharf ran from these doors, once flung open to wheel hundreds – nay, thousands – of bales a day from the shed to the waiting freighters, tied up exactly where the old chap sat.

She ignored the main door, and instead turned down a narrow lane that ran around the back of the warehouse. She wanted to enter by stealth if she could; not announce her arrival and walk straight into an ambush.

Halfway along the side wall was a man-size door, the sort you could imagine the watersiders used to slip outside for a fag at smoko. A steel picket fence closed off this side of the property, but a gate set into it tilted on a broken hinge. Posey regarded it for less than a second before slipping through the gap and making a low run for the door. She turned the rusted handle, and it opened with a squeak that set her jaw.

Inside, she pressed her back against the solid block wall, and held her breath as her eyes adjusted to the dim and dusty surrounds. Before her, the wide expanse of the warehouse floor opened out, and she smelt and saw that the wooden floor retained the soft sheen and odour of lanolin from the many fleeces that had passed through the building. Heavy timbered arched bays punctuated it on both sides; the timber squared and monumental, like wharf piles. On top of each bay dangled massive chains, each link half the size of her fist, hanging from heavy iron wheeled pulleys once used, she guessed, to hoist up bales for loading.

A minimum of natural light penetrated through the barred windows, and for a few minutes, she could make out only the broadest outlines of the surrounding space. Wide stairways – enough to accommodate a dozen men – ran up either side to the mezzanine, leaving a gaping two-storey space from floor to ceiling in the mid-section.

Posey dawdled, reluctant to relinquish her cover, terrified at what awaited her. The day carried the silence of dawn. The only sound that penetrated the solid block walls was a distant whisper of water slapping the piles underneath them, and the gentle cooing of pigeons roosting on the roof.

Probably warming themselves in the first rays of the morning sun.

Stop it! Concentrate!

And then, out of the tranquillity, a baby cried.

Posey would know Robbie's cry anywhere. He was close.

She tiptoed out of the safety of the wall and into the shadow of the mezzanine overhang. She peered up and down the space of the wool store floor.

And almost as fast as she absorbed the details of the trap before her, she understood she had no choice but to walk – nay, run – right into it.

Sixty-eight

Robbie sat in the middle of the floor, close to a wooden crate that was the only other object visible over the wooden expanse. He lifted his arms, wanting to be picked up, his cries getting louder and more agitated with every second no one came.

But there was no one near who could pick him up, because his mother stood several feet above him on the crate, her arms tied to her sides, her wrists bound with thick hemp rope. And around her neck draped the same rough rope, tied in a noose and attached to a heavy hooked chain, which hung like Damocles' sword above her. Posey stared upwards, following the snaking of the chain, first through an iron wheel acting as a pulley on the top of a bale beam, and then across to a winch, controlled by a lank-haired, burly fellow in a dark coat with the collar pulled up, partly concealing his face.

She dashed for the child and scooped him up on her left hip, her right hand coming to rest on the outside of her padded right pocket. All she could hear above Robbie's crying was a triumphant gust of laughter as she broke her cover and emerged from the shadows.

Before she could even turn, she sensed a man had moved

from the dimness behind her. She whirled around.

"Well, well, Miss Barclay. You took the bait. I didn't think you would."

His voice carried a northern burr. From Yorkshire, perhaps? A middle-class accent.

This is no pleb.

He stood at well over six feet, and his hands and feet matched the size of his frame. In truth, over-matched it. They looked too big even for his size, clumsy encumbrances that might have been almost comical if not for the threatening power displayed in his every movement. He hunched his shoulders forward, in a boxer's stance. A grimace that could never be called a smile crossed his face. A wolf about to go in for the kill.

Posey raised herself to her full height, tightening her legs and chest in an unconscious threat response.

"You know my name, but I don't know yours, Mr...?" She left the gap and was proud of the insolence that dripped from her words.

You don't deserve to be Mr anything. You're the scum of the earth.

"Mr Nobody to you," he snapped.

She laughed at that. "Well, Mr Nobody. You don't need to hurt the child or his mother any further. They haven't any part in whatever twisted game it is that you're playing. Let them go."

"Oh, no. I don't think so. Our instructions are to make things uncomfortable for you. Verry uncomfortable." His eyes flicked to an accomplice overhead. "Show her what I mean, Griggs. Let her see we mean business."

Griggs slowly turned on the winch, tightening the chain. The slack rope went taut and Sally's body straightened. She screamed and stood on tiptoe, desperately seeking to keep her feet on the crate to take up her own weight.

Sensing his mother's distress even if he didn't understand what was happening, Robbie burst into more frantic howls.

Mr Nobody called "Enough for now, Griggs," and his offsider lowered it for Sally's toes to brush the crate again. Her head fell forward in a coughing fit, and when she raised it, Posey could see deep-red rope welds marked her neck.

"That was torture," Posey cried, loud and furious. "And it's completely unwarranted. Let her go, I say."

The torturer advanced on her, his face beaming with malice. "Torture, was it? Well, now it's your turn." He pulled a knife from his belt and stalked forward.

Sally screamed and Robbie's little arms flailed.

Poppy had prepared for this moment. Her hand, already grasping the pocket pistol, whipped it out of her jacket. The man was only feet from her when, in one movement, she brought up the pistol and shot.

He shrieked as he grabbed at his shoulder and staggered backwards, roaring like a bull. Blood spurted through his fingers. He'd dropped the knife when the bullet hit, and Posey dashed forward and kicked it out of his reach. It skittered across the polished floor.

Sally screamed again, and out of the corner of her eye, Posey saw the man called Griggs raise the winch. Whether deliberately or as an involuntary act, she couldn't tell.

She whipped around and raised the gun to aim at him. "Let

her down right now, or I'll shoot."

At this distance I'd be lucky to do you any damage, but let's hope you don't know that.

Griggs hesitated for a few critical seconds, and then lowered Sally so her feet touched the crate again.

A noise behind Posey alerted her to movement. The torturer was scuttling across the floor on his backside towards the discarded knife.

She was swinging the pistol towards him to take another shot when the main warehouse door burst open. Sunlight poured in, momentarily blinding her as she saw two – no, three – men charge in.

Jeavon halted momentarily to assess the scene. Their driver, Robert, was by his side. Silas raced in, not stopping until he reached her.

"Thank God. You're alive," he said, gasping.

She couldn't take her eyes – or gun – off the man on the floor.

"Get him," she yelled to Jeavon. "He's going for a knife."

Jeavon made his way across the warehouse so fast you'd never dream he'd had mobility problems in recent months.

"Harrow," he said as he hoisted the man up by the side that was not bleeding and snapped his wrists in handcuffs behind his back. "Fancy meeting you here."

Harrow uttered a malignant snarl.

"You know him?" Posey asked.

"Disgraced copper," Jeavon said. "Sacked two years ago. He was bad enough then, but he's fallen to a new low."

As Robert charged upstairs to grab Griggs, Hawk Eye made

his way to Sally. With Harrow's knife, he cut away the noose and her wrist bonds, and she fell into Posey's arms, crying.

"I never imagined…" She stared wildly around her.

"Never mind. It's over now." Posey, still overloaded with Robbie and the gun, half hugged her.

Tears gushed down Sally's cheeks as she reached out for Robbie, who gurgled and pulled one of her long blonde locks over her eyes in joy.

"Ow," squealed Sally. "You little rascal. Don't do that! It hurts Mummy." She glanced up at Posey. "Luckily, not as much as those other creeps, though. Miss Posey, how can I ever thank you?"

"Oh, Sally, forget it. You wouldn't have even been here if it wasn't for us." She glanced at Hawk Eye. "Though what exactly we've done, and who's behind this, I've still got no idea."

Sixty-nine

"Here we were, racing to Posey's rescue" – Silas laughed – "and she didn't need us. She'd already got the situation well under control."

Posey pulled a face and huffed in disagreement.

"Not true. You and Jeavon – and Robert – arriving was the best sight I've seen in my life. If you hadn't come then, I'm not sure what would have happened." She shuddered. "It doesn't bear thinking about. Harrow might have bullied Griggs into pulling up that winch. He could have reached for the knife and thrown it at me. Who knows? And I'm not much of a shot. I'm not at all certain I could have hit him again." Under her breath, she added, "Thank goodness Griggs didn't realise that."

Harrow had resolutely refused to tell the police anything about the assault, particularly who had hired him.

"I guess it's someone who can pay him enough to make it worth his while to keep his mouth shut," Jeavon said.

Griggs admitted Harrow had hired *him*, but he knew nothing about the job except for his part in it.

"I think it was someone who wanted to get at you, Silas. But because we had effective security on you, they went for Posey instead," Jeavon said.

"You might have your private suspicions, but the fact is, there are many people who would like to see the Barclays pay them compensation, so there's quite an extensive field to choose from."

"Spoken like a true policeman, Jeavon," said Hawk Eye.

"But I know my brother. This has all the hallmarks of a Gideon attack. Launched in such a way that he eludes personal responsibility. Always leaving someone else to take the blame. That's Gideon.

"I am in no doubt he was behind this. I accept proving might be difficult. He's made so many direct threats to me over the last few weeks… It would be highly unlikely for him not to carry them out. That's not his style.

"But the thing I most feared – that if he couldn't get to me, he'd attack those closest to me – has come to pass.

"It just happens that Posey was more resilient and resourceful than anyone could ever imagine – and she beat him at his own game."

Seventy

"Lord Brook. Do come in and take a seat." Sir Frederick was gesturing to the single chair set in front of his magnificent brown stretch of oak desk.

Alfred Morgan, the chief justice's assistant registrar, the same Irishman who'd welcomed him when he'd stepped ashore in Sydney four weeks ago, stood aside to allow Gideon Vane to advance into Sir Frederick's office.

Right. So, this is how it's going to be. No brandy or coffee in armchairs around the ottoman this time.

Gideon slumped into the chair like a mutinous schoolboy, hinting at his contempt for the office of Chief Justice by his posture.

Sir Frederick lost no time in getting down to business.

"Nice of you to come, Lord Brook," he observed with a wintry smile that communicated just the opposite. "In the few days since we last talked, fresh information has come to my notice." He paused and let his eyes roam over Gideon's sour face.

"I'm pretty certain you will know what that may be. Does the name Primrose Hetherington mean anything to you?"

"That chit—" Gideon protested.

"Please, Lord Brook. Don't make this any more embarrassing than it is already. For either of us. I'll never air this matter publicly because of the need to protect the young woman concerned, but I expect a Supreme Court judge to exercise discretion in his private life, and this you have clearly failed to do. At the very least, you should have declared your good standing compromised and your reputation being in jeopardy."

Gideon's eyes flickered to the gilt-and-mother-of-pearl clock that sat on a bookcase shelf to the right of Sir Frederick's chair. If he wasn't wrong, it was in the Austrian style. His mother had one rather like it, he recalled. The minute hand clicked round, moving with miniscule speed, as Sir Fredrick's voice droned on, like a blowfly up against a closed window pane.

"And of course," the chief justice was saying, "if you had done that, it is highly unlikely I would have appointed you in the first place. We both understand that, but there we are…"

Done what? Oh, yes, fessed up to my sins. But they are too many for anyone to want to listen. He almost laughed in the old crone's face at the thought. *You don't know the half of it…*

"You have also been less than honest in other aspects of your declarations to me, as we discussed in our earlier meeting. In the light of everything, I'm requesting that the Court of New South Wales be released from its undertakings towards you.

"I want this to be achieved with a minimum of upset on both sides, so I ask that you resign your post for one of the standard reasons: family illness or death, unexpected tragedy at home. Please yourself how you word it."

Gideon's attention switched back to the clock.

How much longer is he going to bang on? It reminds me of when I got chucked out of Eton.

"You should understand that the Australian newspapers don't observe the same cultural restraints as the English press, as far as their treatment of the nobility is concerned. We're a more equal society. And the Sydney papers are onto this. They're likely to run an account of some sort in the next few days, so I am giving you the chance to move on before you face the music."

Gideon stood abruptly.

"I quite understand, Sir Frederick, and I apologise for putting you in this situation. I've just remembered my father, the earl, is on his deathbed, and I have been suddenly called home.

"As a matter of fact, I got a telegraph this last evening to that effect, and I was going to ask you for leave of absence anyway. Depending on what happens, I may have to assume my duties in the family estate."

He clicked his heels and gave a stiff bow. "That should do it, I presume?"

Sir Fredrick rose from his chair with the air of a man relieved of a nasty burden.

"That would fit admirably. And, Lord Brook, I wish you well in your future."

I bet you do. Hypocritical old goat.

Seventy-one

"He's asking me to see him off." Silas flicked his observant single eye on her and raised a quizzical brow.

"Really? And will you?" Posey teased.

"Only if you come. We can stand there together and let him see who won and who lost."

***

The chief justice lost no time in announcing to the world that, with great regret, the newly appointed Supreme Court judge was seeking indefinite leave of absence from his post because of a family emergency and would depart Sydney immediately. And within another twenty-four hours it was general knowledge in the upper circles of society that Lord Brook's father was on his deathbed, and the soon-to-be Earl of Worcester had booked a first-class cabin on the latest clipper, the RMS *Celestial Winds*.

As Posey and Silas waited to board the sparkling black vessel with its distinct white band around the hull for their last dinner with Silas's brother, Silas pointed at the lifeboats hanging above deck. As an official carrier of Royal Mail, the *Celestial Winds* could fly a special Royal pennant and use a crown insignia on dinner services, stationery and other facilities.

"See the crown insignia? Approved by Queen Victoria. That will appeal to Gideon." He gave a quiet chuckle. "I must say, I'm much gratified by the way this has all played out. Two weeks ago, I was on my knees." He grinned again. "In more ways than one. Praying, and capitulating."

Posey gave his arm a gentle squeeze. "But you came through. You regained your spirit."

A steward in a smart royal-blue jacket beckoned from halfway up the gangplank.

"Sir? Madam? We're sailing in four hours. Dinner service is beginning soon. Please allow me to escort you on board."

"We're farewelling Lord Brook," said Silas. "Lead on."

***

Gideon met them at his cabin door, arms outstretched, all expansiveness and bonhomie.

"So good of you to come," he said, hugging Silas. He shot Posey a curious sideways glance. "And Miss Barclay! How unexpected and delightful."

His tone was distinctly droll, and Silas and Posey dared not make eye contact.

"I didn't realise you and my brother had become so…" He allowed for a theatrical pause. "Close."

"Oh, read nothing into it beyond a highly successful working relationship," said Silas airily. "Naturally, we've spent a lot of time together working on the family's case. And now you won't be here to see the outcome. A shame." He made a suitably sad moue with his lips.

Two can play at false sentiment, mon frère.

"Of course. But with Father so desperately ill…"

"Yes, that was sudden," said Silas. "But of course his health has been poor for some years now."

"True, true," Gideon said in an offhand tone, ready to move along. "Take a seat. I apologise for the cramped quarters, but with such a last-minute booking, I was very fortunate to secure first class."

They paused for a moment to admire the decor. A first-class cabin on the *Celestial Winds* included a comfortable double bed dressed in fine linens, a small chaise longue under a porthole, and a compact round table with three dining chairs already set for dinner with the crown insignia dinnerware.

The opening porthole was a particular luxury, allowing for natural light and fresh air – if desired – to flood the cabin. A washstand with a porcelain basin and pitcher – similarly royally marked – stood in one corner. Today, it also had crammed onto it a bottle of red wine and three glasses.

But even first-class passengers had to share bathrooms, and Silas doubted the dining table was a permanent fixture.

As if sensing his thoughts, Gideon gestured to it. "They brought this in especially, and removed the writing desk, just for now. I can't complain. It will do me till I get to India."

"India?" said Silas. "I thought you were hurrying back to London."

"Oh, I will be," said Gideon, waving an airy hand as if it was all the same to him. "But via Madras. It was the quickest way."

Silas and Posey exchanged a quick glance.

Sure it is.

"So, what's actually wrong with Father?" Silas asked. "I've known nothing about his health for a long time now."

"Oh. His heart," Gideon said. "Cardiac dropsy, the doctor says."

"I see," said Silas. "And how do they treat that?"

Gideon shrugged. "Digitalis and rest, I believe. And brandy. He likes his brandy. Anyway, sit and we'll get started." He stepped towards the washstand. "I hope you enjoy red wine. I'm afraid wine stewards are in short supply, but at least we've someone to serve our food." He grabbed a bell pull by the washstand and, back turned away from them, took the wine bottle in hand.

Silas and Posey slipped into their seats.

Gideon stepped forward, a glass in each hand, and served first Posey, and then Silas, his hand trembling as he stretched across to deposit it in front of him. He retrieved the third glass, and Posey shot Silas a meaningful look before then looking at the glass and then back up at him.

'Be careful,' she mouthed.

Gideon sat down opposite them, jerking his head in the nervous tic she'd noted overtook him when he was ill at ease.

"Cheers," Gideon said, raising his glass. "Let's drink to better times. A new beginning. I haven't been the best brother, Silas, I know that. But I promise, I'm changing my ways. Can we make peace?"

Silas regarded him wryly, adjusting his black eye patch as he did so. "Make peace? If it's important to you, Gideon, of course. But I think we work best when we're on different continents, don't you?"

Gideon gave a self-conscious barking laugh. "Different

continents. That's a good one. I'll have to remember that next time I think of coming to Australia."

"So, you're not planning to return then?" Posey eyeballed him with a hard stare. "Sir Frederick's announcement just said, 'Extended leave of absence'."

For a second, Gideon dropped the bon-accord persona. He bared his teeth in his first show of aggression and then flattened his lips.

"I won't be returning to Sydney. I find the air doesn't agree with me." He left a long pause and then added, "Nor the women."

Clearly seeking to regain the hail-fellow-well-met mood. He shook his head and laughed. "I'll have my hands full as Earl of Worcester. Looking after the estate and all. It's a big job. I doubt I'll even have time to practise law."

He looked at their glasses, which were still on the table in front of them. The wine glittered with an iridescent sheen.

"Last chance then. All forgiven?"

"If you say so," said Silas.

They raised their glasses just as there was a knock on the cabin door and a voice called, "Your dinner, Lord Brook."

Gideon rose and lumbered to the door to meet a steward with a heavily laden tray.

Quick as a flash, Posey reached across the table and swapped Silas's glass for Gideon's. Then they both made a play of bringing their lips to the edge of the glass, but drank nothing.

Gideon's attention was fully taken up with the process of unloading the food; three servings of roast beef already carved and plated, and then the dishes of roast potatoes and pumpkin, spinach and gravy.

"Pumpkin," he groaned. "I've never understood the way Australians eat pumpkin. It's one thing I won't miss. Cattle food. That's what we call it." He gulped a mouthful of wine. "Come on then. Eat up!"

***

"So, have you been to India before, My Lord?"

Posey peered over her half-empty glass. Every time Gideon's attention was distracted with eating, she'd slipped a little of the wine into the gravy boat, while Silas made a show of drinking his slowly.

"No, I haven't. It will be interesting, I'm sure. And I am on the lookout for business opportunities while I'm there."

"Oh, yes? What sort of business did you have in mind?" Silas worked hard at appearing interested.

Gideon shrugged. As his consumption of the wine continued, he appeared increasingly scattered in his thoughts.

"Cotton, tea, spices? Who knows?" He laughed. "Maybe even a little opium. Jasper seems to think a bit of the blue smoke is what a gentleman needs."

"Jasper? Jasper Blackwood, do you mean?" Silas asked.

"Yes. Jasper Blackwood. What other Jasper is there?" Gideon's voice took on an irritated edge. "A fine fellow Jasper. Until he turns nasty."

"Turns nasty?" Posey echoed. Her voice oozed sympathy. "What did he do?"

"He tried to blackmail me, if you must know. But he got his comeuppance."

"How did he do that?"

"He got bitten, didn't he? By some giant dog. Serves him right, I say, for not getting things done."

"Oh? Getting what done exactly?"

Gideon's brow corrugated into worry lines. "Um… I can't remember," he said.

"And what about Harrow?" Posey asked gently. "Did he let you down too?"

"Harrow? How did you know about him?" He stared into his glass, and then at them. "I don't feel well…" He stared into his glass again, and he went still, as if receiving a message from a distant land.

A long tense silence stretched out… and out… and out…

From the corridor, they heard faint footfalls and muffled voices as passengers and crew went about their business. Drifting up through the open porthole from the wharf below came occasional human cries mingled with the keening of circling gulls.

"Bye… Good luck… See you again…"

His eyes widening, Gideon's face drained into an expression of horror as the light dawned. "The wine…" he croaked. He looked at the glass resting by Silas's plate, his eyes wide with surprise. "You swapped the glasses."

Posey smiled and nodded. "I did. Why? Was there something the matter with it?"

Gideon attempted to jolt to his feet, but succeeded only in pitching sideways and toppling off his chair.

Posey and Silas swapped significant looks.

"Gideon's suddenly taken ill," she shouted for the benefit of no one in particular. "It can't be the wine. We all drank the same brew."

Gideon croaked gibberish and fell back on the floor.

Posey lent over him and took his wrist to check his pulse. "Your heart's still beating," she said. "We're getting a doctor, Gideon. Immediately. I hope you recover before you get to India."

THE END

ACKNOWLEDGMENTS

Right from my first book – with Graysie and Nathan in Poisoned Legacy – I had in mind to do stories about Nathan's half-sisters left back in Sydney when he was restoring the family's fortunes in the Golden State.

Originally, I intended to have them come to California to join him, but when I began to plan the series, I felt much more drawn to the idea of spreading my Pacific wings and of having them stay in Sydney and to locate the story there.

I'm very aware of that Pacific Ocean circle that binds the US West Coast with both Australia and New Zealand. I love the thought of those waters touching all of our lands, and of the very close links we have all shared over two hundred years or more.

I have lived and worked in Australia – spending more time in Melbourne than Sydney, I admit – but I did have a wonderful summer in Sydney before moving to Melbourne. I have two sisters who live in Queensland who I visited regularly before Covid, and I have always felt a great affection for that remarkable continent.

I've interviewed many Australian authors on my Joys of

Binge Reading podcast, and greatly admire their vibrant publishing industry. And I have Australian readers, so it didn't seem like a big jump to set the series there.

But I hadn't planned to have one of the bad-boy characters from *Poisoned Legacy*, Willoughby Martens, pop up in the new story. That just happened as part of the creative process and I hope you agree that it makes a satisfying link between two series.

Researching Australian history at this time of the late 1860's was a whole new adventure.

I particularly enjoyed researching the early days of the women's suffrage movement. As you will soon discover when you read *Posey's Peril*, Posey Barclay is an independent thinker, a woman ahead of her time. Formal organisations for women's voting and property rights were launched in the later 1870s but there were some remarkable women like Rose Scott, Dora Montefiore, Vida Goldstein, Louise Lawson and many others who helped set the stage for united action.

I am grateful to editor Lauren Finger, who kept me in line when I went astray with both some facts and scoping out a timeline for this story. She also was a great help with colloquial speech in 1868 Sydney.

Formatting for digital and paperback books was once again handled with skill, good humour and alacrity by Marina and Jason Anderson at Polgarus Studios in Tasmania.

Many thanks to them and all my newsletter subscribers for supporting me and walking alongside in a sometimes bumpy publishing journey.

ABOUT THE AUTHOR

Jenny Wheeler is the author of the ten-book Of Gold & Blood Old California historical mystery series, the Home At Last series, and the new Sisters of Barclay Square series, set in Sydney, Australia. She's also the host of *The Joys of Binge Reading* podcast, with more than three hundred interviews with fellow popular fiction authors posted online at thejoysofbingereading.com

Posey's Peril, #2 in the Sisters of Barclay Square series, is the second in an Australian series. The story of Poppy's and Posey sister Petunia, is coming in early 2025.

When I'm not writing I adore getting out in nature. I'm a dedicated exercise freak, gardener and bee keeper. Most of all, I cherish living with joy in my heart every day I'm alive!

I love to hear from readers and listeners and what you enjoy reading, particularly in historical fiction.

CONTACT ME

You'll find me online at:

Websites:

Jennywheeler.biz

Thejoysofbingereading.com

Email Jenny@ jennywheeler.biz

Or on social media:

Facebook: @JennyWheeler.Biz

Instagram: @jennysbingereading

Pinterest www.pinterest.nz/Jennywheelerbooks

And YouTube: @jennywheelersbingereading6886

www.ingramcontent.com/pod-product-compliance
Lightning Source LLC
Chambersburg PA
CBHW030927120726
47906CB00002B/522